FIRST WORLD

To Lola Eve, who taught me the true meaning of unconditional love

FIRST WORLD
A Walker Saga Book One

Jaymin Eve

First World: A Walker Saga Book One

Copyright © Jaymin Eve 2013

All rights reserved

First published in 2013

Eve, Jaymin

First World: A Walker Saga Book One

1st edition

No part of this book may be reproduced, stored in a retrieval system or transmitted in any form or by any means, without the prior permission in writing of the publisher, nor be otherwise circulated in any form of binding or cover other than that in which it is published and without a similar condition, including this condition, being imposed on the subsequent purchaser. All characters in this publication other than those clearly in the public domain are fictitious, and any resemblance to real persons, living or dead, is purely coincidental

Chapter 1

I glanced over my shoulder at the approaching darkness. *Move your butt, Abby, you're almost safe.*

Safe. I was fooling myself but I needed the pep talk. It should surprise me that this was happening again, but unfortunately it didn't. Lately it'd become a regular part of my daily routine. Get up, go to class, escape the compound and get chased by gangers all afternoon ... sure, just standard stuff. I really needed to find someone with a normal life, kill them and take their identity. I'm kidding, of course. In my seventeen years, I've yet to meet anyone with a normal life.

I ran across the road, tense as I waited to hear the footsteps that had been echoing my own hurried pace for the past twenty minutes. But there was nothing. Where had my pursuers disappeared to?

I hesitated, scanned the area. The street was empty. Shadowy and unnaturally silent. I looked again, more thoroughly, in the last rays of the setting sun. Shattered shop windows – junk piles. Courtesy of the current world crisis. But the gang of tattoo-faced thugs that had struck such fear in me when they'd attacked in Central Park was missing. Four on one hadn't been the best odds, but I'd managed to shake them off and almost ... almost was back at the compound.

I crept along the street; the slower movements broadcasted my discomforts. My side was particularly painful. Lifting my raggedy sweater, I breathed in, it was immediately obvious I hadn't escaped the attack undamaged. In the fading light I could just make out the dark bruises shadowing my ribs. Purple already? That was going to be a pretty sight by morning. But being no stranger to pain, I dropped the top back down and focused on the street. One could never forget the dangers.

My eyes were the only part of me still moving.

A rodent scuttled by – but that wasn't causing the tension filtering into each of my muscles. I couldn't see the source – or hear it – but I could feel it – I wasn't alone. Without taking more than a few shallow breaths I expanded my senses, trying to determine where the ambush was coming from.

The world was eerily quiet, but I was missing something.

Unable to stay still any longer, I started to move again. It's an understatement to say I'm not patient. I acknowledge that. I'm ready for lunch the moment I finish breakfast – though that might have more to do with a love of food rather than impatience. So action of any kind was my preference. I've always worked on the theory that in dangerous situations there's little point sitting around waiting for the axe to fall – a theory expertly formed through my formative years spent watching pirated old-school horror movies. Ah, yes, the loss of television was one of the things I've mourned since the fall of New York. Stupid really, considering how many other things lost, but escapism was hard to come by.

So back to my current predicament. My instincts were urging me to get off the street; something dangerous was coming my way. Better to avoid the gangers until they moved on to some other nefarious business – which preferably wouldn't involve me. I was banking on their notoriously short attention spans. So, making a split-second decision, I ducked into a nearby alley.

Almost no light penetrated this far off the main road. Even with excellent night vision I crept cautiously. The dusky light barely highlighted the short, dirty alley. It contained just a few rusted-out dumpsters scattered close to a brick wall dead-end.

Bad idea, Abby. Retreat. Retreat.

My instincts don't usually let me down, but it seemed the danger on the street was preferable to being caught in a dead-end alley.

I turned to leave, but only took two steps before the faint sounds of feet scuffing the footpath halted my escape. My heart skipped a beat.

Great.

I was about to become that idiot movie-star-heroine, you know the one: stupid, stacked, blond, and dead. The film industry doesn't exist anymore, but I had watched enough old movies to know the general plotline. Considering I was neither stacked nor blond, I decided I'd pass on that career choice.

I moved further into the shadows. There were exactly two suitable dumpsters. The rusty faded red, which was emitting suspicious rat noises; or the other, a delightful brown color, which, judging by the smell, was home to at least two dead bodies.

I flipped a mental coin before sliding in behind the red one. There was just enough space to hide. Leaning back against the wall, I ignored the rustling and forced my muscles to relax.

While listening for an ambush I also tried to contain the flood of unpleasant memories. But as always, if I sit still for too long, all the negative crap piles in on me. It still amazes me that people of the early 21st century thought Earth of the future was going to be awesome. By the year 2020 we'd have flying cars, talking dogs, and somehow live in houses suspended in the sky. The reality – 2035 and we live in a dead zone.

Technology and communication systems – gone.

Malls – gone.

Schools and sports – gone.

Fossil fuels and transport systems they powered. Sigh. Gone, too.

Yep, pretty depressing.

The Brutal Gangers – currently chasing me – were one of the many gangs fighting for survival and power. All striving to dominate control of food sources, drugs, human trafficking, and, of course, the ever-prevalent battle for more territory.

It was during my lifetime that the rebels tried to regroup, to take society back. But the militias and gangs had a strong hold. They controlled the majority of weapons, food and the only communications system left – archaic two-wave radio. We were the rebels. We had less numbers and no choice but to barricade ourselves into compounds, only leaving when necessary.

Kicking back against the dumpster, I thought briefly of raiding it for food. There wasn't much point. I hadn't found anything remotely edible for months, but we were dangerously low on supplies.

We barely survived, but we were good at biding our time and being smarter. *Smarter* – sitting in various types of gunk on the freezing ground, waiting to be beat down by some thug – *Yep, smarter*.

It was about time I initiated a safer escape from the monotony of the compound. Next time I felt a need to jog I'd just stay home. Strike that, I'd just stay in bed. This wasn't my first experience with the Brutal Gangers and probably wouldn't be my last. I hoped my luck wasn't due to run out anytime soon.

It was pitch black in the alley now and my legs were almost asleep. I'd exhausted enough patience and spent way too long brooding. Time to make a break for it.

Easing myself free, I brushed down my jeans, dispelling the dust and the other disgusting items I'd been sitting in. It was a small comfort that the darkness hid the ground. Shuffling along the alley, I headed toward the street front, discernible in the faint spectra of light cast by one of the few working street lamps.

I paused at the end of the alley and focused. A secret to my survival was 'trust your instincts and use common sense'.

Yeah, it wasn't much of a secret, more like common sense – whew, hard to come by. Lucy always told me she'd come running with me when I was at the survivalist level of Bear Grylls. On a scale of one to Bear Grylls, I wasn't even close. Sigh. I missed television. No new shows had been made past 2015, but I'd always enjoyed the oldies. No more, though. Our television unit now housed mice and quite a few cockroaches.

I waited patiently in the darkness, absorbing the silence. It was a good sign, time to make a run for home. Easing around the side of the alley, I breathed deeply. No time to hesitate. I took the first step, pushing off hard from the ground. But, before I even landed, my right arm was jerked roughly, flinging me to the side. The pressure didn't ease. *Shit* ... I'd been caught. Twice in one day was a record, even for me.

A large masculine hand was wrapped tightly around my arm, long fingers overlapping on my right biceps.

Experience taught me that I had seconds to escape.

He was alone now, but that wouldn't last long.

Going limp, I slumped against him.

He grunted at the unexpected force of a hundred and thirty pounds of dead weight, and his grip eased slightly. Using my leg muscles for leverage, I wrenched myself backwards, landing in the alley. Pain exploded through my body as I hit the ground hard, but at least I had some space. Brushing my long hair from my eyes, I scuttled back down the alley. Distance was the key to my fighting style. I'm too light and weak to have much chance if they get their hands on me, but I am fast.

The shadowed figure had not moved from the alley entrance.

Upon reaching the end of the path, I stood carefully with the brick wall anchoring my back. My escape had been too easy; there was definitely an ambush coming. I needed to take him on while he remained unaided. That was my only chance. My much-abused muscles ached in protest and I was grateful for the amazing power of adrenalin.

I took a few steps closer, leaving the safety of my wall. My arms hung loosely at my side, my stance relaxed and ready for battle. I stopped halfway, ten feet from the man, his features shadowed but discernible in the backlight.

An average man, albeit a little weathered. His dark hair was peppered through with silver highlights and cropped close to his scalp in a haphazard manner. Either his hairdresser really sucked or he cut it himself with a blunt knife and no mirror. It was a small relief that he displayed no facial tattoos or clothing insignia from the local gangs. Although, truthfully I was more comfortable with the monster I knew. The motives of gang members I understood.

This man I did not.

His clothing looked tattered, an array of brown and tan fading into each other. The shabbiness didn't disguise their unusual quality and style. He could have stepped off the pages of my history books, elaborate military-style dress with large medals on each shoulder.

What was this mystery man doing on the streets? Out here there were gangers, the occasional lost human – dead men walking – and the crazy homeless beggars. But this man didn't fit any of the profiles. A lone wolf. He emanated a unique strength and power, but more than that, he was strangely familiar. In an almost involuntary movement, I took a step closer. The cooling air sent chills down my spine. Either that, or the energy pulsing in the space between us.

I was now close enough to distinguish the dark blue of his eyes, shrewd and perceptive. On top of that his commanding and charismatic presence dominated the little alley. What a plethora of contradictions. This familiarity was crazy; I'd never known anyone but the rebels from my compound.

And then it hit me.

I'd been probably nine years old, I guess. It was only the second time I'd escaped the compound. The situation in New York was not as bad then, but being a child I'd had more restrictions. The first ten minutes had been fun and uneventful. But then I'd noticed a group of men standing near Central Park. Unsure of the situation and worried for my safety, I decided to make my way home. It had been near this very street that I locked eyes with a man. This man. I was sure of it now.

The same warmth ... the same strength ... the same sense of safety had reached across the space between us. As a child, I hadn't even hesitated stepping onto the road toward him. I'd taken three steps before he'd smiled sadly, lifted his hand in a wave, and taken off into the park.

The memory had stayed with me for years, gradually fading until now. I guess any psychiatrist would assure me he was the reason I ran the streets: searching for him or some such psychology bull.

Standing here, eight years later, he still evoked feelings of warmth and safety. And my curiosity would not be denied. My sensible side was demanding over and over that I move my butt out of there, but, if I hadn't listened for seventeen years, I wasn't about to start now.

He didn't seem dangerous. Just standing there...

So, conveniently ignoring the fact that he'd grabbed me only minutes before, I decided to take the chance. What did I have to lose?

Don't answer that question.

Since my escape from his clutches, he'd made no attempt to approach me again. Usually this would be the old lull-me-into-a-false-sense-of-security ploy. But the vibe I was getting was the opposite. I tapped my foot reflexively. For the world's most impatient person, it had reached the point where I couldn't stand the silent staring any longer.

Time to speak up. *What's the worst that could happen?*

Yeah, I threw that out into the universe ... I liked living on the edge.

"Strange man with horrible haircut..." I said. "Who are you and what do you want?"

There was a subtle change as my words broke our stare-off. His muscles tensed, as if expecting a confrontation. I tilted my head to the side. It seemed important to hear him speak; I felt like I had been waiting my entire life for this moment. His lips turned up at the corners.

"Fiery redhead, with an attitude."

I smiled. He had a sense of humor. How refreshing.

"I am your watcher, *miqueriona*. Tell me, what is the name you are called here?"

His words were thick, his voice rusty and unused. With the combination of unfamiliar accent and gravelly voice, I barely registered the question. I stood there, mouth hanging open. A sudden and unexpected burst of emotion was wreaking havoc with my central nervous system. I had never heard anything as beautiful as that accent. It was lilting, somewhere between speaking and singing, and was old fashioned, like his clothing. It soothed as it flowed down the alley like a river of warm honey.

Any normal day I would think I'd just experienced some type of mild psychotic episode. And, yes, I did say normal day. But it was all to do with that accent. Which was almost more disturbing.

I considered his strangely phrased question.

"My name is Abby, so that's what I'm called here, and everywhere else." I paused for a moment. "What's a *micwa rena*?" The wording, so beautiful in his accent, sounded odd and disjointed from me.

I waited patiently. Well, pretty patiently. My hands were not on my hips yet, and my foot had only tapped twice.

Then he dived at me.

It was so fast I wouldn't have believed it if I hadn't been looking directly at him. My obsession with his voice had relaxed my innate self-preservation. I'd let my guard down and now it was too late. Standing next to me, he was huge, towering over my five-foot ten-inch frame. He held my right arm again, gently this time. Don't ask me how that happened. My movements were in slow motion compared to his. He flipped over my wrist and we stared at the diamond-shaped mark just visible in the dim lighting. Curved around the small of my wrist, the smooth purple mark looked larger than usual.

"*Miqueriona*, my little one. Have you ever wondered why you have this mark?"

Abigail, get the hell out of there.

I wasn't sure if that was my inner voice or an outside force issuing direction. But something was telling me to ignore the inviting warmth and ... well ... get the hell out of there.

I stared up into his piercing blue eyes and continued the conversation. What? I'm a slow learner.

"I know why I have this mark. It's a birthmark." I used my I'm-speaking-to-a-two-year-old tone. "Again, who are you?"

The man smiled. His teeth were straight, white and perfect. Not typical of many street people. He was definitely keeping some secrets.

"Who am I? Not important." He continued, and I admit it, I was in love with his accent. "What do I want? Much more important. But right now there is no time to explain."

Between the randomness of the conversation and his accent, I was struggling to understand.

"But you are the most important of all, young Aribella. Now is not the time for questions. Danger lurks in the darkness. I will locate you again. And as difficult as you will find this, try to be patient. Your time is coming."

No! He couldn't leave yet. My hands tangled in the extra cloth along his sleeves. The material was unusual; it looked rough and coarse, but felt as smooth as silk. I opened my mouth to stall him, but he never let me speak.

"And stop roaming the streets. It's too dangerous for you. *Salutia, miqueriona*."

Then he tipped his head and, escaping my grip, was gone.

More than annoyed, I took off after him, following his path onto the street, but it was deserted.

Impossible!

I'd just met the older, grumpier Superman, because no one could disappear that quickly. Taking a few hurried breaths, I winced. Now that he was gone I noticed the increased pulse of hot sharp jabs under my ribs. If I didn't stop falling down, my body was going to go on strike and refuse all movement. I glanced at my battered old watch. Crap! It was after eight; I was going to miss last class. The matron was sure to kill me this time. I had no idea why people worried about the danger on the streets. *They should live in my house*. It was time to get back there.

I took off along the path at a reasonably fast pace,

the entire way my tumultuous thoughts beating at me. That was such a strange meeting. The man had called me Aribella and *miquw awara* something or other. The first one was a name, for sure, and the second definitely another language. My heart raced. I needed to find him again. I wanted to look now, but he was right: the dark was hunting-time; the predators emerged. Tomorrow, I decided, would be much safer.

I was passing familiar streets; I was almost home. Though, trust me, it was missing a few of the homely essentials. The cold stone building where I grew up was Compound 23, one of the dozens of hidden dwellings where children were stashed. I'd been dumped on this one's doorstep. Figuratively speaking. These under-eighteen compounds are single sex and secluded. The training grounds for future rebels.

Lucy, my best friend, lived there with me. She helped me smack down a couple of bullies when we were three and we'd been inseparable ever since.

I side-stepped a large pile of rusted-out bike frames. It was second nature to run and dodge the random array of trash. Downtown New York was just rubble now. I hadn't seen her in the prime of her life, but I imagined she was magnificent.

Pausing before the compound's front gates, I glanced around to determine I was alone. Crazy vines covered the outside of what looked like an abandoned building. But there was a minute high-tech security panel hidden in the wall. I pressed my palm against the scanner before entering the password and finishing with voice authentication. All of this security plus barbed wire fences, video surveillance ... and still girls disappeared.

The human-trafficking movement had gained strength over the years. We lived in constant fear of ending up in that life.

The gates opened and I slunk inside. The landscape within the estate was barren. The barriers which were designed to protect cast an ominous prison feeling. Old photos that hung in the hallway depicted the manor surrounded by lush gardens, but all that was left now was scuffed dead grass and scattered leaves. Suffice to say, it offered protection but no warmth. Opening the large front door, I stepped inside.

"Where have you been, Abigail Swish? Class has started and I see you aren't in it."

I jumped at the sound of the cold high voice behind me. Spinning around, I hesitated to deliver a smartass reply. Standing, hands on her bony hips, was Patricia Olden, head of Compound 23. Her black hair was short and slicked back, framing her sharp features. She was forty-five years old, one of the youngest leaders among the rebels. Her joys in life included being a controlling bit– witch ... no, I was right the first time – bitch. On top of that, her loathing of teenagers was legendary. This was my mother figure. Hence why I ran in the ganglands.

She continued, arrogance and derision dripping from every syllable: "I don't care if you tattoo yourself, get a face full of piercings and join the gangers, but if I have to see your face under my roof, I expect to receive my full cash payments. You will make it in time for every single class."

"Since I'm tattoo and piercing free..." I glanced at my watch. "And classes have only just started, I'll head that way now."

The resistance planned to take back the city by breeding the strongest rebels. It was a long-term plan. Very long-term.

Education was deemed to be of utmost importance. Future rebels were trained in both academics and combat. They paid the compounds per class attendance, so it was priority one around here. It was also why junior compounds were single sex. Less distractions.

Marching over, Olden grabbed me, her bony fingers pinching my arm. She dragged me across the hall and we ended up in our main classroom. Using my free arm, I attempted to protect my injured ribs. Breathing was becoming somewhat painful.

The teacher paused. She was resistance-

employed, around sixty years old, but it had been a hard sixty years. As Lucy would say, 'The lady has city miles on her'. The pain dulled to an angry throb as Olden released me.

"Mrs Crabbe, note Abigail Swish is present for this class."

The teacher glanced at her watch before nodding. "A little too close, Patricia. I'll let it slide today, but have your girls here on time in future."

As she shuffled off to open her attendance book, Olden rounded on me.

"You will make every class from now until you're eighteen. You've irritated me since the day you arrived. It's a bad habit that will not serve you well on the streets."

"I can imagine," I said drily. "Seeing as I was one when I arrived, must have been all the dirty diapers."

Ignoring me, she continued, her voice dropping dramatically. "You're eighteen soon, Abigail. No one will be around to protect you then. You'll be on those damn streets you love so much." Her thin lips curved slightly, a cruel smile. "You have no idea what awaits you."

Da dum dum. Wasn't she dramatic tonight. With one month till my eighteenth, Lucy and I had been trying to figure out what to do. Most made their way to an adult rebel group. Junior compound leaders were supposed to direct you. And that was my dilemma – Olden was not trustworthy.

Throughout the room, girls were studiously reading their books, hoping her attention wouldn't turn toward them. Not Lucy, though. She was sitting near the back of the room in her usual spot, glaring daggers in my direction. Luckily, Olden appeared to be done for the day. Turning to leave, she was out the door in record time, like she was afraid if she spent too much time with us she'd catch something. In my opinion, her absence was her most enjoyable aspect.

Threading through the room, I made my way toward my desk. I dropped into the chair, ungracefully, of course, painfully jarring my side. Ignoring this, I faced the front. The teacher continued the lesson in her tedious tone. In ten years I'd never had an interesting teacher. I was beginning to think they were myths, like unicorns and comfortable high heels.

Movement to my right caught my attention. Lucy Laurell, best friend, still glaring. Her gorgeous, doll-like features all screwed up in annoyance. Big blue eyes narrowed. Major PMS mode, if you ask me. Lucy was tiny, barely five-foot, and angelic with shoulder-length wavy blond hair and a delicate heart-shaped face. The delicate facade covered a core of steel and determination. I knew that firsthand.

When we were six she'd forced me to perform a blood bond. She'd decided this was the number one requirement of sisterhood. I hated the sight of blood, often throwing up or, in extreme cases, fainting. But somehow, despite her size, she held me down and hacked away. The painful memory will always be with me, along with a crooked scar along my left palm. Lucy was no surgeon.

"Where did you disappear to, Abigail?" Her low voice sounded calm but I wasn't fooled.

"I was unexpectedly delayed, Luce, but I'll tell you about it later."

She'd been in a martial arts class when I'd left for my jog. I'd planned on it just being a quick one. Shaking her head in exasperation, she turned back to face the front.

I tried to pay attention, but the constant droning was sleep-inducing. Right now we were in urban landscape skills class. Module three included camouflage, identifying and containing traps, and some chemical warfare. Important stuff. If only they'd splash out on a teacher who had real life experience or at minimum an actual interest in the subject. I'd been outside the gates more than Mrs Crabbe. If Lucy wasn't such a good student I wouldn't have passed a class. I rested my head on my hand and stared aimlessly toward the front. It was going to be a long hour.

Chapter 2

After dinner, Chrissie, a lanky fifteen-year-old with masses of thick brunette waves, cornered me in the hallway. Living up to her goth persona, she was dressed entirely in black.

"Where were you today, Abby?"

We sat on the bottom ledge of the large wooden staircase, just down the hall from the dining room.

"Went for a jog outside the compound."

It was unusual to spend time chatting with Chrissie; she hated small talk. So I knew there would be a point to this conversation.

She fidgeted a little. "You were gone for a long time. What's it like out there?"

I shrugged. "It's fine most of the time, although I've had a few scary moments."

A calculating look crossed her face. "Not this week, Olden's here, but next time she's away ... um ... can I come?"

My eyes widened. No one ever wanted to go outside the gates. I couldn't even get Lucy to run with me. Chrissie was too young to be allowed out on her own; we'd have to sneak.

"Uh, sure. If you really want to." I wasn't thrilled to have the responsibility of another person out there. But I was curious and I'd hate to think she'd brave the streets on her own.

Nodding, Chrissie jumped to her feet. "I would very much like to see what's happening outside the gates. Let me know."

I nodded as she walked off.

That was strange.

I made my way upstairs to get ready for bed. As an added bonus the delay resulted in an empty third-floor bathroom. The room held an array of toilets, sinks and shower stalls, and with twenty girls currently residing it was rarely unoccupied. I took my time brushing my teeth and washing my face. We had strict water rations, two-minute showers and drop-pit toilets.

Finally clean, I straightened to meet my own green eyes reflected back at me.

As a child I'd been painfully shy, hating any attention. The unique color of my eyes – almost emerald green – and large oval shape assured I received plenty of stares. But now I no longer cared about blending in. I was just grateful I didn't have the freckles usually accompanying red hair and fair skin.

Although my hair was another anomaly. It fell in curls, not quite ringlets except those shorter tendrils framing my face, to my mid back, and it wasn't a standard golden red: it was a deep blood red with undertones of black. It was unusual enough that the girls speculated I'd somehow managed to procure hair dye. But that'd been non-existent for many years.

I gave my expression one last grimace, my full, red lips thinning, before I turned to leave the room.

I made my way down the hall to the room I shared with Lucy. She was sprawled across my bed, wearing her favorite purple flannel pajamas. A thick novel lay open in front of her. Her attention never wavered as I stretched out next to her. It took a few minutes before she flicked a page and spoke.

"Are you actually gracing me with your presence, Abigail? To what do I owe such an honor?"

I smirked. "Honestly, Luce, I just felt a need to give something back. You know, to those lesser."

She raised an eyebrow, flicking across to the next page. "You are going the right way to end up on my list, Abigail."

My smirk fell. Lucy's list was not a place you wanted to be. The last girl who got on her bad side ended up with her hair glued to a school desk.

"Sorry, Luce, I was staring at myself in the training mirrors and my butt looked huge. I had no choice. I had to get out for a run."

Shaking her head, she sighed. "As if your tall lanky butt would ever look big. Try being five foot, Abbs. I look at a picture of a donut and it attaches to my thighs."

I laughed. Lucy was curvy in all the right places, without an ounce of fat anywhere else.

"Did you have to mention donuts?" My mouth watered. I was eight the last time we had their sugary goodness. But there was no way to forget.

We'd had canned beans and an unidentified rodent stew for dinner. We had learned to never expect junk or fresh food; they were the rarest of all. We didn't starve, but much of the joy from food was missing.

I attempted my nightly routine of taming my curls into a braid. Lucy took pity on me, helping out when my ribs screamed loudly at me. After she finished, I relaxed back into my pillows.

"So what happened today? I'm assuming you didn't plan on being out until the middle of the night, worrying your blood sister to death." Lucy could lay on the guilt with the best of them.

"You were in self-defense. You know how boring I find the basic classes. I can't even believe we still have to attend them."

"They seem to think we'll forget everything if we don't repeat absolutely every class." Lucy shook her head. "And don't diverge from the topic. What happened?"

I skimmed over my day. Most of it was unimportant.

Except the encounter in the alley.

It was foremost in my mind. I spent the most amount of time describing every little nuance.

Lucy shook her head, confusion warring with humor and fear.

"Who are you, Abigail? You jump from one dangerous situation to another and yet somehow escape unscathed. I'm afraid one day your luck will run out." She glared at me. "If you die, I'm going to find you, bring you back, and kill you again. Understand?"

"Understood, psycho!"

She patted my head.

Ignoring her condescension, I continued. "I need to go back and find him. I need answers. The curiosity is killing me."

I hadn't planned on telling her – she was a worrier – but keeping secrets is not my strong suit.

She nailed me with her 'look', freezing me to the spot.

"We should consider ourselves lucky that you

escaped today without losing any body parts. He said he was your watcher? Do you really want to chase down weird alley stalkers?"

"I can't stop thinking about how he made me feel."

She shook her head. "I swear worrying about you is giving me gray hair."

I wanted to reassure her that everything would be fine, but we lived with zero guarantees.

"I'm eighteen in a month and, as Olden so kindly pointed out, onto the streets we go. It's not exactly my dream to join a resistance group. I don't want to be a foot soldier in this pointless war."

Lucy nodded, unease plying her pixie features.

"I feel restless, Abbs. I'm getting no sleep, and wrinkles, I think." To reiterate her point, her forehead crinkled. "My thoughts are that we should get out of New York. There's no future for us here. We have nothing to lose by checking to see if it's this bad everywhere."

I shook my head in frustration. "I know I say this every day, but what the hell is wrong with people? War is so short-sighted. They're destroying the very world they have to live in."

"Yep, people are stupid. That we established long ago."

"Word." I shook my head. "And stupid's an understatement. Not nearly strong enough to describe this idiocy. Slow, dim-witted, dense, moronic..." I trailed off and Lucy picked it up.

"Brainless, thick, dumb-ass."

I laughed out loud. "I think you nailed it. They take dumbass-ness to an entirely new level."

A wave of exhaustion flowed over me. "And you're right. New York is just too dangerous. If only we had family to go to."

Lucy lay back against the pillows, her expression grim. Her tone had far less bounce than usual. "Well, my parents are dead. Car bomb saw to that. And I guess if no one has come forward for you after eighteen years, then yours are either dead or somewhere far from here."

It was incomprehensible to me that my parents were dead. I knew they were out there somewhere. I shrugged, flinching as the movement tugged on my ribs. "We've never relied on anyone else before. Plus, we're smart enough to figure this out. Surely."

Lucy laughed and, reaching over, fist-pumped me. "Smarter than the average rebel."

I yawned loudly, barely keeping my eyes open.

Lucy saved my ribs the painful effort by switching off the main light for me. She dived into her bed, whilst I pulled back my covers and crawled under. There was a real chill in the air. A little more effort to insulate these old buildings would be much appreciated.

"Night." I yawned again.

"Night, Aribella."

I groaned. "Seriously, not you too! Was that the only thing you took from today?"

She laughed. "Aribella suits you."

"Go to sleep, Lucy Laurell."

"Sure, use my full name. Totally scary."

"I still think we need middle names, you know, for dramatic effect."

Lucy laughed. "We're abandoned teens, Abbs, we can't afford middle names." She dropped her bottom lip.

I snorted with laughter. "Word."

She let a few chuckles escape. "The other day I was trying to remember when we started using 'word'."

I paused for a moment. "You know, I have no idea either, but we can't give it up now, the memories. Remember that day we answered every one of Olden's questions with 'word'?"

Snorting laughter sounded from Lucy. "Totally worth the week of scrubbing floors."

Smiling, I switched off the bedside lamp. Darkness flooded the room. Sleep claimed me instantly, and there I was, in my dream world. It had taken a few years for me to realize how unusual it was to have the exact same dream – every week – for as long as I could remember.

Dream-me started her adventure in an immense forest. Ancient gnarled trees and dense overgrown green foliage spanned as far as the eye could see.

As usual, I found myself wandering aimlessly through the peaceful expanse. Waiting for them to find me. The woman arrived first, stepping out of the vast tree-line to stand before me. She was beautiful – tall, with straight black hair that hung almost to her waist. She looked to be in her early thirties, but her eyes held the weight from many more years.

She radiated intoxicating warmth. Generally we stood there, simply staring. I soaked up the feeling for as long as I could, and, just as I was expecting her to move on, something changed. A sense of urgency filtered through the forest. Clutching my hand, she pulled me closer. Leaning in, she spoke.

"We love you." Unlike the usual dream fuzziness, the words were soft but clear. "Find the blue stone."

Then she was gone.

Reaching out, I fought to keep the warmth, but my hands clutched empty air. Sorrow flooded through me. I'd lost something vital.

At that point, a distraction stepped through the forest – which had turned strangely misty – capturing my full attention. My stupid heart galloped away in my chest.

He isn't real, I repeated over and over.

He was astonishingly perfect, and, unlike the woman, had only started appearing a few years ago. I had long reached the conclusion that he was too amazing to exist anywhere but in dreamland. Broad-shouldered and tall – well, more like giant – he had messy dark hair that fell around sculpted features. My favorite part – his eyes. Surrounded by thick sooty lashes they were a deep rich brown. When they focused on me everything else faded away.

We stared, the moment powerful. Energy hummed in the short distance between us. I wanted to move even closer, but something held me back. His lips turned up in a quizzical smile, and he was the one to close the distance. His large hands engulfed my face on either side.

Leaning down from his great height, he rested his forehead against mine. We fit together in that moment, two puzzle pieces that until that point had been clattering around in an empty box. And then he was gone. The emotions in my dream world were so intense; the sense of loss was sharp and biting. Eventually, as always, the world faded and the darkness of a dreamless sleep consumed me.

Much too early the next morning I found myself jarred awake. Glancing over to the small side window, I saw heavy sunlight streaming through. I had slept long and soundly for the rest of the night. In typical dream murkiness, the details were already fading, but, lying back, I contemplated the latest addition from last night – the woman had spoken to me. And in the bright clarity of morning, one detail stood out: she had the same accent as the alley man. Excellent! One more thing to add to my list of strange.

My first attempt at rolling out of bed was pain-filled. I'd forgotten about my ribs. Lifting my flannel shirt, I grimaced. Still an ugly dark purple, although some spots had yellowed. I must admit that I take my ability to heal in a quick manner for granted, but this injury was worse than usual. With a deep breath for courage, I sat up and pulled myself out of bed.

Hobbling down the hall, I pushed my way through the girls in the bathroom to find a spare sink to brush my teeth. No way was I waiting in the shower line this morning; I had a man to find. I took a few minutes to re-braid my hair, needing it off my face.

Back in my room I grabbed some clean clothes from my drawers. The current world crisis doesn't allow for a high-fashion life. Which is fine by me. I like comfortable. Tattered slim-fit blue jeans, low cut enough to sit below my bruises, and a simple white t-shirt.

Dragging on battered black boots and grabbing my hooded dark-gray coat, I left the room. The weather was reasonably mild this time of year, but with the cold season around the corner the wind could cut right through.

Lucy would be at breakfast; she was an early riser. I have a personal vendetta against all hours before 10am. I didn't bother with any cosmetics, not that many existed. Lucy's contact on the outside did procure a few things, such as mascara, which she was addicted to. She was the only person who managed to get clothes and cosmetics smuggled in. Worked out for me too – occasionally a new shirt would magically appear on my bed. But my lashes were already naturally thick and inky black – and with my talent of getting more of the mascara in my eye than on my lashes, I never bothered with it.

Starting down the stairs, I made it to the first landing. As usual I rounded the corner far too quickly. I found myself in a collision. We teetered comically on the ledge before managing to untangle ourselves. I recognized the mass of blond hair: it was Lucy. As she pulled back from me, I noticed she was dressed to impress today.

"Cute shirt, Luce. Who did you bribe to get that one?"

Her love of clothes was well known. She'd teamed a funky purple vintage t-shirt with short denim shorts, long socks and sneakers.

"I've told you before, Abbs, if you knew what I did for these things I'd have to kill you. Or myself," she muttered. Glancing down at her watch, she gasped. "I don't want to alarm you but ... wait for it ... it's only 8.30 in the morning."

Groaning, I massaged my temples. "That's why I feel like this. I hate mornings. Remember that fight years ago? We haven't talked since."

"How could I forget? It was the falling out of the century." Lucy has sarcasm nailed.

"So, I was coming to find you..."

I would work on the little white lies later. In my determination to find the alley man, I'd completely forgotten about Lucy.

Watching me, eyes narrowed, she shook her head. "Liar!"

I smiled. The girl knew me well.

"You were heading out to find your alley man."

I laughed. A little too well.

"Can't get anything past you, but I'm just a tad excited." Bouncing on my feet, it was probably obvious. "Last night in my dream the woman spoke and, holy mother of gold, her accent was the same as the alley man. I kid you not."

Her eyebrows hit her hairline. "That's a strange

coincidence. You had any 'I'm a crazy person' thoughts, Abbs?"

"Every day, every damn day. But this feels different. Or maybe I just wanted to hear the accent again so badly that I made her speak with it. I don't know." I was afraid to get my hopes up.

"It does make sense. You obviously feel a connection to this man and his wicked accent." She shrugged. "But since I've misplaced my army tanker, there's no way you're getting me out on those streets."

"Chicken." I knew her instincts were to rise to a challenge.

Her brows narrowed, blue eyes flashing her annoyance. "You know my requirements, Abby. Do you possess the skills to use a decaying dead animal as shelter? And would you recognize the right plants to eat should we get lost?"

I snorted. "Did I miss the memo? Was the compound shifted to Africa overnight?"

"You can never be too prepared. Just saying."

"If Bear Grylls bred with Chuck Norris, I would be their love child. That's how skilled I am."

Lucy's face remained carefully blank. "Thank you for that disturbing imagery. But we both know Chuck Norris needs no one. He creates children from thought alone."

"Agree to disagree, Luce. I'm a Bear fan all the

way."

Crossing her arms, she leaned back to observe me. "Despite the fact it's lame to still discuss shows from twenty years ago, you will never defeat Chuck."

I shrugged. "Twenty years? You're being a little generous to old Chuck. And some shows are just timeless."

"And why are they timeless? Oh, that's right – the television industry imploded on itself and no more shows were created."

"Valid point." I changed the subject. "So are you ready to leave now?"

Running shaky hands through her blond curls, she groaned. "You're lucky you're my best friend and those people are hard to replace, Abby."

"I knew you'd cave. Let's go."

She rolled her eyes, but followed me as I skipped down the last few stairs.

I looked back. "Your life would be so boring without me."

"Imagine that, a boring life, one where we both lived to, like, thirty. Definitely overrated."

"I know, right. What would we possibly do with all those extra years?"

Unlocking the door, we left without any drama.

Exiting the compound, we both performed security checks and then were on the street front.

We hadn't been given security clearance until after our seventeenth birthday. I have no idea why they decided that was a good age, although most of the girls don't leave the compound until they're kicked out at eighteen.

In the deserted morning streets I couldn't sense any trouble. I guess gangers like to sleep in too. Lucy followed my lead as I started jogging.

Hurrying along the dirty, desolate streets only reminded me how much had changed in my life.

"This is what New York looks like now?" Lucy was aghast. "What the hell happened?" She hadn't been out since we were kids; the city was almost unrecognizable.

I shook my head, my breathing even as we powered along. "People happened. And, like history, they keep repeating themselves. These power-hungry dumbasses just keep on sucking the world dry."

"It feels wrong. There's something really off; I'm holding my breath waiting for the end of days or something." The strain showed across her features.

"I thought I was imagining it, but a definite undercurrent of malevolence has been growing steadily over the last few years."

During human relations class, a subject I

struggled to endure, our teachers went on about how people are just animals deep down. Decency and morals were merely (and unsuccessfully) cultivated to keep society running smoothly. But once the dark depression started, that pretense disappeared. Even the rebels don't particularly care about using people. They might not be as blatantly cruel and destructive, but I guess that perspective simply depends on whether you hold the power or are the victim.

Shaking off my dark thoughts, I led Lucy across the last road and into the alley.

"Wow, Abbs, could you have found a creepier alley?" She jumped, wrenching painfully on my bruised side.

"Did you see THAT?" she screeched in my ear.

I shook my head. "I'm not worried about seeing anymore. It's my hearing that's been severely compromised."

She shoved me. "There is no way you missed that. It was a giant bat ... or ... no – it was a rat, with wings."

I laughed.

She glared and yanked me further into the alley.

"Just hurry the hell up. I feel much more comfortable at the compound. Our own little piece of terror and despair."

She then refused to budge from her spot near the

entrance.

As I moved into the alley, small particles of daylight penetrated the gloom. It was clearly empty. Remembering my hiding spot, I double-checked the dumpsters on my way back.

As I walked toward Lucy, a strange sensation trickled up my spine. Spinning around, I searched for the source. This was familiar, an early-warning system. But the alley was still empty.

As the cold shivers continued to traverse my spinal cord, my vision wavered. I shook my head to clear it when a sudden headache stabbed at my temples. The alley was trembling, spinning. I struggled to remain upright; I couldn't pass out and leave Lucy alone. Screaming sounded from far away and the pounding continued. Dropping to my knees, I cradled my head in my hands. Unable to take the pressure anymore, it was a relief when consciousness faded.

Awareness returned quickly. I waited, eyes closed, but the pain didn't return. *Excellent*. I probably had some rare brain tumor.

"Well, that was the strangest..."

As I opened my eyes, my heart stuttered a few times. Looking around frantically, I tried to comprehend what I was seeing. Instead of ankle-deep in alley scum, I was sprawled in immense fernlike bushes.

Alright, this is fine, no need to panic yet.

There was an explanation for this. It was eluding me at that moment, but there had to be one. Like, I hadn't woken from my little blackout in the alley and this was a dream. A fantastically realistic dream, where for the first time there was a distinctive and pungent pine scent in the air.

In a daze, I pulled myself up. Stepping over to the nearest plant, reaching out, I gripped the shrubbery. The green foliage broke off easily in my hand. It was slightly crunchy, contributing to that pine scent. I let out a short burst of hysterical laughter.

Keep it together.

The sound of strong wind, like the noise of an immense cyclone powering through the forest, had my head whipping around. Breathing shallowly, I ran through the possibilities in my head. Crazy beast, angry native, axe-wielding lunatic.

As it moved closer, I knew I had to get out of sight.

I glanced around. There was nowhere to hide.

The crashing was louder now; I was running out of time. Hopping on the spot in panic, I dived under a large-leafed plant with unusual red spiky foliage. The itching started immediately, my eyes watering as I struggled to stay quiet. Through a small gap, I caught a blur of colors. They dashed past me. Masculine laughter trailed off.

Waiting an extra moment, unable to stand the itching any longer, I wiggled out. My ribs were on fire as I dragged myself backwards from the bushy plant. What the hell was with that? I'd never felt physical pain in my dream world before.

I froze at a crunch behind me, but by the time I spun around it was too late. A heavy body crashed into me. I stifled a shriek as the impact sent both of us hurtling toward the ground. At the last moment the huge lump twisted and managed to land next to instead of on top of me.

My head was throbbing where I'd slammed it into the ground and my first attempt to open my eyes had spots dancing. I flinched as hands began a methodical investigation along my body. He was either checking for injuries or groping me. He paused, his hands resting on either side of my face. This gesture felt strangely familiar. Sanity returned in pieces and my eyes flew open. The light still burned but I ignored my tearing eyes to pound on his rock-hard chest.

"Get your hands off me. I expect to be bought dinner before I'm felt up." I sounded snarly, but it had been a rough day so far.

As my eyes adjusted, his concerned features came into focus. Blinking stupidly, I shook my head, once, and then again. The picture didn't change. And I knew why those hands felt familiar.

Rich brown eyes examined me in a disquieting manner. The warmth of his body was soon replaced by a chill as he moved away. Which was worthy of noting; the weather was sunny and warm.

"Sorry about that. Did I hurt you?" There it was again, laying assault to every sense I possessed.

That accent.

Although, his was a little different again.

As shocking as it was to hear the potent and lilting sound, that wasn't the craziest part. How could it be when the man of my dreams, literally, was crouching before me? Well, maybe it wasn't so strange. This was a dream. Well ... that was my explanation, and I was sticking with it.

Seeing him in three-dimensions was … intense. I ran my eyes over his strong masculine features, short dark hair that fell in a mess across his forehead and perfect full lips. He was at least six-and-a-half-foot tall, with delicious expanses of golden tanned flesh showcased in well-worn jeans and a fitted shirt.

I was speechless.

And the eyes, those amazing eyes, fringed with incredible, and probably unappreciated, thick black lashes. Every time he blinked, the lashes cast shadows along his defined cheekbones. I bit the inside of my cheeks as I continued to unashamedly gawk. I needed the pain to distract from him. He was aesthetically beautiful but somehow still masculine. I felt extremely inadequate in the face of such perfection; it wasn't natural.

"Sorry again. I didn't expect anyone to be in the forest. Well, other than Lucas." His words brushed over me soothingly.

Lucas must have been that first person, the one I had actually avoided. I attempted to pull myself together. As a distraction, I began brushing off the leaves, pulling a few strays from my braid.

"I'm fine, no harm done." Avoiding his gaze, I couldn't help myself. "What's your name?" Information I'd been waiting years to know.

"Brace ... Brace Langsworth," he answered in a relaxed manner. A smile spread across his face.

Of course he had flawless white teeth; a blemish wouldn't dare mar his perfection. I had the uncanny feeling that he was somehow connected to the man from the alley. In small ways he reminded me of him. Something about the cadence with which he spoke and manner he held himself.

"Feel like returning the favor? Your name?" His gaze never wavered.

"I'm Abby."

There was so much more to say. Questions flew through my mind. But he had me stunned. I'd never met any person as instantly appealing as Brace. And it wasn't the looks, which, don't get me wrong, were a hundred percent sex appeal, hotness. No, it was something more. Like the man from the alley, there was a comfort that shouldn't be possible from a stranger. Shaking my head, I attempted to act like a normal person. I doubted Brace was privy to our dream familiarity.

As he stood, I couldn't help but notice his grace and coordination. He offered me his hand. His eyes were daring me to trust him. Briefly hesitating, I placed my hand into his. He smirked as he engulfed my palm and pulled me to my feet. Expecting to be set free, I was stunned when he wrapped his right arm around my back and pulled me closer. Looking up into his perfect face, I knew there was nothing romantic in this embrace. Nope, more like kidnapper.

"What are you doing in the royal forest, Abby?"

His tone was suspicious, which in no way detracted from the appeal of his accent. *Who is this guy when he's not making dream appearances, the forest police?* Wiggling impatiently, I worked to free myself. The entire time Brace scrutinized my features.

"I'm going to say this one time only, you giant behemoth. You have, like, thirty seconds to get your hands off me or we are going to have an issue." I attempted to throw an elbow into his gut, but somehow he anticipated the move and managed to avoid it.

As I continued my pointless struggle, his expression remained stern, but his eyes had lightened slightly. Strangely, he relaxed his grip.

"Your accent is foreign. Where are you from? Surely you know it's a crime to be without displayed papers, especially in the royal forest."

As he locked me in his stare, I forgot to breathe. Damn those amazing eyes. His brow was wrinkled slightly. Reaching forward, he brushed a lock of hair from my face. One of those wayward curls had escaped my braid.

"Who are you?" He said it as more than a simple question.

Realizing it was either breathe or pass out, I sucked in some air.

"I don't understand your ques–"

I didn't get any further. Pain and darkness pressed in on me again and the disorientation was back. My vision blurred and I was pitched forward. Landing on my hands and knees, the concrete bit painfully into my palms. Where had I landed now? I opened my eyes just in time to be pulled to my feet.

"Where the hell have you been, Abby?" Lucy was furious, staring down like a tiny demon.

She was shaking and tear tracks were defined on her cheeks. Her blond curls stood up, as they did when she was stressed and had been running her hands through them. She looked like hell.

"What do you mean?" I said. "I was here, just passed out in the alley." *Delusion, thy name is Abby.*

"No, Abigail, you disappeared right before my eyes. You disappeared." She confirmed our combined insanity. "I've gone crazy..." She trailed off before bursting out again. "What the freaking hell happened?" She clutched my arm.

"You will not believe me." I barely believed me and I was there.

"Try me." Her tone was dry. "After the last twenty minutes, my mind's wide open."

I sank against the alley wall, Lucy slumped down beside me.

I shook my head. "It started with this wicked head spin and pain, so much pain I blacked out. And what do I see when I open my eyes – forest."

Lucy's expression remained calm but her eyes turbulent.

"Forest ... there are no forests near New York."

I exhaled loudly. "I know what I think happened. And if some type of hallucinogenic gas wasn't just released in this alley–"

"And we can't rule that out," Lucy interrupted.

"Then I was just transported to my dreamland,"

I finished in a rush.

Silence echoed throughout the alley.

"Right," she said. "Wait, what?"

Her eyes were wide enough that I was worried they were about to fall out of her head.

I nodded a few times. "Yep, your expression right now says it all."

"We're insane, Abby. This doesn't happen in real life. People don't disappear or transport to dream worlds."

"Well, what's your explanation?"

She stood and, with hands on her hips, looked around.

"We both died, dead as a doornail, and now we're living in some type of weird alternative dimension of purgatory."

Tears of laughter ran down my face. The shock had caught up to me. Lucy wasn't really that funny.

Pulling myself together, I stood and attempted to straighten my clothes. As I brushed at my shoulder, three leaves drifted to the ground.

"Do you see them?" I said in barely a whisper.

"Holy mother of gold, Abigail. Are they leaves?" She turned to me in horror before clutching me close. "Tell me everything."

I started slowly, but my pace increased as I moved through the story. "I woke in the forest. It was the same as my dreamland, but so much more real. It was tactile. I could hear, smell, and touch. More three-dimensional than any dream I have ever had. And he was there, Luce." I winced at the painful memory. "It wasn't exactly the first-meeting I anticipated."

She knew precisely who I was talking about.

"You mean ... your dream-world hottie?" She stomped her foot. "This is crap. All I ever dream about is horses dressed as knights, who are riding horses into battle, and weird little worms building mud houses. But Abigail gets to have full-on man-candy fantasies – which then come to life."

"Seriously, Luce? Let's be grateful your dreams don't come to life. Horses riding horses? How exactly does that work?"

"So the hottie finally has a name."

"Yep, Brace Langsworth. And no man-candy fantasy was re-enacted. Although ... it was sweet." My smile dimmed slightly. "And just a little confusing."

"Disappointing, more like – if he's as good looking as you say, then you wasted a perfect opportunity."

And just like that I was grinning broadly again. "He was better, Luce."

She pouted. "That's just mean. I want one, Abbs. Get me one."

"Oh, yes, your majesty, I'll get right on that."

Hot damn, I wanted one too. "But, more seriously, did I mention that he has the accent too?"

She shrugged. "Everyone you meet lately seems to have this accent."

She made a valid point.

I grabbed her hand, holding on tightly. "You want to know what I think? Something really strange is going on."

She laughed. "Did you come up with that all on your own?"

Wrenching her arm as I bounced on my feet, I attempted to keep my voice low. "I think this place actually exists. Somewhere that's peaceful with green plants and hot jerky guys who run you down in the forest."

"A secret, peaceful place that has escaped this war and we need to find it immediately."

I levelled a glare on her, before realizing she was dead serious. No sarcasm at all.

She continued speaking. "We also need to find the alley man. He said he was your watcher, and I'm going to loosely interpret that to mean guide slash taxi to dreamland."

"Well, holy cold day in hell. I did not predict that reaction from practical old Lucy." While she was an optimistic person, she didn't do fantasy very well.

"Hey, I'm open-minded. I've believed your craziness for years. What's one more thing?" She smiled, her expression thoughtful. "I knew how much you love your dreamland and I never said anything, but I'm secretly a little jealous. You had this whole world I could never be a part of, even if it was just in your crazy mind. But now, well, I'm going on a little bit of faith."

"So we're agreed: stalk this alley until the man appears again."

She bopped her head a few times. "Agreed. And let's call him Ralph. Alley man is not working for me."

"Agreed."

Ralph was not manly enough, not even close, but it would work for now.

We were both bouncing. Never for one moment had I believed my dreamland was real. But now ... well, for the first time I was excited to turn eighteen.

Chapter 3

It was reckless, but we hung around that alley as much as possible over the next three days. For once the streets were eerily quiet. No gangers or rebels crossed our path. There was probably a rebel mission somewhere, which was a big-time gangers' distraction. That morning we waited as long as feasible before we had to leave to make it back to the compound in time for fight class.

Relishing the chance to work off some of my frustration, I stepped onto the blue mat with Chrissie. As one of the few girls near my height, we were often teamed up to fight. That day it was Muay Thai. Which was one of my favorites. It suited the long-limbed and toned litheness of my body. I might lack Lucy's curves, but I utilized what I had.

I flexed my fingers. I may have wrapped my wrists a little tightly that day, but they would loosen during the round. We fought no-holds-barred; they prepared us well for the possibility that we would get our butts kicked as soon as we stepped onto the streets.

Chrissie and I faced off before bowing in the traditional manner. Our instructor nodded, and as soon as Chrissie slammed her knuckles into mine I started to dance. Muay Thai is light on your feet and constantly moving. She came straight at me; her style was direct.

I dodged the first jab from her left and kicked out. I managed to make contact with her thigh before she darted away. I followed close behind, throwing my own right hook, which she blocked. We continued in this manner, but with my unrelenting direct attacks Chrissie was starting to slow. I had so much extra energy; there was no way she was taking me down.

After a few minutes of blocking, jabbing, back-and-forth sparring, I managed to pass her guard, throwing out my right elbow and connecting soundly along her cheek. With a squeal she went down and appeared to be staying there. Looking up at me, one hand to her face, she grimaced.

"I concede. Abigail's on fire tonight."

I laughed, rubbing a painful spot on my arm. "You got quite a few good hits in yourself. I'm just glad that elbow missed your nose." Reaching down,

I pulled her to her feet.

She shook her head. "Tell me about it, plastic surgeon. I like my nose just the way it is."

It's not the nicest nickname. I've rearranged a few noses in my time. I might be a little competitive.

Bouncing off the fight floor, I dropped down next to Lucy. I proceeded to unwind my straps, before throwing them aside.

"Well, you enjoyed that a little too much." She was lying on her stomach, arms tented in front of her with her face resting on her hands. Two other girls had stepped up for their round.

"I love fighting. I'm just glad my ribs are finally pain free. It was so frustrating sitting out for the last few days."

"I wish they would change the blue mats. They smell like sweaty ass." She screwed up her tiny nose. "Although it is incentive to stay on your feet."

Blue mat.

Cursing loudly, I shot to my feet. Gesturing to Lucy, I ran from the room. She was right behind me. How could I forget something so important? The moment she'd mentioned 'blue mat', the memory had been triggered. Reaching our room, I waited for Lucy to step inside and then slammed the door shut.

"What. The. Hell. Abbs?" She gasped each word out.

"I'm such an idiot." I tried to keep the panic at

bay. "I forgot until you mentioned 'blue mat'. The woman in my dream, Luce, she told me to find the blue stone."

"What! How could you forget that?" she screeched. "Next time, write your dream down or something."

She stopped scolding; her expression was now shrewd. "Because if you had mentioned it before I could have told you that recently I've heard reference to a large sapphire rock." She paused. "During some innocent eavesdropping. What are the odds that this is the very stone you're looking for?"

I narrowed my eyes in disbelief. "Innocent? You? Don't be ridiculous. What were you really doing?"

"Never you mind, Abigail. More importantly, it was Olden I overheard, on a communication radio. I only caught the last part, but she said the sapphire's location had been compromised."

Well, that was interesting. "Do you think it could be the same stone? Why would Olden have it?"

"No idea. As far as I know, Olden hasn't left New York in twenty years. Maybe she's from dreamland." She shrugged.

"Yep, that would be my luck. Knew there had to be a catch."

Lucy laughed. "Maybe the stone's not significant

to your dream world, just something we need for our journey there."

"Need, as in we need to sell it and make lots of money, or need as if it will lead the way like a giant bat signal?"

Lucy shrugged. "Either way, we clearly *need* to find it."

"Easier said than done. Olden doesn't exactly advertise her secret hiding spaces." A sudden thought gave me some hope. "Possibly, though, if her last hiding spot was compromised, then she may have moved it here for the interim."

"Although I'm finding it suspiciously convenient that it was only last week she mentioned it."

Very convenient. *Wait* ... I bit my lip as a flare of excitement flooded me.

"Luce, what day is it?"

"It's the twenty-sixth day of the eleventh month."

My voice rose in pitch. "And what does Olden do for the last five days of every month cycle?"

Her face lit up.

"She leaves the compound to meet with the resistance. Giving us all a much needed break from her delightful presence." She smiled. "And we'll have our best chance to find the blue stone."

"New plan – blow off all of our classes till we

find the stone."

Lucy smiled and nodded. "Awesome, I like this plan. First thing we should do is pack a getaway bag." She was way too excited about a possible mission.

Rushing around like a crazy person, I managed to gather my meagre possessions and haul them into a bag. Lucy was on her side of the room, surrounded by clothes and shoes, moaning about what to leave behind.

I couldn't help my chuckle. "Just wear five sets, one over each other."

She glared. "You're not taking my pain seriously. It's like leaving my children behind."

She held up a pair of faded denim shorts with an intricate white cotton patterning over the pockets.

"These shorts are from 2015, Abigail. Do you know how difficult it is to get hold of vintage clothes?"

"Probably less difficult than trying to run through the streets with two tons on your back." I was still grinning. "Just saying."

"You only 'just say' that because you have no idea what I do for them."

I knew exactly who her contact was, but I let her have this little mystery.

"Toss a coin, Lucy, and let's get this show on the road."

I left her grumbling about being an orphan, having no coins to toss, best friends who have no idea of fashion, and went to have a quick shower.

Feeling so much better, I was jumping out just as Lucy appeared.

"You'll be relieved to know I'm now packed and have said my goodbyes."

I heard a few sniffs as she closed the frosted glass door to the shower.

"That's a relief. The stress was almost too much to handle."

There was no answer as I dressed in comfortable black sweats and runners. Either she was ignoring me or hadn't heard above the sound of the water.

Standing in front of the mirror, I ran a brush through my red hair, although when it was wet it was dark enough to look black. Once again I went for my trademark braid down my back. Lucy was finished now and dressed. She pulled her curls back into a high ponytail.

I met her gaze in the mirror and she grimaced. "I'm so glad we got clean, only to start searching through God-knows-what to find a hiding spot."

I laughed. "If we're lucky, the stone will just be sitting on her bed." I held open the bathroom door for us to exit. "So, first obstacle: where do we begin looking? I was always under the impression that

Olden sleeps in the rafters like a bat."

Lucy snorted. "Actually, Abbs, her room is on the next floor."

"Good to know you're clued in to where evil rests."

"No special evil radars here. I helped her move some junk up there once. And by help I mean she stood to one side and gave orders while I lugged her crap up three stories."

I laughed drily. "Sounds like Olden."

Dumping her towel down the chute, Lucy nodded. "I cannot wait to be rid of this place."

"Word."

Leaving our packs on the bed, we shut the door to our room. It was easy to make our way unnoticed through the halls. And not because, as Lucy put it, we were stealthy. Everyone was still in class. Lucy led the way up a narrow staircase, before pausing at a small landing at the top.

"This is her suite." She waved both hands in a grand gesture to the doorway.

"Of course Olden would have a suite," I muttered. "Is the door locked?"

While lock-picking is in my repertoire of skills, I didn't have a kit on hand. Lucy leaned forward and twisted the knob; it rattled but was definitely locked up tight. Reaching up, she brushed her hands along the doorframe. There was a tinkle and a small key fell into her palm. Smiling in triumph, she held it up.

"Olden's laziness finally came in handy. She didn't bother changing her hiding spot."

She clicked the lock, pushed open the door and bravely stepped into the unknown.

"Taking one for the team, Luce?" I followed her in.

"I got this one but you can have the next." She smiled. "Which is sure to be much worse," she finished under her breath.

Over her head, I was visually exploring Olden's suite.

"One thought has immediately sprung to mind." My voice echoed around the room.

"Is it 'What a thieving bitch'?" Lucy snarled.

It was a big room, huge actually, and it was full of very valuable food ration boxes.

"What is she doing with these ration boxes?" Lucy's outrage was clear.

I shook my head. "I don't know, but if we find donuts or coffee in any of them, Luce, Olden's a dead woman."

At least thirty boxes were scattered haphazardly around a humongous four-poster bed. There was also one other door.

Threading my way through the boxes, I yanked

it open. Dull white tiles reflected back at me from the empty bathroom. There was a sheen of soap scum and dust layering the entire room. I opened the few drawers on the washstand, but they were all empty. Poking my head out, I saw Lucy was checking out the bed.

"I don't think Olden stays here much. The bathroom's empty."

"And there aren't any sheets on this bed. So where does she sleep?" Her voice was strained as she lifted the heavy mattress off the frame.

"My 'bat in the rafters' idea's not so crazy now, is it?"

Moving toward the closest rations box, labelled in large black letters as 'noodles', I ripped off the tape. I stared at the contents. Shaking my head, I moved back to see the side again and then the contents again. There was something very wrong going on here.

"Uh, Luce, you better get over here and see this." Finished her inspection, she moved across the room to stand next to me and we both stared down. "There appears to be some labelling mistake here," she drawled.

"Yep, I've never seen noodles quite like these."

The box was full of hundred-dollar bills. Neatly bundled into huge chunks. Money still ran the rebels and gangs, so it was an incredibly valuable commodity.

She gripped my arm tightly. "Holy shit! We have to get out of here, Abbs. This is bad, very, very bad. People kill for much less money than this." Panic threaded through her voice.

I shook my head at her. "We need to check the rest of them. I have to make sure the stone is not here."

"Well, only one way to find out." Lucy let go of me and without pause upended the box onto the floor.

The bundles tumbled out in an avalanche.

"Nothing else in this one," she said. "Let's move on."

Okay, well that was one way to do it.

We continued throughout the room.

"Why would she keep all of this money here? Not exactly a safe spot." I wiped back a strand of hair that had fallen in my eyes.

Lucy snorted out a harsh laugh. "Where could be safer than in her bedroom that has a spare key sitting above the door frame? Hey!" She gave a shout. "I found something."

Looking up from my box, I saw Lucy had a chain dangling from her hand.

"It's an engraved pendant. *To our darling Lucinda. We will be back for you.*"

"Lucinda, as in the blonde with the smart

mouth?" I remembered her from martial arts class but I'd never really spoken to her.

Lucy lifted her shoulders in a massive shrug. "I would assume so. Didn't she leave last year?" It sounded like a rhetorical question, so I didn't bother to answer.

With a heavy exhalation of breath, I continued to the next box. "Of course Olden would steal from us. The woman has no soul."

"So, if you're lucky she has the stone because she's a dirty rotten thief. Not because she's connected to dreamland." Lucy winked at me. She might just have found the silver lining.

With renewed determination, we finished checking the boxes. The floor was covered in wads of cash. Slipping along a large pile, I stumbled onto the last box. Ripping off the tape, I opened it.

For the first time there was no cash. Instead she'd been storing stones: precious and semi-precious.

"Yo, Luce. Olden's been stealing stones from more than me."

Finished with her boxes, Lucy made her way to me.

"Do you see any blue ones?"

I sifted through them, letting the multitude of silky smoothness run through my hands. They looked like a combination of valuable rubies and less precious diamonds. The market had been flooded with simulated diamonds through the years, lowering the value.

There was a loud thump from behind.

I swung around, expecting Olden to be standing over us with a baseball bat. Instead, it was … my mouth fell open.

"Tell me you are seeing that?" I managed to splutter out.

"If by *that* you mean the large blue stone which seems to have magically appeared in the center of the room…" Lucy didn't even sound surprised.

We were getting good with the strange.

I stepped closer. "Is this a joke? What are the odds the very stone we're looking for would just appear?"

She laughed. "This fits perfectly for the weirdness lately."

I reached forward, hesitantly, to pick up the stone. I was waiting for the hitch here. I paused a moment before my hand was about to graze the smooth side. Taking a deep breath, I scooped it up. It was warm, as if humming with its own life-force. Holding it close to my chest, I glanced around waiting for the ambush. The room stayed quiet.

Lucy laughed and started humming her favorite 'end of day's' theme song.

The stone was heavy, about the size of a large baseball. A dark, depthless blue. There was an odd indent on one side, but the rest was perfectly round. I jumped as a swirl of color spliced through the deep blue. I sucked in hard, the dusty air tickling my throat. This was so not a stone. This was ... well, not a damn stone. I could feel it to the depths of my being: this was power.

"That's freaking gorgeous, Abbs. We should cut it up and make jewelry."

I shook off my sudden premonition and threw a light-hearted smile at Lucy. "Of course you would want to take our one chance to escape and turn it into a fashion statement."

The girl should have been born when there was still a fashion or design industry.

Luckily my sweats had some decent pockets – I stored the stone. I didn't want to waste time dealing with it until we were out of Olden's lair.

Glancing around the room, I flipped the end of my braid over my shoulder.

"Let's get out of here. I don't particularly feel like rumbling with Olden."

Lucy snorted. "I think she's going to know we were here." Her sarcasm was not needed. The hundred-dollar bills coating the floor painted a clear enough picture.

"She's got to be involved with the gangs." A niggling thought was annoying me. "Head of a compound – millions of dollars – you thinking what

I am, Luce?"

She nodded. "Yes, Abbs, I believe I am." She looked around the room before turning in my direction again. "Actually, I don't have a clue."

I snorted and continued. "I always knew there was a reason I didn't trust Olden with directions to the adult compound." I clenched my hands together tightly. "The bitch sends us to the gangs. It's the most logical explanation."

Comprehension and horror dawned in Lucy's eyes.

"Are you saying that when we turn eighteen, she directs us toward the gangs? Why haven't the resistance discovered this? They pay her to look after us, oversee our training and education, and still they never notice that not one of her girls ends up in the adult compounds."

My anger was burning inside of me, threatening to spill over. "It's not really surprising. The adult compounds are even more secretive than ours. One junior compound is nothing in their great scheme." It was disgusting. "And on that lovely note, let's get back to our bedroom and get this stone safe. We'll have to deal with Olden later." God I hoped I got to deal with her.

We left without a backwards glance. The halls were still empty. We were back in our room in no time. I placed the stone into an inner zipper of my pack.

"Well, Abbs, we have the stone. Now what?" Lucy had shouldered her pack. "I'm standing by for our next instructions."

"Very funny, Luce. You're determined to turn this into a ninja mission."

"Hell, yeah, might as well have some fun with it. And I am dressed all in black. What better reason for my lack of color palette?"

"We need to get out of here now. Sorry, I know this is your worst case, but we're going to the streets."

She shrugged. "The alley can be our home base until we figure out what to do."

I nodded. "Good idea, but we can't wait around there for too long. If Ralph doesn't show up within, let's say, two days, we bail on New York. It's just too dangerous."

"Word. But we have to warn the other girls before we leave."

"We'll hit the classroom on our way out."

Shouldering my pack, I followed Lucy from the only bedroom I'd ever known. And I couldn't have been happier. The girls would be in language class, so we headed down the stairs and toward the school hall. Reaching the double doors – there was no need for discretion – Lucy shoved both doors wide open. They smashed into the back walls and every face swung in our direction. Stepping up next to Lucy, I surveyed the other girls. A variety of ages, ethnic backgrounds and cultures stared back at me. The years of turmoil on Earth had lessened many of the things that used to divide people. Now it was more rebel versus gang or militia. That was at least one small positive. Miss Crabbe was furious, hands on her bony old hips at the front of the room.

"What do you two think you are doing? Either come to class or don't, but I don't appreciate the interruption."

"We just needed to let the other girls know something and then we're gone." I turned to the room. "Don't trust Olden. If you trust her, you're as good as dead. And don't take her instructions after you graduate from here."

We had no time to sugar-coat it.

The girls were silent, their expressions saying 'What the eff?'

The teacher's eyebrows rose slightly, which for her was a huge display of emotions. "What are you saying?"

"Olden's room is on the third floor. Lucy and I just came from there and the place is full of money. So much cash she could only have received it from the gangs. We think, instead of giving us directions to the compounds, she sends us off to the gangers."

Lucy added, "And on a side note, some of the

boxes had jewelry and personal items. You should make sure she doesn't have anything of yours."

Shock, disbelief, and fear flashed across the silent faces. Then chaos erupted. Chairs went flying as the girls shoved past us to head for the stairs. Angry voices raged as they exited the room. Chrissie paused next to me.

I met her eyes, my lips tilting in a warm grin. "Chrissie, sorry I never had a chance to take you out of the gates."

She shook her head. "I'll figure it out, Abbs. I've never trusted Olden. Long story for another time, but I was planning on going my own way."

She waved to her friend, Chandra, who was paused in the doorway. "I can't leave Chandra, and she's not ready to take the plunge out on to the streets yet. But good luck out there. I think we'll see you soon."

I grasped her hand briefly. She gave it a quick squeeze, before walking out the door.

"Girls! Girls! Stop right now." Miss Crabbe's screaming was largely ignored. She spun to face us. "This is completely ridiculous. There's no way such an operation could happen. Not under the rebels' notice."

Lucy scoffed. "Really? And when was the last time someone, other than teachers, who couldn't care less, actually visited this compound?"

Some of the speech registered with her – probably the part about teachers not caring less. She gave us each a long look before leaving the room.

I turned to Lucy. "Best case scenario, she reports this to someone higher up the rebel chain, and they may do a little investigating."

She shrugged. "Don't hold your breath. We're never going to be a priority to them. But we might have created some trouble for Olden."

"Hopefully we gave the girls a chance. It's better than nothing."

It was time to leave.

There were a few nerves. I was just hoping we lived long enough to enjoy our adventure.

"Do I look like I'm freaking out, Abbs?" Lucy turned her perfectly serene face in my direction.

"Um, no actually, you look very calm."

She smiled. "Awesome. I was wondering if it showed. A ninja never reveals their emotions."

"You're not a ninja."

"Go rain on someone else's parade, Grinchiness."

As we left the room, echoes of smashing objects could be heard in the distance. Music to my ears.

Chapter 4

As we walked out of the compound, the sun was encased by dark ominous clouds, casting the streets in shades of gray. Shrugging my pack higher, I led the way to the alley. We needed to set up base before nightfall. Lucy's shorter legs struggled with my pace, so I slowed. Still, it only took a few minutes to reach the alley entrance.

Lucy puffed hard. "Damn, I'm unfit. I need to start jogging, if this running-for-our-lives thing continues."

"Told you escaping the compound was useful. I'm always running for my life."

We moved along the alley. When we reached the red dumpster, I threw my pack down beside the wall. "We should move this away from the bricks, get in behind it."

Lucy dropped her pack too. "Abbs, I'm wearing

Vuitton runners. One doesn't move bins in Vuittons." They were bright purple runners, with large yellow stars on each side.

I shook my head. "Luce, you have two seconds to start moving this dumpster or I am dropping you back to Olden."

Sighing, she moved at a snail's pace around to the side.

I ducked to the front. As I braced my hands to push, I sensed a disturbance behind me.

I spun and cursed. *Oh hell*. We were in trouble.

Three men stood in the alley entrance, blocking the exit.

Dark-blue facial tattoos were evident against their light skin. Tribal in design, the minor members' were simple, the higher ups more intricate, identifying them as Brawler Gangers.

"Abby," Lucy whined from behind the dumpster. "Are you helping? What the hell? Ouch! Broke a nail ... I'm okay. Don't panic."

Her attitude would be funny if we both weren't about to die.

"Uh, Luce, you might want to step out here."

She appeared next to me, cradling her right hand. Noticing the looming men, she sighed. "This is bad, right?"

The shortest of the three stepped forward: someone of such average appearance he'd go unnoticed in regular society. Dirty blond hair, weedy build, small angry eyes. Before the war he'd definitely have been part of the stimulating field of accountancy. It's always the ones with short-man syndrome.

"Look what we have here, brothers, two delicious morsels ducking into this little out-of-the-way alley." He had a distinctive New York accent, clipping off the ends of the words.

The man on his right was darker and more solidly built. His tattoos less prominent, he sat somewhere in the middle of the gang totem pole.

"Ya, Jass, they have conveniently wandered themselves into our territory. Now, what should we do with them?"

"Is it our territory? Wasn't youse just saying yesterday that the Kleps had this one?" With biceps the size of mini trucks, the third was the epitome of brawn over brains.

"Shut it," Jass spat.

They fell silent.

"So, Abbs, I'm starting to think there's an excellent chance these are the last faces we'll ever see?" Lucy and I were creeping back. We had about ten feet to the wall.

"Fate could not be that cruel. Shouldn't it be beauty at the end, not 'thing one, two and three'?" I said.

Judging by the drawn eyebrows and blank stares, my words confused them. Guess Dr Seuss wasn't on their reading list at gang school.

"We're going to fight, right, Abby?" Lucy said breathlessly.

I nodded. "Hell yeah! I'm going all eye-of-the-tiger, pose-like-a-crane on their asses." I smiled – never let them see you sweat – it's the principle.

"Crane? Seriously? You should at least choose dragon or spider, you know, something that might actually scare them." She flexed her hands, tightening them into fists before releasing again.

The men continued to advance toward us, their expressions smug and satisfied.

"I'm pretty sure they've been studying menacing behavior in *A Morons' Guide to Gang Member*." Lucy had decided taunting them into submission was the way to go. She shook her head. "Stop me, Abbs. You know when I'm nervous my mouth runs away."

"Jass, did you hears what the short one said? Jass? She called us morons. Let me have her. C'mon, Jass."

Jass didn't even glance his way. His fist simply swung out and smashed straight into Stupid's face. Which barely moved.

Great – his face is made of rock.

"There goes our hope they'd beat each other to

death," I snorted at Lucy. *Focus, Abby.*

Stretching my wrists, I stepped back to settle into my favorite fighting stance.

Lucy met my gaze her smile widening. "Calling 'plastic surgeon' to the ring." She turned to the men. "Hope you aren't planning on keeping your noses in their current shape." She shrugged. "I guess anything would be an improvement."

Despite her continued taunting, I knew Lucy was ready too. She was bouncing lightly and her eyes were focused.

A cruel smile crossed Jass's face. His anger filled the space like thunder rolling in over the plains. I knew then he would not be taking me alive. Rape and torture awaited us at his hands.

"We'll teach you respect before this day is done. Trust me on that." Jass low voice spoke for all three gangers.

Lucy's word-vomit continued. "Okay, I'm about ready to panic now."

In that moment, a flash of green clothing crossed my peripheral vision.

I ducked.

My training kicked in and I threw a right hook before diving out of the way.

"Oh, for the love of Klaus."

I heard cursing. I'd connected solidly.

A shadow towered over me and strong hands

gripped my arms.

"Aribella! Hasn't anyone told you not to attack people here to help?"

The moment his accent registered, I stopped struggling. I locked onto a pair of brilliant blue eyes. "Ralph? Where did you come from?"

He looked confused. But Lucy knew immediately who was standing between us. She engulfed him in a huge hug. Well, the best she could, only coming up to his waist. He froze, glancing down in confusion.

"Thank God you're here, Ralph. I thought we were goners." She pulled back. "Damn, you're tall."

Laughing, I yanked Lucy free.

"Meet Lucy – best friend – insane." Lucy glared for a moment, before sighing in acceptance.

The gangers were standing not far away, looking extremely irritated.

Jass spoke for the trio "What the hell is going on here? Where did he come from?"

Lucy whipped around to glare. "Quiet, morons, we'll get to you in a minute."

'Ralph' laughed out loud, infectiously. "I like her, Aribella. She's a keeper."

Lucy preened a little.

"And my name is Quarn," he grimaced. "Not Ralph."

Lucy shrugged. "Close enough."

He rubbed his jaw. "That was a nice right hook, Aribella. But it might not be enough to get the job done."

Before I could reply, he pulled a thin sword – the length of my arm – from somewhere in his clothes.

"What the crap? Is that a sword?" Lucy was wide-eyed. "Where did he pull that from?"

"Probably better we don't know."

He was impressive, looking ten years younger – warrior and his weapon.

"I haven't had a decent battle in a while. Should be fun, don't you think?" His blue eyes sparkled.

"Damn, I'm glad you're on our side. You're a little crazy," Lucy said bluntly. "You know that, right?" She turned to me. "Surely someone's told him before."

I shrugged. She smiled now. "And totally loving the accent. I know what you're talking about now. It's pure magic."

Quarn quelled his smile, but I'd still seen it.

Lucy was cute – she was one of those people that grew on you – like fungus.

He faced the gangers, his expression calm and serious. Without saying a word, he raised his right hand, palm up, and gave the old 'come and get it' signal.

"What gang are you from? Display your markings," Jass called along the alley. He wasn't retreating yet, but the sword had given him pause.

Quarn remained quiet. The men shifted nervously.

"Where are their weapons, Abbs?" Lucy was bravely cowering in Quarn's shadow.

I kept my voice low. "In my street experience, most gangers carry knives, but not guns." The gun shortage was implemented to prevent inter-gang fire. Ganger leaders used to be taken out regularly. Now only a trusted few have the 'hardcore' weapons.

Quarn moved then, advancing toward the men.

Jass, Other, and Stupid held their ground for a moment. Their hands twitched at their sides, but in the face of Quarn and his sword they must have decided against using knives. Jass, expression deadly, gave me one last look before he gestured to the men, and they scurried out of the alley – like rats.

"They'll be back, with many more," I said to Quarn's back.

He turned and smiled. He'd already sheathed his sword – somewhere.

"I have been on these streets for a long time, Aribella. There is nothing here that I fear."

Lucy challenged him. "You know her name is Abby, right?"

"Outer names are nothing. They can change with

the winds of time."

Uh ... what?

"Nice work, Quarn. Once again I have no idea what you're talking about. But before you disappear, we want to find dreamland. Can you help us?"

He smiled. "Your words are just as confusing to me. Dreamland?"

Oh, right.

"Sorry, that's my really original name for this world I dream about. There was a woman, she spoke with your accent so..."

Something close to worry – disbelief maybe – crossed his features. "You dreamed of home? How is that possible on Earth? It's a dead zone."

I shrugged. *Dead zone?*

"You should have gone to 'dreamland' many years ago, Aribella. It has other names, but once again I find myself with too many stories and not enough time."

"Why...?" I looked around. "Why am I still here then?"

Lucy interrupted then. "Could someone speak in English? Just for five minutes." Annoyance replaced her usual cynicism.

Quarn's already strong features hardened further. "We need to get Aribella back now. The countdown is on for both of these worlds. And it's too dangerous to be roaming New York." He sighed. "The reason you've been here for all of these extra years is ... I don't have the power ... and I lost contact."

Lucy glanced at each of us in turn.

"I'm really hoping when you say *Aribella* needs to go to dreamland, you mean Lucy and Aribella, and you just forgot about me." She crinkled her nose at me. "He just forgot me, right, Aribella? Crap. Sorry..." She grinned. "It's a catchy name."

I shook my head and sighed. "I'm not leaving without Lucy, no matter how annoying she is."

Quarn had paced a few steps away toward the alley entrance. He spoke over his shoulder. "You cannot go, Lucy Laurell. It is no place for an Earthling. You must stay here."

Did he just say–? Hell. NO.

"I'm going to ignore that. Your not-very-veiled implication that I'm some type of alien ... well, it's just rude."

"Are you kidding me? Don't ignore it." Lucy interrupted me to glare at Quarn. "What do you mean: 'Earthling'?" Her voice dropped to a whisper. "*Is* Abby an alien?"

I groaned. It was time for the conspiracy theories.

"I knew it." She was triumphant. "There's no way someone gets to be as gorgeous as Abigail and *then* is also tall. On top of that her lips are full and perfect and naturally red without one ounce of lipstick. Come on, it's not natural."

"You're not natural," I retorted weakly.

Lucy was always harping on about how unusual my lips were. I was just happy they matched the blood-red of my hair and not the black.

Lucy glared. "Oh, I'm sorry, Extraterrestrial. Did you forget to put your happy skin on today? What, is green not your color?"

Quarn interrupted. "Sorry to cut this short. As amusing as the pair of you are, we need to move before the gangers regroup. I'm good, but even I have my limits." He was still near the entrance to the alley, scoping it out.

"I'm. Going. Nowhere. Without. Lucy." I had to spell it out.

He looked between us for a second before nodding. "It does not matter. I don't have the power to send one of you there, let alone both of you."

"How do we get more power?" Lucy looked around eagerly. "I'm ready. We digging for coal ... oil?"

I laughed. Fossil fuels. We'd have more chance of finding a magic wand.

He shook his head. "Nothing on Earth. The dead zone is more encompassing than we'd ever anticipated. I'd need a storage amulet, which is rare.

A sacred stone, even rarer. And, as a last resort, a power on the other side to assist."

I smiled. It spread broadly across my face. "Quarn, this may just be your lucky day."

Moving to the wall, I retrieved my pack before reaching in to unearth the stone. Cupping it with care, I held it out in front of me.

"Is this a sacred stone?"

It was impossible to describe his expression. A sense of reverence fell over him. He stepped forward, laying a hand lightly, respectfully, on its blue surface.

"No, this isn't, Aribella. This is something much more than that – it's one of the royal pair, the most important stones in our world. Your ... mother sent it with you ... I thought it was lost." He whispered the last part.

I interrupted. "*Mother?* You know my family?"

He nodded. "Your mother, Lallielle, is one of my oldest friends."

I shuddered, trying to fill my compressed lungs with air. "Does she have long dark hair? Green eyes a little lighter than mine?"

He nodded again.

I swallowed loudly, my throat suddenly dry. I'd guessed right for once.

I was filled with a strong urge to find her. "She was in my dream. She told me about the stone and then it just appeared. Could she have anything to do with this?"

He shook his head. "I don't know. Which is not a comfortable place for me. I would have said not possible, but with the dream-spanning Lalli must have found a way." A thoughtful look crossed his features. "The stone has power. It may have decided that it would come to you."

He was reiterating my previous feelings: this stone was powerful. Still, I wasn't that comfortable with its sudden appearance after so many years absent. In my world the very things you either want or need do not just appear before you. I'd proceed with care when it came to this stone.

"So now you have enough power, right? To get us to dreamland. Abby needs to meet her family." Lucy's blue eyes were huge.

Quarn held out a hand for the stone. At the last second before it left my hands, I realized I didn't want to part with it. Despite my hesitation, I released it. We were out of time; I was surprised the gangers weren't back already.

He cradled the solid weight to his chest. "I don't know if this will work. My aim is to open a doorway, long enough for two energies to cross. Then it will close. No one will be able to follow and you will not be able to return."

I grabbed his arm and, yes, may have stomped

my foot like a child.

"Two? How many ways do I have to tell you? I'm not leaving without Lucy."

He stepped away, dispelling my hand. "No, Aribella, it's I who cannot leave." His demeanor changed. "There's something I can't ... won't ... leave yet. The time-frame has been accelerated and I'm not prepared."

He seemed oddly vulnerable; the normal piercing of his blue eyes were dulled. I would have pried further, but a sense of panic consumed me.

"How will we survive without you? We have no idea what we're doing."

"You're stronger than you think, Aribella. Don't doubt your instincts. I have seen them serve you well on these streets. The same skills are required when you step through the door."

Lucy linked her arm through mine. "Abbs! You haven't told him about the forest incident."

Oh, right. I'd momentarily forgotten about that odd little trip.

"The day after we met, I came back to this alley to find you. This crazy pain, like knives carving into my skull, struck, and when I opened my eyes I was in the 'royal forest'. I trailed the last word. "How could this happen? What does it mean?"

Quarn gripped my other arm, pulling me closer. Lucy wasn't budging, so her tiny frame flew as she was dragged along.

He spoke with intensity. "What happened there? Did you meet anyone?"

"Well, there were two people there. Someone named Lucas, who I didn't meet, and Brace. He ... uh ... crashed into me in the forest."

He drew his slightly bushy eyebrows in to form confused lines across his face. "I don't understand, Aribella. Of all the people that could have pulled you there, people far more important, why was it Brace?"

"I don't know," I murmured. "But Brace and Lallielle are the two from my dreams."

Quarn shook his head. "There must be a connection there. Something I do not know." He looked uneasy. "You need to tread cautiously with Brace. He had not been around long when I left, but he has always struck me as odd ... unnatural."

"Probably Brace's sexy hotness. From Abby's description, that's unnatural." Lucy turned to look at me. "Kind of like Abby's hotness."

"Luce, shut your trap."

She saluted me. "Yes, your majesty."

Quarn shook his head. "How did you know, Lucy, that the sexy-hotness of Brace is always the first thing on my mind?" His voice was deadpan.

I spluttered out my laughter. Quarn's sense of humor was unexpected.

Lucy simply nodded, as if she was not surprised.

"Lucas is the emperor's son. He is the last of his line. That might be important information for you."

I looked at Lucy. "We're so screwed."

She nodded.

Sadness shot through me as I examined Quarn's weathered features. "Will I see you again?"

"I don't think your time in New York is finished, *miqueriona*." He gave a half-bow.

It was so old-fashioned, I couldn't help but smile.

Cradling the stone in his hands, Quarn stepped away, and within seconds his lips were moving, speaking quietly. From the bits and pieces I was hearing, it was not English.

A shimmer like a thousand fireflies descending in sync to form a veil, setting the alley wall alight. But it was gone as quickly as it appeared.

Quarn shook his head, his lips moving even faster, the intensity building.

It started slowly this time, like a whirlwind building strength.

The misty glow fell over the alley again. I stared in fascination at the beauty of the shining wall.

"It's just like those old Christmas trees covered in fairy lights," Lucy whispered.

I nodded, captivated, unwilling to move.

Quarn moved closer, disturbing my love-fest.

"Safe journey, little ones. Find Lallielle. She will help you to embrace your destiny."

He zipped the stone into my pack and, stepping around, his blue eyes were surprisingly gentle. His stern features softened as he leaned down and laid a kiss on my forehead. Tears pricked my eyes, but with a deep breath I kept them at bay.

"Keep the stone safe and secret, Aribella. It will seem peaceful there, especially compared to New York, but don't be deceived. These worlds are more parallel than you think."

"Well, that's comforting. Thank you," Lucy interjected, hands on her hips in impatience.

He smiled. "You two look after each other. It's rare, in all of the worlds, to have someone you trust."

Right ... all of the worlds ... wait, what?

He nudged me forward, toward the shimmering wall. Taking a deep breath, I grabbed Lucy's hand. But I didn't have to worry about her backing out. She was out in front, dragging me through. I closed my eyes at the moment of crossing.

I wasn't sure what to expect, a tingle, some type of whooshing sound, but it was calm, like stepping through an opaque mirror. One step and we were on the other side.

Chapter 5

I sucked in a few deep breaths. Wafts of cool, fresh air drifted lazily through my lungs. It was intoxicatingly clean, no soot, smoke, or pollution. I wondered how I had missed this the last time I was here.

"Oh, my God, Abbs, are you breathing? Tell me you're breathing." Lucy was next to me, eyes closed, face raised. "Un-freaking-believable."

I shook my head. "I keep waiting to wake up and find I've been in a coma for the past week."

Lucy's quick grin should have been my indication, but she was too fast, reaching over to punch me – a solid hit to my biceps.

"Ouch! What the hell was that for?" I growled at her, rubbing my arm.

"I was just testing your theory. You don't feel pain in dreams, or coma-dreams."

"Oh, right. And you know this how?" I rubbed harder. *Where was she hiding those muscles?* "You just wanted to punch me."

She shrugged.

I shook my head before taking a moment to look around. I should have been freaking out. I knew it. But instead I felt this great sense of relief. "There must be elevated oxygen levels here."

"So, are we going with alternate universe? Another planet?" Lucy's voice was calm. Deceptively calm.

"I have no fracking idea. I'm still trying to get my head around the fact I'm standing in dreamland."

She snorted and widened her eyes at me. "Did you just say 'fracking'?"

I shrugged. "I'm trying to clean up my potty mouth. You know, meet your mother, get mouth washed out with soap."

"And you think ... fracking ... is the way?" She threw me a look of dismay. "That's effing terrible. Just stick with swearing."

I couldn't help the chuckle that escaped. "Are you kidding? It's the best. There are at least three different curses in one."

She disregarded this with a wave of her hand. I knew how she felt – arguing with a crazy person could get tiring.

"So this is your dreamland, Abbs? It's very ... green." She was swinging her head around trying to take it all in.

I laughed louder. Lucy must have been expecting her dream land – shoe stores.

"It's so wild and ancient looking." She craned her neck. Her blond ponytail ruffled in the light breeze. "These trees are out-of-control tall. I think the clouds are floating through their branches." She dragged in large deep breaths. "And this air – ah-ma-zing."

I nodded. "God, yes, especially compared to the crap we were breathing in New York."

Dust lived in New York air, like some type of symbiotic relationship. Of course I'd never really noticed until right then just how bad it was.

"Does it feel like home? I can't believe your mother is here ... somewhere. Think about it, Abbs, you're not from New York – maybe even Earth." Her face fell.

I nudged her gently to break the mood. "So I'm an alien from the jungle," I said, looking around. "Technically, here – you're the alien."

Lucy's expression lifted. She nodded. "Word. Let's pick a direction and get this show on the road."

Through the towering treetops, glimpses of the sky shone through. White fluffy clouds dotted around the dark blue-ish purple. Yes, you heard right. Purple. Shaking my head, I tore my eyes from the sky to stare at Lucy.

"Can we take a minute to address a few things?" I held a finger up. "One – it was afternoon and freezing in New York. Here–" I squinted into the sun. "I'm guessing mid-morning and hot, hot, hot."

I lifted the hem of my shirt, trying to rediscover the cool breeze. The heat was different to any I'd felt: heavy and damp. Drops of moisture already beaded my forehead. I raised a second finger.

"And the sky is freaking purple."

Lucy shook her head at me. "Purple – seriously, Abby? Have I taught you nothing? It's indigo." She sighed. "I might have to get out my color chart again."

"Purple – indigo – maroon. The important part – the sky should be blue." I took a deep breath. "And I live in constant fear of having to sit through 'what color suits Abby?' again." I raised my voice in a high-pitched imitation of Lucy.

She proceeded to both flip me off and stick her snooty nose in the air. "One day my skills will serve us well. You just wait and see. And I got nothing with the sky. I'm just going to pretend it's normal."

I looked around. We were standing in the center of a jungle that was denser than I remembered from my last visit to crazy town. I couldn't determine any path through the vegetation. From our compound stash, I'd packed a few energy bars and three bottles of water, but that wouldn't last long. We needed to find shelter first, followed closely by food.

"Is that a slight pathway through there?" Lucy pointed out a small gap between what could have been two bright green ferns.

That was my guess, anyways. We had no plants back home to compare. And pictures did not give a great representation.

I tilted my head, trying to see around. "There doesn't seem to be a path anywhere. We'll have to push our way through and see what's on the other side."

I moved first, the foliage hugging close on either side. Once we were past the initial large bushy plant, a type of path did appear, widening enough for us to move more freely.

"How old do you think this forest is?" Lucy swatted away at some small flying bugs as she followed. "These trees are as tall as skyscrapers."

I looked up again; the trees were massive and intimidating. I felt like a dwarf walking amongst the giants. And the noise – life echoed throughout – a chorus of insects, birds chirping and sporadic rustling throughout the undergrowth. There was nothing stagnant here.

I brushed my hands through the shiny silkiness

of some leaves. Sticky sap coated my fingertips when I pulled back. "This entire forest looks ancient. Back home, long ago they'd have demolished this for a housing complex or something equally useless. "

I wiped my hands on my pants, all the while thinking of how bad Earth's over-development problem had been in the early twenty-first century, throwing its entire eco-system out of sync. Now New York had thousands of abandoned buildings, but zero food – priorities, people.

I gestured to nearby flowers, gorgeous orange blooms. "Imagine how pretty New York would be if there were still flowers and trees. This is the way a world should look."

Lucy was also brushing her hands through the leaves as she walked. Before she suddenly started to shriek. "Eeeeeek ... eek ... crap! Get it off." She was jumping up and down, spider webs trailing along her arm and in her hair.

Laughing, I helped de-web her. Luckily, there was no sign of the web owner, although Lucy made me spend an additional ten minutes double- and triple-checking her hair.

Finally she relented, shuddering as she looked around. "You know, at least when there're less plants there are less bugs, and that's fine by me."

Lifting my face, letting the sunlight bathe me in

its glow for a moment, I shook my head. "Not me – I love plants. When I was younger I'd sneak around the compound burying seeds, but the soil was too dry and leached of nutrients. Nothing ever grew."

Lucy's eyebrows rose in astonishment. "Are you freaking kidding me? How could I not know that about you?"

I laughed. "Gardens aren't exactly your thing, Luce, so I just kept that little quirk to myself."

She nodded. "True, I can appreciate the beauty of nature as much as anyone, but I'm more about the clean sheets and walk-in wardrobe." She pulled at some missed web and leaves in her hair. "Although it's growing on me. There's something recharging and peaceful here. It's hard to describe."

After trekking for thirty minutes, I paused to mop up some of the sweat. We had taken our coats off but it was still stifling hot. Retrieving a bottle, I took a huge gulp of water, letting small amounts run down my chin. I handed the half-full container to Lucy and looked about in misery.

"Is this a forest or a sauna?"

Lucy peered around me as she stashed the now empty container in her bag. Her hair hung in damp clumps, pale skin slightly pink and flushed.

"Does the undergrowth look like it's thinning over there?" She pointed to the tree line about fifty feet away.

Shifting my pack higher, I changed direction. As we moved closer, I could see what she meant. The undergrowth was tapering off to reveal a small clearing in the forest. My eyes took a few minutes to adjust. The canopy was thinner, the light extra bright. I noticed a strange reflection near the back.

"Tell me you're seeing that house?" Lucy whispered, practically climbing my back to see over my shoulder.

I squinted again. Finally the scene came into focus. "Holy moth– shut the door," I managed to splutter as I stared.

There was a house tucked into the trees, and I'd almost missed it. And no, my sight wasn't failing – the entire house was camouflaged. It looked just like the forest.

I moved into the small clearing. Four steps in and I was standing at the left side of the house. I glanced around furtively before leaning in closer. The material was unusual, smooth with no visible joins. I reached out to examine the texture, but did a double take as my hand reflected back at me.

"It imitates its surroundings, Abbs." Lucy leaned her face closer, laughing as her blond-haired, blue-eyed image reflected back perfectly.

"That's pretty damn clever. It allows the building to blend into the forest." I was impressed. "This is so 'not in New York'. The gangs would be all over this to hide their lairs or whatever they call them."

Lucy nodded. "So this is an extremely advanced part of Earth – right?"

Even I could tell she didn't believe that, but she'd reverted back to denial, the best kind of ignorance.

I shook my head. "You heard what Quarn said. Do you really think we're still on Earth?"

Grimacing, she stuck her tongue out at me. Before I could retaliate, a bang shattered the silence.

We both jumped.

My heart galloped in my chest, threatening to burst out like a weird alien baby.

Lucy crouched low. "Ahhh – what the hell was that?"

"I think we might be about to see our first inhabitants," I whispered back. I was pretty sure the noise had been a door slamming open.

Lucy gripped my arm and gestured toward some large trees framing the back of the house. They weren't going to offer much cover, but better than being caught in the open.

Moving quickly, we made it just in time. Through the branches I spotted a man standing in the exact spot we'd just vacated. And – wait for it – he was tall. Notice the pattern: Quarn was tall; Brace even taller. Even I was reasonably tall. I looked down at Lucy; she was going to hate it here.

"Guess I know where your ridiculously unfair height advantage comes from," she whispered indignantly.

I was determined not to laugh at Lucy's predictability. She was so touchy about her height.

As we watched, he turned on the spot, surveying the forest from all angles. He looked to be around thirty, with blond, shoulder-length hair tied back against the nape of his neck. He was good-looking, but in that boring guy-next-door way, with lightly tanned skin and a few laugh lines framing his eyes.

My attention was suddenly drawn to a large black baton resting over his shoulder. I shuddered, thinking about being smacked around with that. It looked kind of lethal. I was distracted from this by movement close to his feet. Emerging from near-by ferns, an enormous gray animal padded over to sit beside him.

What is that? I turned questioning wide eyes to Lucy. She was mesmerized, her mouth open. I turned back. The only comparison I could think of were pictures of a pack of wolves from my animal textbook. The basics were there: body shape, four legs, pointed ears. But everything else was slightly off, its features more elongated, its eyes extra-large and intelligent.

I'd always wanted a pet – what kid doesn't? – but

animals were rare in the city – practically non-existent. And don't ask me why. Trust me, it's better you don't know.

"Bady, I don't see anyone, but the alarm did sound. Can you take this side of the zone and I'll patrol the west end." The man looked down as he talked to the animal.

Lucy nudged me, not that she needed to. I'd heard – same accent again. There was a smooth quality to this man's, something Quarn's lacked, although I preferred the throaty quality of Quarn's voice. It was more real.

Taking into account how foreign this land was, I wondered again about their ability to speak English. I shook my head. Yet another question to add to the growing list.

Bady took off at the command. Either he was well trained, or animals were far more intelligent than I'd been led to believe. The man disappeared around the front of the house.

"Got a plan yet, Abbs? That animal thing is heading our way," Lucy asked worriedly.

I peered back through the bushes. Bady was running in diagonal strips, sniffing the ground as he went.

I spoke quickly. "Either we speak with the man, play dumb and see where we've ended up ... or we make a run for it and hope to find a town nearby."

Lucy looked around nervously. "Not really a fan of the stick he was carrying. Let's make a run for it."

I nodded. That was my preference too.

Holding hands, we backed through the trees. Ten feet later, we turned away from the house.

"That way." I pointed to the less foliaged area.

Freeing my hand, I pushed Lucy to move first. She sprang out of the bushes. I was right behind her. We hurtled through the dense growth. I couldn't see a thing in front of me and winced as the low branches and vines whipped and stung. Glancing over my shoulder, I was relieved to see no pursuers yet. My gaze snapped forward at Lucy's yell.

I immediately saw the cause of her alarm: a strange gleam suspended in the air.

We were too close. No way to avoid the impact.

Lucy hit first and flew back past me. Closing my eyes, I threw up my hands and cushioned the collision, before a loud thump catapulted me backwards. With no time to panic, darkness claimed me.

Chapter 6

A heavy pounding reverberating through my head was the first indication of a return to consciousness. I drifted through the haziness for an unknown period of time before disjointed memories intruded.

Oh, right – dreamland.

Gasping, I sat upright and forced my heavy eyelids to open. Biting back panic, I looked left and right.

What the eff?

Not even a sliver of light broke the endlessness. I'd either recently gone blind or I was somewhere in complete darkness. I fumbled around with my hands. I was tucked into what felt like a soft bed. I clutched at the edge of the fluffy covers, pulling them up to my chest.

I was clearly no longer in the forest.

This place was cool, with none of the damp heat

from outside.

I tried to remain calm, but without being able to see Lucy it was difficult to fight back the rising panic.

Reaching to my left, I choked on a scream. Jerking my hand back, I sucked in a few deep breaths. Someone was lying next to me. Reaching out again, I felt a small relief as familiar fluffy hair grazed my fingers.

That hair belonged to Lucy. Not some weirdo in bed next to me. Lucy.

Grasping her shoulder, I shook. "Luce ... Lucy ... wake up. We have to get out of here." My voice echoed.

But she was still, only her deep and rhythmic breathing indicating life.

I had no idea where we'd ended up – in the camouflaged house – or somewhere else. The man probably had my backpack and the stone, which, something told me, was not going to look good as I pleaded our innocence. And besides that, I hadn't even been its keeper for a day and I'd already lost it. Good job, Abby.

A groan distracted me. Hair brushed my arm as Lucy shifted.

"Luce – get your butt up, sister." I reached out in the general direction of her shoulder again.

Lights flared in the room.

The brightness forced my eyes closed.

Taking a moment, I re-opened them slower this time. The disorientating black dots disappeared quickly as the room came into focus. I could finally analyze our surroundings. Lucy and I were on a huge bed, covered in a fluffy white throw. A bedroom – furnished simply. A large wooden dresser stood against the wall and a dark brown, high-backed armchair was squashed in the corner.

The reason for the sudden light show was standing in the doorway: the large blond man with a crowded tray perched precariously on his left hand.

We stared in silence.

He broke the moment by stepping into the room and placing the tray on the foot of the bed. He then sat in the armchair.

I jumped as a hand landed on my arm. I looked down to find Lucy staring at me. She was paler than normal and her blue eyes were huge and questioning. I shook my head: *stay quiet*.

"I suppose neither of you will speak first. So let me begin – why were you attempting to plow through the iso field? You're lucky you weren't killed."

His voice filled the small room and, despite the situation, the accent was still soothing.

I examined his features. They seemed kind, fine

laugh lines softening his hard planes, but there was no way I would trust him. Despite a few questionable decisions, I wasn't a complete idiot.

His calm expression was soon replaced by a stern frown. His brow wrinkled, and the very dark nature of his eyes deepened as he again attempted to question us.

"I need to know what you are doing here. This is a restricted area for all except Royal Guardians, which I assume you're not." He looked at us pointedly.

With an annoyed sigh, Lucy pulled herself to a sitting position. She'd actually been quiet longer than I'd expected.

"You're doing an awful lot of assuming, buddy. You know what they say about people who assume." She drawled her words.

He looked completely blank-faced while he waited for her to continue.

Lucy looked at me, eyebrows raised. "Apparently he doesn't know."

He spluttered a little. "Well, I know you didn't enter through the screening gates, because you're without displayed papers. Give me a reason not to throw you straight to the Guardians."

Something about what he said stirred a memory. Right, the papers thing. Brace had mentioned that too. Glancing down at my hands, I found I was unconsciously twisting them over and over. We were in trouble. Lucy had already spoken, so he knew we weren't native to this land and we had nothing with which to defend ourselves.

"Say something, Abbs," Lucy hissed at me.

"What do you recommend that won't have us thrown to these Guardian people?" I whispered back hotly.

"They're taking these matters very seriously at the moment. The recent attempt from insurgent groups to infiltrate the palace has everyone on high alert."

Since I doubted he was just going to open the door and let us leave, we had no choice but to attempt to talk our way out. Before I could follow through with that, a loud rumble from my stomach echoed.

Shhh, I mentally berated my tummy. It appeared to be ready to eat my spleen, judging by the battle noises.

Lucy snorted with laughter, shaking her head.

I threw a haughty glance in her direction. "The food is a huge distraction and it's sitting right there." I pointed to the tray, from which tantalizing aromas wafted in my direction.

The man interrupted us again. "I apologize. My questions can wait a few moments. Please eat. You must be starving. You've been unconscious for many hours." He looked thoughtful. "Perhaps you'll be more inclined to converse once you're more comfortable."

Comfortable. Yeah, okay.

I love food, but not even the smell of warm freshly baked bread was enticing enough to forget we were being held prisoner.

Lucy had a different opinion. She dived over me toward the tray. "Out of my way, Abigail," she muttered on her way past.

I shrugged. "Sorry about that. Love of food wins out over manners."

Lucy stuck out her tongue but didn't break stride in her mission to uncover every dish.

"I wouldn't throw stones, Abigail. Often when I sit next to you at dinner I worry about the safety of my limbs."

Lucy had a point, and that was with the crap they liked to call food in the compound.

She distracted my retaliation by handing me a bowl. It was filled to the brim with a dark, thick stew that sloshed a little over the edges. I picked up the utensil, which Lucy had dumped to the side, and my mouth watered in anticipation. I sank the rough spoon-shaped device into the bowl and lifted the first steaming scoop to my mouth. A variety of colored vegetables and a dark meat filled my mouth. I couldn't savor that first bite long enough.

"Holy mother..." My eyes closed in pure love. "I want to marry this food."

There was no reply and, looking over, I did a double take. I couldn't see Lucy's face. It was half submerged in the huge bowl as she slurped down the stew.

I watched fascinated for a few moments. It was like an animal documentary, where the lions hacked into a zebra.

Shaking my head, I went back to my delicious stew, letting the freshness tantalize my tongue. The flavors were strong, full-bodied. I had no idea food could be seasoned with anything other than salt, but there was so much more going on here. There were small floating green pieces which, had we been back in the compound, would have been greatly concerning, but here might actually be–

"Luce, I think these green floaters are *herbs*." A sense of reverence coated my words.

Lucy pulled her face from the bowl to examine the contents. She nudged the surface of the bowl.

"I've heard of these so called 'herbs' from the older rebels' fairy tales. You know the ones that start with 'Back in the good old days.'" She shrugged. "I think they may have been right, though. This is a whole other level of tastiness."

I shoveled repeated spoonfuls until my initial hunger subsided. At that stage I had no choice but to slow and catch my breath. Lucy handed me a chunk of roughly textured grain bread, the source of the delicious scent. Using this, I soaked up the last of the liquid. I took the first bite. It was gritty, but delicious.

Chewing, I looked around. I was fascinated to see Bady padding silently into the room. Against the white walls, he appeared even larger and more bizarre than he had outside. Stretching out on the blue woolen rug, he went straight to sleep.

Blondie shifted in the chair. We locked eyes. It was time to speak up.

"Sorry, I'm a little disoriented from face-planting into your ... force-field." Can't beat the brain-injury excuse. "We're trying to make it to town ... I'm guessing we didn't quite reach our destination."

There had to be a town nearby. How else would he get supplies?

He raised his eyebrows. "No, you didn't make it to ... which town were you heading to?"

I shrugged my answer.

He continued anyways. "You're at the eastern castle outpost. I'm Deralick, custodian." He glanced between us. "Where are you from? I don't recognize your accent."

Lucy dropped her now empty bowl back onto the tray. I'd just shoved the last of my soaked bread into my mouth, so she answered for me.

"We live really far in the north, but we aren't welcome back there. Nothing too crazy, just problems with our parentals."

Her words were awkward. I don't know why we hadn't practiced a cover story before we found ourselves in this position.

Deralick looked dubious. "You don't look much like sisters."

I swallowed my bread. My throat felt irritated, scraped by the rough texture. "Different fathers," I rasped out.

He looked confused.

Come on, what planet was so perfect that there was no divorce or death? That was a family staple on Earth.

"I'm sorry to hear of this break in your family unit." His mouth lifted in a half-smile. "But that doesn't explain why you've ended up here. Since the emperor's illness, the three sides of the surrounding forest have guarded fields. It was announced via satellite uplink that anyone guilty of unauthorized trespassing could face the maximum penalty."

I guessed we didn't want to know what the maximum penalty was. *Thanks, Quarn – straight into the fiery pit.* Although, having been on Earth for seventeen years, he probably didn't know about these new 'laws'.

I looked at Lucy. She shrugged. She's always so helpful.

Well, we needed information. Time to play dumb.

"Honestly, we had no idea we were even in the royal forest. I don't know where we went wrong."

I should have left the dumb-blonde routine to Lucy. She played it perfectly. Hair curling and everything. Although, in its current disarray...

Sighing, I continued. "We, uh, like, don't even know where we are right now."

He raised his eyebrows, expression suspicious. Pushing the feeling of dread away, I wondered how much more trouble we could get into. We were already facing this unknown 'maximum penalty'.

"You're in the land of the emperor, the Isle of Itowa, which is part of the Jana province."

I remembered Quarn's words. *Lucas was the emperor.*

Deralick continued, adding to my confusion. "The council's in session at the moment. Hence the extra patrols. Grandier's security is top rate."

"Grandier?" Lucy questioned.

His face was expressionless as he stared at her. "The name of the planet." He shook his head, muttering quickly, "Field addled their brains." He smiled without much emotion and spoke. "I'm sure you just use 'First World'. I know most, under the age of a hundred and fifty, prefers Grandier's decidedly unoriginal nickname."

I looked at Lucy. She had the same 'oh shit' expression as I had. *Longevity of inhabitants – unknown.* But one thing confirmed. We were most definitely no longer on Earth. Dreamland was Grandier, with the apparent nickname of First World.

Deralick straightened, his features creased in worry.

Not liking his expression I distracted him with a subject change. "I'm Abby and this is Lucy."

Lucy waved, her blond hair sticking out in all directions, some type of dirt caked along her forehead, along with a light scrape on her right cheek. But she still had that sweet trusting face. Her deceptive looks were handy.

I shoved the tray back to the end of the bed. As I rubbed the bridge of my nose to release some sinus pressure, I realized the pounding head pain was back again.

Attempting to gather my woolly thoughts, I spoke without thinking. "I'm here to find dreamland. And my mother."

Did I just say dreamland? I shook my head in an attempt to clear it.

Deralick stood and retrieved the tray from where

it was haphazardly flung at the end of the bed.

I sank back into the pillows.

"Something is happening..." Lucy's words were slightly slurred. Then, without warning she collapsed into the pillow.

He stopped in the doorway. "I hope you can understand. I have a job and I take it seriously. Whether I believe you or not, I have no choice but to report all intruders for assessment."

I waited for panic – or any emotion – but nothing.

"You'll be interrogated by the royal council. If they find you innocent, you'll be free to go."

I was slipping further into unconsciousness.

With my last functioning neurons came the thought: the stew was drugged. Well, that was rude – if you can't trust strangers bearing food, who can you trust?

"It's only *laven* juice. It won't harm you. In fact, you'll have a restful, healing sleep," he said as he exited the room.

Well, at least we weren't dying – a faint shimmer of relief before I drifted off.

The dreams hit me fast. I was standing in the throne room of a castle. People were collapsing all around me, crying, begging and clinging to one another. I walked through the white marble hall unnoticed, seeing nothing to cause such chaos. I made my way up to the large chairs and stopped at the center pedestal. Resting on top was a purple pillow cushioning a pair of intertwined stones. One was my blue stone with a smaller red one sitting perfectly in its large side indent.

The royal pair.

The room disappeared. I found myself standing at the base of a black mountain. It took me a few moments to figure out why everything looked so dark. It was all dead. Withered black plant tendrils curled around my boots. I shuddered. Even in the dream an oily darkness coated the air. My instincts were telling me to run, to leave, and never return. The world started to move in fast-forward, swirling before me. Backing up, I tried to escape, moving and falling...

I regained control of my consciousness.

As I sat up, my eyes flew open. A low light threaded the room. Lucy was still asleep, or passed out. I knew, instinctively, we needed to escape from here now.

Reaching over, I shook Lucy a few times, with the same result as the night before: no movement, just deep breathing. I had no time to delay.

Looking left and right I spotted a large opaque jug on top of the nightstand. I grabbed the vessel. Water splashed over the side, onto my hand. Feeling a little desperate, I flicked some drops at Lucy. She didn't stir. Looking down at the jug, I sighed, she was going to kill me. I dumped the lot over her head.

"What ... where ... what the hell?" she muttered, sitting up quickly.

Her eyes were wide, but still held the haze of sleep. She wrinkled her nose before sneezing loudly, and then she fell straight back into the pillows.

Oh, for the love of...

"Get up, Lucy. We need to get out of here before Deralick 'drug-pimp' hands us over to the guards."

One eye squinted as she shook her head a few times, water droplets flying off in all directions. Pulling herself up to sit, she eventually opened both eyes. It took a moment before she turned to me calmly.

"Abby ... there'd better be an outrageously good reason for why I'm wet."

I shrugged, attempting to unobtrusively nudge the jug off the bed. "I have no idea why. You were like that when I woke."

Lucy closed her eyes. "Do not kill Abby ... she's your only friend."

I laughed in a loud rasp, almost choking. She opened her eyes and her answering smile was not nice. I jumped in before she could tear strips of me. "So, speaking of killing ... Deralick ... I'm going to kill him when he comes back to the room."

Reminding her of our common enemy had to be a good distraction.

"I'll help you hide the body." Lucy attempted to run her hands through her wet, ragged curls.

I laughed again. One of her hands was completely entangled. It took numerous attempts and a few torn chunks of blond strands before it was freed.

I snorted at her second attempt to tame the mane. "My recommendation – shave your head." Her hair was so tousled now it stuck completely out on the right side

"I probably wouldn't give 'recommendations' until you check your own reflection," she said, sticking her tongue out at me. She then hit me with a quick subject change.

"So, did you have some whacked-out dreams last night?" Her eyes widened. "I was locked in this freaky old-fashioned cell. There were people everywhere – some dead – dying. It was grisly."

I bit my lip and attempted to keep my expression neutral. "That's comforting. Bet you can't wait to sleep tonight." Jumping off the bed, I stretched my limbs. Despite the drugging, I felt great. I had no aches or pains from yesterday. "I did have some pretty vivid dreams, but nothing like that."

I pushed the black mountains from my thoughts. They were wrong and it would take many therapy sessions to delve into that one.

Lucy shuddered. "It barely felt like dreaming. I was there; the emotions were real and raw. I could smell the sweat and that salty tang of blood."

I gagged at the thought. She shook it off, her pixie features relaxing back into their usual cheeky grin. "Never mind, it was just a dream." She hopped off the bed. "So what's the plan? I'm not waiting around to be handed over like common criminals. Firstly, I'm anything but common. And, secondly, I need to brush my teeth. Urgently."

I ran my tongue around my mouth. Deralick's drug had left a powdery residue like a skin over my teeth.

I nodded my agreement. "Let's get out of here. We'll just have to forget our packs. If we can make a break for it, just go."

The only important thing I had was the stone, and either it had already been confiscated or Deralick, with all his rules, would send it back to the castle.

I moved toward the space where I remembered the doorway had been. There was just a blank wall.

"Where the hell is the door?" Lucy was next to me, running her hands along the wall.

"It was open last night." I squinted, but there wasn't even a join to indicate a doorway ever existed.

I hesitated at a low whirring sound. A split

second later, the wall disappeared, like a panel sliding out of the way.

An automatic door that vanished somewhere into the wall cavity.

Expecting to see Deralick, I gasped at the person filling the space.

Lucy stepped close to whisper in my ear. "Oh. My. Hotness."

I spun around, stunned at the burst of rage flooding me.

He is not yours, Abby. Step back, Miss Bitch.

Someone needed to slap me.

Brace, his expression serious, stood with his arms crossed across his broad chest. Even in my astonishment, I still found a moment to revel in his fallen-angel beauty. What was he doing here?

From the corner of my mouth, I mumbled, "Brace."

Lucy's mouth dropped open and, stepping back, she craned her head for a better look. She was incorrigible.

"I figured that one of the two 'unusually' accented females my father found wandering the forest was probably you." His features softened slightly as he smiled.

"Deralick's your father?" There was absolutely no family resemblance.

He gave a sort of half-nod.

Lucy smiled. "It's such a pleasure to meet you." She looked at me. "Abby told me about colliding with you in the forest."

"Did Abby also tell you that she disappeared? Into nothing."

He was glaring at me – locking me in the intense stare of his amazing eyes. It was always like this, whether in dreams or weird alley teleportations. The chemistry between us just about brought me to my knees. And always took my breath away.

Lucy interrupted our intense stare-off, allowing me a few ragged breaths.

"Been there, done that. Abby will give you gray hair. Trust me." She flicked her blond hair, as if to prove her point.

Striving for a pretense of normality, I kept my eyes off his gorgeous face, and away from his stupidly captivating eyes. That way I could speak and breathe.

I waved my arms a few times in their direction. "Alright, if you two can resist the Abby-bashing, maybe we should get out of here."

"Why are you here, Brace?" Lucy asked before I could step around her.

He turned to answer Lucy, and once again I was drawn in. Despite Quarn's warning, it was hard to defy the magnetic pull.

I ran my eyes over him. He was dressed for the

outdoors: a short-sleeved, fitted shirt and army-style pants. In shades of black and dark green, the material looked expensive.

I shook my head. *You don't know him.* Brace could be as stupid and shallow as he was breathtaking.

He was still speaking, so with effort I stopped devouring him with my eyes and focused on the conversation.

"... from patrolling last night, and talked to Father," Brace explained to Lucy.

His eyes flicked in my direction as he ran them over my features. The slightest smile drifting across his face.

I rolled my eyes. No way could he know I hadn't been paying attention.

"He does believe your story of being lost, but he's responsible. He'll hand you over to the royal guards." He ran his hand through his dark hair.

It looked slightly longer than he generally wore it. As if he was due for a cut but hadn't gotten around to it yet. I liked it much better than the military style he sometimes sported during our dreams.

He turned a bothered gaze toward me. "I'm not confident of the royal guard at this time. So I'm about to cause some real trouble."

"Forgive us if we don't exactly trust you or your

father." I shrugged, reminding my traitorous heart that he was a stranger. "Probably something to do with being drugged last night."

Lucy nodded. "Exactly! Just because you're standing there stupidly tall and unnaturally gorgeous, flashing those dimples and muscles, doesn't mean we're going to fall at your–"

I put my hand over Lucy's mouth, muffling the last few words.

"Sorry, Lucy's missing an essential filter between brain and mouth. I try to stand within arm's reach, because there's no 'off' switch."

He smiled. "Reminds me of Lucas. Someone should look into an off switch for them both."

He peered out the door. His voice was slightly muffled. "We need to leave. Father was out on patrol but he'll be back soon." He shrugged, facing us. "I'll accompany you to town. I might be breaking you out, but I better make sure you don't cause any trouble."

I exhaled loudly. Someone save me from bossy control freaks.

I looked at Lucy. "I say we trust him for now. We can ditch him later."

"You know I'm standing right here." His brow furrowed over the velvety brown of his eyes.

Lucy ignored him. "Tell me you're using your brain for this decision, Abbs. Remember what

Quarn said."

Brace reacted minutely at the mention of this. Or I may have imagined it. Either way, it felt like it was time to remind him who he was dealing with.

I stood to my full height, hands firmly on my hips. "Don't mess with us, Brace. Lucy is super talented with a razor and glue gun."

Lucy nodded. "That's right. Your eyebrows will never be the same again." She smiled. "And with that threat hanging over your head, let's go, gorgeous." She sauntered past him out the door.

As I watched him follow her I realized something. Which, if asked, I'd deny until the ends of time – I was feeling some very strong emotions; I wanted him around.

Also, I was determined to figure out his secret. And why he, of all people, ended up in my dreams.

Brace paused in the hall and nodded toward two familiar packs on the floor.

"I retrieved your bags. Deralick said he didn't go through them, so everything should be there."

Dropping beside my pack, I furtively checked for the stone. Everything was in its place.

"Thank God he didn't touch my shoes." Lucy had a pair in each hand, her favorite vintage pink Chucks in the right, and purple wedges in the left, which I personally found too ugly to exist.

"That would have not ended well for anyone,"

she finished, shoving them back into the bag.

"Were you actually worried that Deralick would have a use for your size five pink and purple shoes?" I pursed my lips as she rained glares on me. *Guess she had.*

"Let's go." Brace paused. "Do you need any help with your packs? It's quite a walk to town."

We both shook our heads; this was my second attempt at protecting the stone. And apparently Lucy trusted no one with her clothes.

Shouldering her pack, Lucy had a new distraction as she hopped on the spot. "Tell me the bathroom is close?"

Confusion crossed his features, but he answered. "It's just down the hall."

We followed him along the plain white hallway. He paused at an intersection; frosted glass doors were the only break in the endless white. Once again there were no latches, handles, hinges or any indication an openable door existed. The panel just slid into the wall.

With his right hand, Brace gestured for us to enter.

"Five minutes," were the last words he said as we stepped inside and the door slid closed.

I moved quickly into the small room. It was stark and clean, with zero character. Large white tiles lined the floor and walls. A glass-walled cube sat in the corner – beside it was the toilet.

Lucy sprinted in that direction, dropping her pack on the ground. My own discomfort growing, I distracted myself by walking to the large mirror running along the wall.

"What. The. Hell." I gasped at my reflection.

Half of my hair was still braided, the other half was teased into curly tendrils all around my head. Damn, I let Brace see me like this? I smirked at my reflection. *There goes any chance of him returning my attraction.*

Lucy snorted behind me. "I told you. Good luck fixing that."

Dropping my pack, I scrabbled around until I found my hairbrush. It was tied together with gel paste and toothbrush. Under the mirror rested a small clear bench. A glass bowl perched on top. As I reached into the bowl, cool water flowed from under the glass.

No faucet. Apparently we were lucky enough to have magic doors and magic water. I shrugged, plunged my toothbrush in and coated it high with paste. I hated an unclean mouth. I had a slight obsession with minty freshness.

Finishing quickly, I spat before rinsing clean. Then I attempted to tame my red mane. Untangling my braid, I attacked with my brush. It stuck at first stroke. Struggling to free it, I groaned as strands tore free.

A flush sounded. Lucy moved to wash her hands next to me.

I moaned my frustration at her. "I'd say two days from dreadlocks."

"Word." She again attempted to run her hands through her own snarled curls, which again ended in failure.

"It's not really fair, Abbs. I have bruises everywhere, and this awesome scrape." She gestured to the pink graze on her cheek. "But besides messy hair you look perfect, and too gorgeous as usual." She glared in mock annoyance. "What's your secret? Do you have a hidden fountain of hotness?"

I stuck my tongue out at her in the reflection. "You're insane, Lucy." I would kill for her curves and blonde beauty.

She shrugged, but didn't comment further. It was a circular argument we'd been having for years.

I worked hard and eventually my thick hair caved to the vigorous attack. Braiding the shiny curls off my face, I smiled. It was stupid, but my braid gave me a sense of normalcy. Lucy grabbed my arm as I moved to the toilet.

"There's no tissue. You'll have to use a few from my stash."

I looked down at the two small pieces she was

waving at me.

"Your generosity knows no bounds," I said drily.

She smiled sweetly. "It's that or your hand. We're on rations – I will not be using leaves, thank you very much."

Shaking my head, I moved to the toilet. It looked ultra high-tech, buttons and gadgets running along the right-hand side. The exact type of thing I would have broken in minutes. Ignoring the buttons, I was going with the hope it worked on the same basic principles as back home. Finishing quickly, I stood. Without any assistance from me, a loud flush sounded. Well, that was a nice change from the drop pits which had replaced flushable toilets in New York. Not enough running water for that little luxury.

Moving back to the sink, I washed my hands. Lucy was finished, dressed in fresh clothes, her two layers of mascara applied and everything. Grabbing my pack, I unearthed a new shirt and underwear before dressing quickly. This was one of my favorite black vintage band tees, last year's birthday present from Lucy.

Shouldering my pack, I followed her over to the door.

"How do they open? It's not a sensor. We're standing right here." Lucy jumped up and down, waving her hands.

Her bag just about toppled her backwards. She grabbed my arm to rebalance.

"No idea. I can't figure how anything works on First World."

Lucy leaned closer. "Oh, and by the way, you totally understated Brace: hot, hot, hotttt." She drew out the last, fanning herself.

I shook my head at her dramatics. "I told you he was gorgeous. It's a waste. I wouldn't know what to do with him."

Lucy opened her mouth. I interrupted before I could hear her sure-to-be suggestive ideas. "Remember, virgin here, almost eighteen and never been kissed." I wiggled my eyebrows. "Unlike Lucy – who makes out with the extremely good-looking Josh, the delivery dude – for shoes."

Her mouth dropped. But before she could respond, the door slid open.

Brace was standing exactly where we'd left him. His lilting accent filled the small bathroom.

"Let's go." His eyes lingered for a moment.

My face warmed as he turned away.

Lucy, already past my teasing, nudged me and whispered, "You're staring at him the way I stare at my vintage Manolo Blahniks."

I shook it off. I was stronger than this attraction. I'd seen Lucy actually drool when she stared at her shoes. Reaching up, I stealth-wiped at my mouth.

Thank the gods: drool-free.

We lagged behind. Even I struggled with his long-legged pace.

Finally we caught up to him.

He stood outside a half-size door and gestured for us to step inside. It was a laundry – not the room I expected to be staging an escape from.

Brace faced us, his white teeth flashing. "Well, Abby – and Lucy – since we're friends now, I'm about to trust you with a protected childhood secret."

He moved to the back wall and with little effort shifted a large white machine to the side. Bending over, he flicked a latch and lifted a trap door.

"This is an old laundry chute; it drops out into the forest." His grin was a little evil. "I used this to sneak out when I was young. The only problem was figuring out how to get back inside."

Judging by that smirk, Brace had been a terror of a child.

I peered into the wide space of the chute opening. "How long since you've used it?"

He laughed quietly, a sparkle lighting his deep brown eyes. "Quite a few years. My father pretty much lets me come and go as I please now."

Lucy pushed me aside to carry out her own inspection. "It's still safe, right? What if it's rusted away in places?" Her voice echoed down the length.

Brace shook his head. "Rusted? It's made from Destruck, and isn't even through a third of its thousand-year guarantee – it's safe."

Lucy snorted. "A thousand years ... I guess that's good enough for me."

Brace squinted at her as if he didn't quite understand the source of her sarcasm, though his lips did quirk into a half-smile.

"I'll go through first and see you at the bottom." He pulled himself into the opening, long legs hanging down. "Don't worry about the alarm and fields. I'll disable them." Then he pushed off and was gone.

"You're next, Luce." I pushed her toward the chute. "I'll be right behind, so get out of the way."

Lucy took a deep breath and climbed in. Then she too was gone.

I waited till last, I didn't want them to see me freak out. I was a little claustrophobic.

It's this or prison, Abby.

I shut my eyes tightly. No way could I get in with my eyes open. Hands out in front, I felt for the opening. Misjudging the distance, I found myself tumbling forward before plunging headfirst down the chute, my heavy pack powering me even faster. I screamed the entire way. Bracing myself, I managed to force a hand over the top of my head as the slide tapered off and I plunged out. Tumbling a few times, I ended up face down, my pack thrown to the side.

I stayed like that for a moment of reflection – and to determine what was broken – something sure felt broken. My pride, I think.

Strong hands gripped my arms and pulled me up effortlessly.

"Are you okay?" Brace asked, his eyes wrinkled in concern and amusement.

Lucy, on the other hand, had collapsed in laughter. "That was hands down the funniest thing I've ever seen," she managed to gasp out.

Brace set me back on my feet before handing me my pack. His lips twitched, but he saved himself an ass-handing by changing the subject.

"Since we are trying to avoid the guard, I suggest we move from here."

I scraped Lucy up off the ground as she continued to let out snorts of laughter.

"Stop replaying it or I will kill you and hide the body somewhere in the forest." I gestured to the masses of greenery around us. "No one will find you."

The laughter subsided for a moment, before she lost it again. I shook my head. Brace was already moving along the path, so, dragging Lucy with me, I hauled it to catch up.

Chapter 7

We walked in silence for a while. Except for the occasional chuckle from Lucy that made it clear – I was never living that entrance down.

Even with my bumpy start, I was relieved to be free. And back in nature. This area of the forest was different: less dense and more traveled.

And whilst we had a little more information, there were still so many questions.

Why was Grandier's nickname First World? I couldn't help but wonder. Was this an old world, much older than Earth?

Lucy broke the silence.

"What are those hugely round trees everywhere?" She pointed to the bulbous tree trunks surrounding us. She was a little breathless, her shorter legs struggling with our pace.

Brace flicked his eyes toward to the tree-line.

"The *sycaim* tree?" He shrugged. "Don't tell me there are no 'thud trees' where you're from?"

I wondered what he would think if he knew that, before yesterday, I'd seen about five trees, and not one was healthy or green.

We shook our heads.

He gave me a half-smile, before he answered drily, "They're First World's native trees."

Whoops.

He stopped suddenly and I almost collided with his bulk, but managed to avoid him at the last moment.

"They've been around First World since the beginning." Reaching down, he gathered a few loose stones.

Without any warning, he flung them into the trunk of the closest tree. As they connected, a loud thud echoed. Nearby, birds screeched before evacuating the treetops. I stared for a moment, fascinated by the huge animals as they flew out of sight. They were so bright, two blue and yellow, and one dark pink.

Brace distracted me by throwing another set of stones. He seemed to enjoy the noise.

I smiled at him. "They're hollow?"

He nodded. "When I was young, Father carved me a tree house in the hollow of a large trunk. They'll still continue to grow, even after that."

As we started along the path again, I realized I was enjoying having Brace as our guide, and my instincts urged me to confess our secret. We needed someone on our side; we needed answers. And if we continued with our obvious lack of local knowledge, he was going to figure it out soon enough anyway. As he led us through the forest, I couldn't help but follow him with my gaze.

For a big guy, Brace moved almost silently – his strength was clear – and my traitorous heart already trusted him. I shook my head.

You don't know him, Abby, I reminded myself for the tenth time that day.

"So, Deralick mentioned yesterday that things have been pretty rough around here lately." Lucy had her innocent face on. She was digging for information.

Brace nodded as he continued ploughing through. "The last twenty years have seen changes I never expected from First World. Of course, after a hundred-year peace during the rule of Emperor Christian and Empress Elisnarra, it's been extra hard to adjust." He paused to move a large branch off the path.

I took that moment's pause to contemplate how anyone ruled for a hundred years.

When we could move along the path again, he continued. "Now, with the emperor's illness, it won't be long before responsibility falls to Lucas and, at this stage, he's not ready."

Quarn hadn't been kidding when he said these worlds were parallel. "It's been chaos back home since ... well, our lifetime," I added.

Brace grimaced. "Darkness continues to spread throughout the land. It started at the black mountains." His eyes dulled, his expression grim. "The pure energies are being leeched away."

Lucy looked at me in confusion. She wasn't the only one baffled. I understood about a third of his words. But I knew the black mountains from my dream.

I had to ask. "Pure energies?"

"The energy of our land. The energy of our people. Those with active gifts have found a huge depletion in their abilities." He glanced toward me, holding my gaze. "Have you noticed the change? Or has it always been this way for you?"

"We're seventeen—"

Lucy interrupted. "Almost eighteen."

I eyed her. "Yes, Lucy ... almost eighteen." I let the sentence trail off.

A thoughtful frown crossed his features. "Well, I'm ... around twenty-two ... and I vaguely remember when things were better. But I'll say you've never known the best of First World. Do either of you have a specialty?"

Around twenty-two? Who spoke like that?

I focused on his questions and, thinking quickly, replied, "Well, we aren't really into 'categorizing' ourselves. What're your favorite specialties?"

I'd go with the same half-truths and diversion tactics he was using.

He laughed. "Quite the individuals, aren't you? There are many, but I do have a few favorites. Animal Affinity: they're usually out in nature with their animal guides. A little scary when riled – you don't want to take on the animal kingdom."

I exchanged wide-eyed glances with Lucy as he continued.

"Nature Spirit: plants bloom in their presence. Moonlighters: walk only at night to use the energy of the moon." He shook his head. "They're quite the strange ones." He looked around. "What else? The Flecho: love anything manmade. They're generally the inventors of our gadgets. Felens: read the emotional resonance of any place ... its history ... memories ... past emotions. And speaking of that, Emoters: manipulate all forms of emotion, best to be avoided."

I shook my head for a moment. Information overload. I wasn't going to remember any of this. But I'd love some paper. The nerd inside me wanted to jot all of this information down.

Brace continued. "Another group to avoid are the

Mesmerizers. Hypnosis is their skill, depending on the strength of an individual's mind and shield." His voice lowered. "You should always be wary of the gifted. Power corrupts."

I speculated whether everyone on First World was 'gifted' in some way, or only a select few.

"Word." Lucy nodded at Brace, her head bobbing vigorously. In typical Lucy fashion, she was just going with the flow, no qualms about people with powers. "Our entire city was corrupted, and there isn't anything special about them."

"Well, I'm glad you escaped." There was intensity behind his words.

I liked that.

"So what's your gift, Brace?" I was curious. There was no way he wasn't packing something serious. I could feel ripples of electricity every time I was close.

And again I copped the full force of his eyes. Silky strands of his thick hair fell across his forehead.

"I have an affinity with energy. It's not an interesting or common gift." He shrugged as if to say, 'no big deal'.

Yeah, right.

Brace smiled, but not with his eyes, just his lips. "I'm curious, though. I haven't been able to get a read on either of you. Do you choose not to communicate telepathically?"

Lucy's mouth fell open. In that moment she probably swallowed ten bugs.

"Shut. The. Door. Seriously? Telepathy?" She laughed.

Shaking his head, he opened his mouth to retaliate – I opted for the distraction.

"So what's with the dark mountains?" Their oiliness was weighing on my thoughts. I couldn't ignore them any longer.

His confusion was replaced by a forced exhalation of air – his anger enhancing his dark beauty.

"They were an amazing natural wonder. First Worlders traveled from all over to ski, mountain-climb and camp throughout their wilderness. But something happened many years ago; their energy changed." He shrugged. "I have no idea what's going on. There are thousands of miles of tunnels underneath. If it was me – and I have suggested this to the guardians before – it's the perfect place to build and house an army."

He said this without hesitation or doubt. I shivered thinking of the dead plants. An army of zombies maybe.

"Where are they located?" I was going to make sure we avoided that area.

He looked back the way we had just walked.

"They're not too far from the royal castle. Less than a day's walk and only four hours' drive."

I sighed in relief. We were heading in the opposite direction.

The landscape was changing as we walked. The forest had thinned.

"So, tell me ... is Lucas single?" Lucy winked at me as she pranced along.

It didn't even look as if the heat was bothering her anymore. I sighed. If she'd been closer, I'd have kicked her.

Brace simply laughed. "Lucas is one of my closest friends. But I wouldn't send him on a date with anyone. Being next in line for the royal throne, he's been completely pandered to."

I chuckled. What a picture those words painted. "We're reading you ... Lucas is a spoiled brat."

He shook his head. "It's not exactly his fault. He was raised to believe he'd end up with his chosen empress. But it's never happened. So now he likes to ... be indulged."

"How is Lucas expected to rule all of First World?" I found that odd. Even on Earth different countries had different leaders.

The corners of Brace's lips lifted slightly. "I'm not sure anyone is expecting him to rule at all. We're all kind of hoping Emperor Quest hangs on for many more years." He ran a free hand through his hair. "Fortunately, six of the seven lands have a competent Mayoral Head. No way could Lucas keep control of two billion inhabitants alone."

Mirth danced in his breathtaking eyes. Apparently the very thought was amusing to him.

"You said you're from the north, right?"

A quick glance toward Lucy told me she couldn't remember what we'd said either.

"Uh, sure, sounds right." I bobbed my head a couple of times.

His jaw tightened. "Yeah, well I think Mayor Johansson might be the one we need to keep an eye on. Lucky for us, even as a stand-in for his father, Lucas is mostly a figurehead and he can't make any decisions without majority vote of the council. They're actually meeting at the moment."

A loud rustling in the bushland to our right distracted me from my next question. I stopped and craned my head higher. This section of the forest was almost barren, with lots of dead twigs and leaves. I shifted my pack, trying to ease the ache in my shoulders.

An echoing roar shattered the air around us.

Lucy pretty much dived into my arms. "What was that, Abby? Abbs. Seriously, did you see it? Is it a bear ... lion ... bigfoot?" Her panicky questions were rapid.

Brace stepped closer and took Lucy's pack from

her. "Keep moving. It could be any of the native animals. I've got your back." He ushered us forward, bringing up the rear.

We set off at a dead run. I always thought I was fast, but now I know – Lucy is faster.

"Angelisian is not far.' Brace's voice came from behind me. "But we need to get out of the forest now. It's a *burber*." His breath came in rasps as we sprinted.

My pack felt like a feather, shoulder aches gone.

"What's a burber?" Lucy gulped, her tiny legs flying.

Brace's voice came in gasps. "Let's hope you don't find out."

The thundering grew louder. I was losing momentum. Despite the adrenalin, the stress of the last few days was catching up to me. Brace kept pushing our pace. He was close behind me. I could smell his clean masculine scent.

I looked back, my curiosity demanding to know what was following us.

A large creature was barreling along about twenty feet behind. It was huge, like a bear crossed with a moose – with massive antlers. I focused again on the path. A second too slow.

My foot caught under a branch and I went sprawling along the dusty trail, just missing a few exposed tree branches. The impact sent shockwaves through my body; I couldn't breathe.

"Lucy, keep running. Wait at the end of the path. I'll help Abby," Brace yelled over my head.

She hesitated, as I knew she would. "Go, Lucy!" His tone brooked no argument.

"Save her or I'll kill you!" Lucy screamed as her footsteps pounded away.

"Abby, are you okay?" He crouched down next to me.

I couldn't answer. My chest burned as I gasped for air.

"Come on, Red. Let me know what to do?"

I managed to suck in a gulp of air as an impatient Brace yanked me into his arms, heavy pack and all.

Spinning around, he stopped.

The creature was five feet away, staring but not approaching.

Despite the fact it had chased us, right now it seemed to be cautious. We were an unidentified threat.

Brace dropped me to my feet and shoved me behind him.

"It's too close. Don't run, little Red."

I shook my head. *Was I a fairy tale character?* "Red?"

"I like your hair." Then he glanced out of the corner of his eye. "You question everything, don't you?"

I sighed. Now was not the time for an argument. But revenge would be sweet – he was getting a nickname.

The beast roared. It arched itself up onto its hind legs. It was dark brown and shaped like a moose, its four legs tipped by large hooves and a short thick fur. But its head, despite the antlers – that was all bear. Including the mouth full of massive, razor-sharp teeth.

Brace stepped further forward. "I'll try and scare it away. Maybe my gift will actually be useful today..."

I waited, wide-eyed, to see what was about to happen.

"*Mandalla altrecia conquesca zue.*" He stood tall, hands held in front of him. Those four words flowed from his lips over and over. "Leave!" he roared in between the phrases.

As he continued to speak, I noticed the leaves, twigs and rocks in close proximity to Brace were lifting to hover around him. I rubbed my eyes. And when I looked again, everything was back in its place on the ground.

Seriously.

The animal paused. Sniffing the air a few times, it snorted into the space between us. After a few more scrapings at the ground, and snorts, it backed away from us, never taking its eyes off the one it viewed as the greatest threat – Brace. Then it turned tail and galloped away. The thundering of its hooves and its echoing roar tapered off into the distance.

"What did you say?" I whispered to his back.

What the hell kind of energy power did he have? My heart pounded in my chest.

He turned and looked down at me. "Just some of the old language – energy words." He shrugged. "Sometimes it works. This time we were lucky."

I gasped a few times; my pulse wouldn't slow. That beast was worse than ten gangers. I knew how to handle *them* – but wild animals – no idea.

Brace cupped my face with his large hand. "You did well. Don't worry so much. I won't let anything happen to you," he said with quiet words and narrowed eyes.

He dropped his hand then and turned away. And in that moment I calmed. Don't ask me why. It was some type of Brace magic.

He shouldered my pack as well as Lucy's, and we took off.

I set a quick pace – worried where she'd ended up. It took us ten minutes to traverse the distance.

"Oh, thank eff." Lucy was pacing frantically at the end of the path.

She ran to me. I swept her up in a hug.

"I thought for sure you were bear-kebabs." Her voice was muffled against my arm.

I shook my head. "Nah, Brace went all Chuck Norris on its ass and it scampered off." I turned to Brace. "And you just earned your first nickname. Chuck."

Lucy's relief was apparent, especially as she failed to contain her laughter.

"What the hell is a Chuck Norris?" Brace had the cutest confused expression on his face.

Lucy sighed dreamily. "The man of my dreams is Chuck Norris. He can rescue an orphan, build a fire and escape a bomb threat, all with his utility knife and a paper clip. He is all kinds of awesome."

Brace looked impressed. "In that case..."

Scrap that. He was too cocky already. "So where is the town?" My impatience forced the words out.

Lucy smiled. "Don't mind Abby. She starts getting a little cranky when we don't get regular food."

That wasn't it. I was frustrated by Brace's ability to both entice and annoy me. Okay, and maybe I was hungry.

He smiled at me. "Don't worry, Red. Angelisian is just over that crest. I have good friends there who'll provide food and lodgings for the night."

"Stop calling me Red." I sighed. "And you're staying for the night as well? Won't your father be waiting at home, to crack you a good one?"

He definitely needed a right hook at times. Lucy

was grinning hugely. I looked at her. "Don't even say it."

She shrugged, but kept her trap shut.

Brace answered me. "I spoke with Father this morning while we were walking, and he also thinks I need to be cracked a good one." He raised an eyebrow in my direction. "But he knows how I feel. The Guardians think you escaped on your own. He sent them in the opposite direction."

I had to assume this was the telepathy he had referred to, because there'd been no conversation in my hearing.

"So do you want to spend the night in Angelisian?"

Even now, when I wasn't prepared for it, the accent still stunned me. It should be registered as a weapon against women. What did he just say?

"Uh ... what?"

Lucy, still grinning wildly, answered. "Yes, that sounds perfect."

We were out of the forest. There was a path running parallel with the tree-line, and beyond that rolling fields of green, so bright they looked false.

Brace looked around. "I probably should have taken Deralick's off-road vehicle. Would have been a faster journey."

I hadn't thought twice about transport. There

were very few functioning vehicles on Earth. And those that did work were in the hands of the Gangers.

He continued. "Vehicles just haven't been the same since the empress banned all polluting machines and converted everything to renewable clean energy."

His crestfallen look was that of a boy who'd had his toys taken away.

We started along the cobblestone road. In the distance, trees were dotted around, and fenced-off areas held large herds of grazing animals. The grass was almost a lime green, so much more vibrant than anything back home.

But where were all the people?

The path was wide and, despite the appearance of large pebbles, smooth. The forest stayed on our left for some of the journey, but we veered off as the path dropped over a small incline.

As we walked up the other side I gasped in awe. As far as the eye could see was the most incredible sight. Something I'd only ever dreamed I'd have the chance to experience – the ocean.

Its majestic and vast beauty stunned me. Crystal blues, aqua greens, burnt reds – the most unbelievable colors threading through the crashing waves. In the distance a small town bordered the white sandy beaches. Angelisian, I assumed.

Lucy grasped my hand. "Can you believe...?" She trailed off.

"Better than shoe stores, Luce?"

She just shook her head, before taking a deep breath. "You know, I think it actually is."

A single tear descended along her cheek. Her face was alight with an innocent joy I hadn't seen for years.

"Are all of the towns here this beautiful?" I asked. "They certainly aren't up north," I tacked on the end, to keep up our charade.

He shook his head. "No. Angelisian is special. It's actually the only town to exist on the royal Isle of Itowa, besides the castle that houses the royal family and the castle subsidiaries. Angelisian is exclusive and filled with many of the higher powered families." His lips lifted in a half-grin. "That scene you can't take your eyes off, that's Bellus Ocean. One of our natural wonders."

I couldn't believe we were going to experience this city on the ocean. I nudged Lucy as we ran along the rest of the path, both of us filled with renewed energy.

"We should go swimming," I called.

It was hot and sticky and the water was an oasis of temptation.

"Abby, we don't know how to swim," Lucy laughed. "But we can go for a drown, if you want."

"Spoil-sport," I muttered.

Either way, I couldn't wait to get closer. And I was so ready to meet more First Worldians ... Worlders ... whatever they were called.

Chapter 8

We reached the end of the path but were blocked from entering the town by a large set of gates. It looked really odd. The gates appeared to be sitting in the middle of the path, but without a fence on either side. I was wondering what the point was, until I noticed the shimmery force field surrounding the city.

Brace stepped forward and spoke to the large brown structures. "Brace Langsworth – to see the Frayre family."

The voice that boomed back was so loud both Lucy and I jumped.

"Who accompanies you, Brace Langsworth?"

I craned my neck trying to see where it was coming from.

Brace gave us a sideways glance. "They are friends of my family. Lucy and ... little Red." He winked at me.

Turning my head away, I chose to be the bigger person and not punch him in the kidneys.

There was a pause, as though the gate was considering the request, before it slid open.

These words echoed as we stepped through. "You have been granted entry. But beware: there is no tolerance here for mischief of innocent or evil nature. The Frayres have vouched for you. Do not mislead them in their trust."

I looked back. I still couldn't see who was speaking. Shaking my head, I turned to Brace.

"I have to say, the gatekeeper kind of has a stick up its–"

Brace wrapped a hand around my mouth, cutting me off, and leaned in close. "There is no keeper, just the enchanted gate. Be careful what you say. The very walls have ears. Angelisian has top-level security; it's one of the older towns, rich with history. Like I said before, very powerful families reside here." He gestured to the emptiness. "No one enters unless a founding family vouches for them."

He finally released my mouth. I ran my tongue along my lips. They felt strangely swollen.

Lucy raised her eyebrows, a sneaky smile on her face. She mouthed. "Abby and Brace – L.O.V.E." She mimed each letter as she said it.

I grabbed her before Brace noticed. "You're a

five-year-old."

She laughed. "Six, actually."

We moved as a group through the outskirts of the small town. It looked like we were heading for the center of the city. Not that it could really be referred to as a city, more like a country town. New York, full of massive derelict sky-scrapers and warehouses held the ugliness of 'big city'.

This town was lovely.

Almost every building was large, but only single or double-story, with incredibly detailed architecture. A variety of colors and styles – very individualized. But it was so quiet. Besides one or two people in the distance, hurrying along, the streets were empty. No vehicles, and not even a stray piece of paper floated past. I couldn't trust any place this clean.

Brace's next comment held an air of dejection. "This town used to be vibrant. They'd have the most incredible street parades, and each family would organize elaborate displays. They worked hard to keep their lives free from the darkness, but in the last year everything's gone to hell."

I didn't know what to say. But one thing was clear: our worlds definitely had some parallels. The last year had seen an even greater downturn on Earth. I felt the same unnatural sense of unease here as well.

We continued through the town. I could hear the waves crashing in the distance, much louder than I'd anticipated. A saltiness in the air coated my tongue. I liked it. The air was also much cooler here. The sun was starting to descend toward the horizon, out over the ocean. This just added to the excess of colors intertwining through the depths.

Brace had noticed my fascination. "Want me to teach you how to swim tomorrow?"

Lucy's eyes lit up, but then worry crossed her features. "I think I'll stick to getting a tan."

I smirked at her; she was worrying about sharks, for sure. I wondered if they even had any here. Not that I cared.

I clapped my hands. "Are there waves – can I surf?"

Brace laughed. "Maybe we should stick with learning to swim first."

I frowned. How hard could it be?

Lucy changed the subject. "So who are the Frayres?"

A true smile crossed Brace's face. It changed his entire persona. The dark beauty he often displayed was softened. He looked different in that moment, though no less beautiful.

"In some ways I grew up in their house. Sammy, their son, is ... was ... my first friend. There were never too many children on Itowa, but we had so much freedom." Sadness shadowed his words. "He's been missing for almost a year now. We were supposed to go fishing, but he never showed. The Frayres are one of the oldest magical lines in First World. They're descended from the royal house."

He cleared his throat. "Disappearances are common, but Sam – he's intelligent and powerful. Considering his family called in every favor, and used their sizeable influence and gifts – I don't want to think about what must have happened to him."

We resumed walking, but the silence was filled with the weight of unspoken thoughts. I was momentarily distracted by a large blue and yellow house which dominated the street. Once again it was made from the seamless material, although it wasn't reflective. Instead, the colors were so vibrant, with no signs of chipping, peeling or fading.

"Whatever Angelisians build their houses from is remarkable. I've never seen such material," I said as I peered closer.

Brace again looked confused; he'd get that a lot around us. "It was my understanding that Alestrite's mandatory in every city now, after winning 'invention of the century'." He laughed a little. "I'm not sure if that really happened, or if it was just claimed by its inventor, Great Uncle Marke."

Lucy laughed. "This material is one of your ... our ... greatest inventions? What does it do, build itself?"

She stepped away from my side, and up to the house for a closer look. I stole a swift glance at Brace.

He looked intrigued ... or suspicious. It was hard to tell.

"Uncle Marke should have considered how convenient that ability would be." He smiled, flashing his gleaming teeth. "The updated environmental laws were passed over two thousand years ago – mandating that the protection of the environment was above all others in importance. Alestrite's a non-degrading and impenetrable plastic that utilizes the power waves of the sunlight to store energy. It powers our lives without the burning or consumption of fuel, just pure sun energy."

"If it's non-degrading, isn't that bad for the environment?"

This world was more enlightened than Earth. Of course, monkeys were more enlightened than most Earthlings.

"Where does it go when you're finished with it?"

"On the rare occasions you need to dispose of your Alestrite, there is a method which dissolves the bonds. It forms harmless crystals, which are used in the powering of many smaller objects."

I stared at him in wide-eyed shock for a moment.

Finally – a culture that understood destroying the organism that kept you alive was a dumb-ass move. Shaking it off, I continued to follow Brace, Lucy bringing up the rear as we moved along our current path. Brace then changed direction, turning smoothly into a small side street, which seemed to be a shortcut to one of the largest residences I'd ever seen. It was in its own little alcove and the ocean almost crested to its doorstep.

Staring up at the beautiful building, I sighed. It was a deep rich blue, a color I'd always been drawn to on Lucy's color chart. Cerulean blue.

Two large pillars ran up the front entrance, elaborately carved with unusual symbols. The walls were Alestrite but the pillars looked like a porous deep burgundy stone. As I observed the magnificence a muffled noise broke the silence.

I turned around to find the source, Brace was standing to my right … but nothing else was around us. No source of noise and no Lucy.

Where the hell was Lucy?

She should have caught up to us by now. Spinning jerkily, I looked left and right.

A horrified cry escaped my mouth. My hands flapped helplessly at my side. Brace was next to me in an instant.

"Red?" he questioned me, before he noticed my frantic head spinning. "Where's Lucy?" His tone was low and gruff.

She'd been right behind us before we took the shortcut. Was she still back on the main street?

The world was going gray around the edges. Pulling myself together, I refused to faint. We had moments before the trail grew cold. I hadn't forgotten the story of Brace's friend. Wrenching myself out of his arms, I ran back through the side street. We had to have lost her in the moments between this street and the house.

"Lucy ... LUCY ... LUCY!" My throat ached, protesting the screaming. I knew deep down I was overreacting. Lucy most probably had just wandered off, but I had a bad feeling, my stomach churning as I ran.

A few of the shuttered house windows showed signs of movement. But no inhabitants appeared.

Brace grabbed me from behind, halting my frantic progression through the town. I spun around, eyes firing, so ready to kick some ass.

"Abby, stop. Our only chance is to get help from the Frayres." His face was all kinds of serious as he gripped my arms. "Trust me, Red."

I was trembling so violently my cells felt like they would crumble apart.

Silent tears ran down my face. I needed to move but nothing responded. Reaching down, Brace lifted me into his arms. Turning, he ran toward the house.

I dried my eyes on the soft material of his shirt, but tears just kept falling.

He dashed up to the front steps of the house. Pulling my face away, I stared at a group of men gathered there.

A search party.

I felt small surge of relief, despite the fact it was impossible for them to have gathered so quickly.

Brace barked out a few instructions and everyone dispersed.

I strongly believed Lucy wasn't dead – yet – but I didn't even know how bad this was.

Brace's strong arms tightened around me as he carried me through the front door. Stepping through the entranceway and into a sitting room, he placed me on a white couch.

His expression was serious. "Don't give up hope, Abby – and please don't run off on a vigilante mission to get her back. They've already locked the town down. No one enters or leaves."

He strode out the door to help search. Closing my eyes, I sank into the soft padding and drifted in my sea of worry, pain and anger.

Eventually, my independence kicked in and I started formulating a plan. I needed to gather information and find some supplies. Then I'd tear this world apart looking for Lucy. I was ready to kick anyone who stood in my way in the face.

Whoever had taken Lucy must have entered through the gates. Surely it kept a record of visitors?

A loud gasp drew my attention – I opened my eyes. A woman was paused in the entranceway, a slender hand pressed to her throat, disbelief on her face. It was Lallielle. My mother, the person I had dreamed of and yearned to meet. And … I felt nothing.

Her wide green eyes, lighter than mine, were blinking rapidly. She ran her other hand nervously through her thick shiny hair. As black as a raven, it hung almost to her waist.

She looked far too young to be my mother. As I examined her closely, I began to understand how wealthy these people were. It wasn't just the amazing house. Lallielle also had that sheen of old-money confidence. She was dressed in a deep-purple calf-length dress, which was draped loosely on her frame. The cut was exquisite. Lucy would be in ecstatic reveling.

I sucked in a ragged and pain-filled breath as her pixie face flashed across my mind.

They had to find her.

"Aribella?" Lallielle's voice shook. Tears filled her eyes but she stayed frozen across the room.

Brace re-entered. I stood and moved toward him. "Lucy?" I questioned.

He shook his head, his velvety brown eyes softening. "I'm sorry. We're still searching, but so far it's just like Sam. She's disappeared into nothing. Not one energy trace or clue left behind."

"Did your men question the gate?" I knew how ridiculous that sounded.

Brace nodded. "That's the first thing we did. No one has entered or left. We were the last ones."

"Could the front gate be tricked?" I was fighting my panic again.

He shook his head. "Technically, no. But we're dealing with magic way beyond our comprehension, so I don't know."

The pain was a dull throb now, a consistent flow. I welcomed it. This I could use. The pain and anger would keep me going.

Brace finally noticed Lallielle.

"Lalli – I didn't see you there. Have you met Abby? It's her best friend who went missing. The men are searching."

"Sister," I said quietly.

Brace turned back to face me.

"Lucy's my sister, my only family." My voice was emotionless, robotic.

Brace nodded once, an acknowledgment that he understood.

A soft sob had him spinning around. He was at her side so fast it was almost instant.

"Lalli, what's wrong?" He draped one of his strong arms around her shoulders. The anger bubbling inside of me increased.

"Where did you find them?" Her tearful features stayed locked on me, but her words were strong and steady.

Brace's eyes shifted to me, a slight wariness in their depths, but he answered without hesitation.

"They were captured by Deralick in the royal forest. He was about to hand them over to the guards. You know how I feel about the Guardians." He looked closely between us. "Do you know each other?" He looked again, for longer this time. "I see a definite resemblance."

I shook my head. I didn't actually see much similarity. Although, if I dissected us a little, the heart shape of our faces was the same. And also our lips – slightly tilted up at the corners and unusually plump. Although Lallielle's were minus my red tone.

And I didn't care. Well, not about anything other than finding Lucy.

"I lost the trail of your essence on Earth," Lallielle said. "I thought the worst had happened." She smiled. "But here you are ... perfect ... beautiful. More amazing than your father and I could have dreamed."

The surge of burning hot anger took me by

surprise. Part of it was for Lucy, but another part – this woman had dumped me on a war-torn planet, abandoning me, forcing me to drag myself to adulthood. She was rich, beautiful and privileged. The only thing her actions had ever given me was Lucy – and now this planet had stolen her too.

I stood across from them, staring daggers.

"You're Aribella?" said Brace, his expression falling.

I found this odd. It didn't fit with the general confidence he exuded.

I shook my head. "No. I told you before: I'm Abby. I don't know who Aribella is." I really didn't.

His moved from Lallielle's side to sit on the couch. He patted the spot next to him. Ignoring this, I perched on the edge of the single-seater.

A slight smile tilted the corner of his lips. "Sammy told me the story of his sister Aribella. She's First World's chosen empress." His eyes scanned my face. "Her death announcement sounded when she was one, the night the royal stones disappeared." He muttered to himself. "Also looks just like Josian."

He turned to Lallielle, his eyebrows drawn together. A lesser woman would have recoiled, but she met his glare. "You knew she was alive, Lalli?"

The look hadn't done anything but the hard tone of his voice had her flinching as if he'd struck her.

"Everyone had to think she was dead. In her short time here there were numerous attempts on her life." She sucked in a ragged breath. "Don't look at me like that, Brace. Sending Aribella away was the hardest thing I've ever had to do. I gave up my baby to save her life. My..."

She paused, her expressive light-green eyes shadowed with pain.

"A soothsayer warned me to not keep my daughter by my side, or she would not reach her fifth birthday. I was desperate; I had no choice. All that is important is Aribella and the survival of our worlds."

She moved forward to sink into a burnt-orange chair, the vibrant color contrasting with the white of the other couches.

I didn't interrupt. I wanted to hear this story – plus, if I opened my mouth, every profanity known to man would be spouting from my lips.

"I decided to use my ability and send you to a youngling planet," she elaborated. "During sleep, I enter a trance state and can dream-span worlds. I was the safekeeper of the blue royal stone, because you're the chosen empress. I used its power to open a doorway between the worlds. I chose Earth because it's void of magic. No one could trace your magical essence."

She smiled sadly. "I assumed your trace would

grow to be really strong, considering who your father is, but it hasn't."

She shook her head.

"My only aim through all of this was to keep you alive – I even sent Quarn, your guardian, and his wife Hallow – to protect you until it was safe to return."

Brace interrupted her. "Quarn and Hallow Lockner? I thought it was strange when the girls mentioned Quarn earlier. I figured there must be another."

Lallielle nodded. "Our plan was simple. They all 'died' in a fiery explosion. That way no one would search for them. Quarn was the best person to send. He's gifted as a protector. He protects his charges until death. The finest there ever was."

Brace looked surprised. "I never knew he was a protector. They're pretty rare."

Lallielle's voice broke as she attempted to continue. Her devastation was obvious. And I realized something else: I had a brother, an older brother.

I shook my head. I'd deal with that later.

Eventually I just had too many questions to continue ignoring her.

Examining the dirt under my nails, I spoke quietly.

"What happened on Earth? I only met Quarn a

week ago. Earth's at war – not exactly a safe place to raise children."

She flinched again, only this time at my tone. But I gave her props, she pulled herself together.

"I don't know. I lost contact with Quarn when the transition took place. I knew that Earth was a magic dead zone, but I thought I could still dream-span and communicate there. I'm a strong Dreamer."

That probably explained my dreams for the past seventeen years.

She took a deep breath before continuing.

"I chose Earth, thinking it was a young, healthy vibrant planet. Evolving slowly but moving forward in a promising manner. The perfect place to keep you safe and the last thing our enemies expected us to do."

I snorted quietly. Sometimes people were too smart for their own good.

She smiled. "Of all the youngling planets, Earth is the closest to ours. You shouldn't have had any transition period. The mistake I made was underestimating the ripple effect."

I looked up from my now clean nails. Around me flecks of dirt marred the pristine white couch.

"You did manage to communicate with me."

Lallielle looked at me blankly.

"All of my life I've dreamt of this world, and in

every dream you were there. And for the last few years, Brace was also in them."

I avoided his stare, although I could see, out of the corner of my eye, he looked bothered.

Lallielle's eyes widened perceptively.

"If you were dream-spanning Abby, then why did she see me?" Brace demanded to know.

She shook her head. "I don't know, Brace. That's highly unusual."

My panic for Lucy was just under control while I gathered information, but the moment the search party returned, and the town was not on lock-down, I was out of there. I shifted to face Lallielle.

"I've never met any Hallow – Quarn was always alone." *Was Hallow the reason Quarn had refused to leave?*

Lallielle shook her head. "We grew up together. Hallow was my best friend. When she married Quarn, we were a close group. They volunteered to watch you. I planned on it being a year at most. Then I would bring you three back and we'd disappear."

She didn't explain how she planned to hide my apparent 'magical essence' when I returned and I didn't ask. It at least partly explained why my mother had sent me to Earth, and not gone with me. If we'd all disappeared at the same time people would have been suspicious. I shrugged. I still wasn't sure if I'd be forgiving her any time soon.

"What's the ripple effect?"

Some of the story made perfect sense, other parts were confusing. But I needed to know. Whatever was happening between these planets involved Lucy now.

She sighed.

"It's a complex part of our history–"

I cut her off. "I don't have time for the entire history. I have to find Lucy. So if you can just tell me what I really need to know..."

The delicate skin above her eye furrowed. Already I had noted this was something she did when upset.

"Your life may depend on you understanding. Please do not leave before I can explain." Her smile was strained. "I just wanted you to appreciate there's no easy, simple explanation." She looked up for a moment. "I guess it begins with First World."

I sighed, resisting the urge to roll my eyes. This was going to be a long story.

Her eyes creased when she smiled. "Our astronomers, space technicians, explorers – whatever you call them – have established First World as the actual *first* planet. Its existence began around the eight-billion-year mark. Give or take a few years."

I sucked in a deep breath. Well, that explained

the nickname.

"There have been humanoid inhabitants for approximately two million years; we are still developing as a species. First World has six younglings."

Her lilting accent was beautiful as she weaved her story. "They're the offspring of our planet, existing in adjacent star systems and connected to First World. Like any young, they're growing and learning to become self-reliant, but they still carry a certain level of ... attachment and connection to their mother. They're unique planets, most extremely different to any world you would have known."

"So Earth is one of these six planets?" Never in my life on Earth had I heard mention of youngling planets.

Lallielle nodded, her clasped hands resting in her lap.

"Yes, the closest related youngling to us. Earth's inhabitants and ecosystems were developing on a similar timeline to ours. That was before the dark days, of course. This is the reason you'll find so many similarities between our planets – culture, language, environment. The younglings develop from our energies."

She smiled at me. "We didn't always speak English. In fact, we used to have many languages, but a universal language developed many years ago and now any other is secondary."

She took a deep breath. "Negative energy will also be passed through the connection, and that is the basis of the ripple effect."

I stood and started to pace around the room. I could not sit any longer – this was like no history class I'd ever been in.

"The six younglings are in the early stages of existence. For example, humanoids have been on Earth for around 200,000 years. They're bright and inquisitive, but with limited abilities. However, we still don't know the reason for the magic void. The other planets all use magic of some description."

She shrugged. "Balance is the entity that keeps the worlds developing. And in the last few years there has been a huge influx of negative energy in First World. Such an imbalance has never occurred before. Everything's in chaos. The younglings feed from our energy, so the chaos ripples."

Tears filled her eyes. "By the time we realized the extent, it was too late – you were already gone and I couldn't find you to bring you back."

It was like a story from some crazy whacked-out sci-fi movie. But, unfortunately, it actually made sense. The escalated demise of Earth had never felt natural. The crazy behavior of the humans had been extreme, even for those who fell into the extra-stupid category.

Lallielle shifted toward me, the sadness in her face pleading with me to understand. "I cannot express my regret for the world you were raised in. Tell me everything that's happened since you left us. Who is Lucy and how did you make it here?"

There was too much. Where would I even start? I wanted to find Lucy, but a quick glance in Brace's direction and the shake of his head told me the town was still locked down. I'd just give her the basics.

Without too much emotion, I described my life to that point. The dismay on Lallielle's face made me uncomfortable. So, upon finishing, I distracted myself by observing my opulent surroundings.

After giving her a few moments to recover from my tales of the life she'd unintentionally gifted me, I decided to ask something I was really curious about.

"What is it that First World people do? You know, for jobs, money?"

Brace shifted in curiosity. "What's money?"

I wondered if I looked as shocked as I felt. I glanced between them.

"You know, little pieces of paper that you use to buy things you need – food, houses, clothes – some people have more and they are rich, others are poor and ... have less."

Brace laughed, like he thought I was kidding,

before sobering slightly. "You're serious, aren't you? How can a piece of paper be worth anything? Does it have some type of magical property?" He shook his head. "No, of course it can't on Earth."

Lallielle shuddered. "That sounds horrid. What happens if you don't have enough of this 'paper' for the basic essentials?"

I bit my lip. In a matter of seconds they'd made something that was so fundamental on Earth sound absolutely ridiculous.

"Before the dark days, if you couldn't find a job and therefore didn't have any money, you ended up homeless and living on the street."

The horror grew on Lallielle's face.

"So if you don't have money, then how did you get this amazing place? And the clothes?" I gestured around me.

She blinked a few times. "Well, we all have talents. Every person is expected to contribute to the upkeep of society. The higher in demand your skill, the more you can barter and trade for other things."

Did she just say barter and trade?

Brace helped her explain. "You remember those specialties I described in the forest? Well, that was just a small insight into First Worlders' skills."

My mind was getting a little blown right now. I couldn't quite wrap my head around the concept. But it would be all kinds of awesome to live in a world where everyone had an important skill to contribute.

Lallielle spoke again, her gentle voice easing my confusion with a subject change. "Would you like to know some of the memories of your baby-life?"

Looking up, I faced her, curious as to what she would say.

"You were born on the first day of the first month, year two million," she said eagerly, smiling in remembrance. "You were a beautiful baby, with these incredible and unique green eyes. They were so large, dominating your entire face. You have grown into them quite beautifully."

At this point, I'm sure my 'unique' eyes were narrowed at her. She was sweet-talking me.

"You hardly ever cried, just stared up at me with your emerald eyes."

And just like that I went from annoyed to this weird urge to cry. Stupid whacked-out emotions. But her words had hit me hard. My life before I was four was a blank, almost as if I hadn't existed before the age where I could retain my memories. But now there was a moment, a memory.

I cleared my throat to help force the words out. "What's the date now?"

"Twenty-first day of the twelfth month," Brace answered.

I was surprised that their time-frame was

comparable to Earth.

He grinned at me. "I presume it's just a few days until your eighteenth birthday."

I had to have Lucy back by the time I turned eighteen. It just wasn't happening without her.

Deciding to sit again, I clasped my hands in front of me. My birthmark flashed at me.

"Quarn asked me about my birthmark." I glanced up again. "Why did he ask that?"

"Aribella, my girl," said a voice behind me, "that's the mark of your mother's royal line. A matriarchal inheritance. But you also have a mark of my family. And I'll bet old Quarn didn't ask you about that one."

I spun around in my chair to find the source of the deep voice echoing through the room. My eyes widened in shock. A man – I think he was a man – stood there, his colossal proportions filling the doorway. He topped out at a minimum of six foot ten, and a glowing light encircled him. He moved further into the room, and I drank in every detail.

He had shoulder-length fiery hair, a rich blood red, even more potent than my own. It was obvious where my hair color had originated. Flashes danced through his eyes, the color of newly turned autumn leaves, burnt gold. He was intimidating, a strength and power unlike any I'd ever experienced. And then, strangely, the longer I stared, the less potent was the glowing, until I barely noticed it. Had he dimmed his glow somehow?

He moved to Lallielle. They embraced, as if they hadn't seen each other in days. The love between them was intense. For a moment I swear an intertwining aura circled them in waves of pink and silver. I shook my head. This 'crazy' thing I was starting to do was a little concerning.

Was this my father? This larger-than-life – possibly glowing – man-giant?

Lallielle's stories implied that she'd made all the decisions alone.

Where had this colossal person been during everything?

He laughed loudly then, a deep husky woof. He even threw his head back as if there was nothing he did that was half-hearted.

"I can read your thoughts, daughter, especially when you are projecting so strongly at me."

I froze. *Did he just say...? What the eff?* "Can everyone read my thoughts?" *Surely not. Brace would have known we were from Earth and that I thought he was the yummiest thing since chocolate chip cookies.*

"No, Josian is special," Brace said laughingly, interrupting my inner monologue.

Josian turned and flashed some type of hand signal I didn't understand. Grinning broadly, Brace reciprocated.

My parents moved closer before they sat on the floor. It looked kind of ridiculous to see such a stunning couple sprawled on the ground.

Josian was even more intriguing close up. His rich golden skin continued to glow lightly. He was like a sunrise. Lallielle snuggled into his side as she talked.

"Josian is your father and he can read your thoughts because he's ... more special than anyone you'll meet on First World." She was dwarfed by him as he clasped her left hand and raised it to his lips to kiss.

"Your mother is being overly generous toward me. I'm not special, just different. I'm not from First World and am far older than any creature that walks these worlds."

Of course he was.

His lips twitched minutely.

Shit ... crap ... stupid mind-reader.

"Stop reading my thoughts – they're private – and it's rude."

He held his free hand up in surrender, but his eyes twinkled with unshed laughter.

"So if you're not from First World, then where?"

His engaging smile never wavered. "I'm a part of an ancient clan of..." He paused, his expression thoughtful. "Deities – for no better explanation. We are Walkers, and for many millennia we have wandered the galaxy, explored worlds and defined cultures. We were the teachers of mischief and mayhem. We do not age or die."

My jaw dropped open.

He grinned broadly. "Now the majority of my family sleep. They wake at different moments throughout history. In many of the key moments of history – throughout all seven of these worlds – Walkers were involved."

His entire demeanor softened as he stared into Lallielle's eyes. "A few of us have found our reasons to settle into worlds."

The autumn of his eyes deepened to a rich vibrant gold as he touched Lallielle's cheek.

I just had one thing to say. "A deity? Come on, you're some type of god?" *Give me a break.*

I've never had much interest in religion.

Yeah, I've heard the stories. I figured they were created to scare people. I'd never encountered any actual evidence of their existence.

Lallielle elbowed him. "He wishes." She looked at me. "There are no confidence problems amongst Walkers."

He winked at me. "Deity's not completely accurate, but it's close. Our people have been worshipped as gods over the years."

"So what are your powers?" I had an amusing

vision of Josian in red-and-blue Superman tights.

His grinning mirth did not waver. If anything, there was an extra twinkle in his molten eyes. Had he just seen my mental pictures?

"We cannot control or create worlds. Our key abilities lie in world-walking and adaption. We can live anywhere and we can walk between any of the worlds. We do not need anything to keep us alive – food, water, shelter, oxygen – nothing." He shrugged. "And we are strong, heal easily and are almost impossible to kill."

Out of the corner of my eye, I glared at Lallielle. Why had she sent me to Earth for safety when my father was this alleged god?

For the first time Josian's face dropped slightly. Lallielle, picking up on this minute change, looked at him questioningly.

"She wants to know why I didn't save her," he answered quietly.

Lallielle patted his arm and smiled. His expression lifted a little. "I was a bit of a scoundrel, moving through the worlds, seducing women and then moving on."

He didn't sound embarrassed; it was said as simple fact.

"Your mother changed everything. Finding her was finding home. But of course at the time I was strong-willed and hard headed. I resisted the feelings, fought against bonding, and left. I had no idea she was pregnant. I had no idea I could even mate with humans. We might look genetically similar, but I'm not human. I was ... I believed it wasn't possible. Luckily Lalli is from the oldest and strongest of First World. No other could carry my power to term in a child."

His mesmerizing eyes flashed. "I will never forget what I've done, the pain I've caused. I left your mother in a deteriorating world, pregnant and alone whilst I threw the equivalent of a temper tantrum across the universe. I'm only grateful my brothers knocked some sense into me pretty quickly."

Lallielle chuckled then. "Keep in mind 'pretty quickly' to these immortals was actually three years here."

He turned his face away and sighed. It didn't in any way indicate a weakness, but there was a sense of tired.

"Time means something very different when you witness thousands of years pass. By the time I returned to First World, Lallielle had already made the difficult decision to hide you. I missed my chance and Earth is a contradiction to any other planet: such a magic void that I could not find you."

He shook his head. "And yet you sit here before me and it's the same as always: you emit no energy signature. You should be shining bright with power, but besides the occasional thought – nothing."

I was relieved to hear that. I didn't need powers on top of everything else.

"I wondered about that," Lallielle said quietly. "And, Josian, love, you must stop blaming yourself."

She turned back to me while leaving a comforting hand on his shoulder. "When I first met your father, I instantly fell in love with him. He was unlike anyone I'd ever met. At the time I didn't know of the Walkers, but it soon became apparent he did not think or act as a human would. He was arrogant with his power – they'd wandered as gods among people for too long."

She laid a gentle kiss against his cheek.

"I've told Josian many times that, in leaving us, he was humbled. No matter his power, everyone has a weakness – his love for you and me – this is what changed him enough that he can live a normal life."

"What about Sam?" I was trying to work out the logistics.

Lallielle's face paled, the life draining from her eyes. "Samuel is your half-brother. He has been lost to us for a year now. Born of drama, he has always walked a rocky path."

I opened my mouth to ask what the hell she was talking about, but she continued.

"Before I met Josian there was a mesmerizer that lived here in Angelisian. He was a master at deception. No one realized he'd been driven insane from his power. He somehow started to believe that I was his destined mate. He held me prisoner for two years."

She swallowed.

"I wanted to die for almost every moment but I didn't. In the end, when Samuel was born, I could not let my baby be raised there, so I waited for the perfect moment, and I escaped. My dreamer abilities counteracted some of his mesmerizer strength."

Josian growled quietly. The rumble filled the room.

"What happened to the man?" I had to ask.

Lallielle started to stroke Josian's back. I was surprised to see how quickly he calmed from that small contact.

"Your father tracked him down. He saved me in more ways than he will ever understand."

The look in his eyes told me the mesmerizer had paid for his crime. I glared as power continued to bleed from the very essence of Josian. It felt as though, if I reached out my hand and touched him, I would be filled with jolts of electricity.

"Why haven't you found Samuel and Lucy?"

His features grew hard; he was suddenly chiseled

from stone.

"I do not know. It should be a simple matter for me to track Sammy. His energy pattern is the same as Lalli's. But nothing. It's as if his entire being has been removed from existence. The same with Lucy. Her essence lingers in town, but there the trail ends."

I sat up straight. "They're on Earth."

Josian didn't look surprised by my genius outburst. "I believe so. I've explored far and wide there, for you and Sammy. But with no powers it's like being blind. I'm not a human there, but far closer than is comfortable."

Lallielle choked back a sob. "I'll not wait any longer. We *will* go to Earth and not leave until we find Sammy and Lucy." She sucked in a ragged breath. "Losing you and Sammy was a punishment for my terrible choices. But Aribella has returned to us. Let's find the others too."

Chapter 9

After twenty minutes of such high emotions, I needed a break, a distraction. I locked eyes with Brace, who was quietly waiting in the wings.

"Has the lockdown been lifted yet?" I didn't know how much longer I was prepared to wait. I wondered what would happen if I attempted to leave.

Lallielle answered. "There will be a siren sound. Until then, no one is to leave their residence. It is unfortunately part of our magical security."

Josian raised his brows, and gave me a grin. "You're welcome to try and leave. As with most Walkers, I'm sure you won't take our word for it."

I looked between them before rising to my feet. With one last glance at Brace I walked to the front door. It opened easily, but as I attempted to take the first step outside my foot hit an obstacle. The entire doorway was an invisible barrier.

With a sigh, I walked back to stand next to Brace. I was struck by a thought as I glanced at Josian with his soft glow. Brace should pale in comparison to this man who was more than human, but he didn't. Okay, his skin wasn't glowing, but there was still something more.

His expression was unreadable as his eyes roamed over my face. "Abby needs food. She hasn't eaten all day," he announced abruptly.

I didn't need food. I needed answers and to get this lockdown lifted and to get the hell back to Earth. I opened my mouth, but Brace moved quickly, hands grasped either side of my biceps as he pulled me up off the floor so we were at equal eye level. As my feet dangled, I felt like a naughty five-year-old.

"Do not argue with me, Red. You're no good to Lucy if you collapse from starvation."

And then, with his gorgeous eyes flashing at me, and the accent-weapon assaulting me, I was no longer a five-year-old.

Josian was on his feet. It looked as if his hair was moving around his face, which wouldn't be that odd, except there was no breeze. Brace glanced at him, but, ignoring the angry god-man, turned back to me. He was waiting for my agreement and wasn't wavering

Rolling my eyes, I nodded. He set me down.

Lallielle stood, placing a hand on Josian to calm him. She had to do that a lot. Gods save us from stubborn, domineering, over-bearing, pompous, ass-hat ... my mental tirade continued as I alternatively scowled at the men.

"I'll organize some food," Lallielle said, turning to exit through the side door.

Josian was still glaring daggers at an unconcerned Brace. A tension that hadn't previously been there filled the room.

Luckily, Lallielle was back in no time. "The girls are organizing a selection. I'm not sure what you like but you should find something to eat."

Everyone sat again to wait. Out of the corner of my eye I could see Brace watching me while Josian continued glaring at him. Lallielle looked between all of us, a half-smile on her full lips. Finally, I decided just to stare out the window to the calm of the ocean. The testosterone was thick enough to choke on. After a few minutes I caught Lallielle's eye and couldn't help returning her smile. Okay, the men were pretty amusing.

A young, blond woman wearing a bright red shift dress entered through the side door. She was pushing a trolley overflowing with food.

The room remained quiet as we moved toward the delicacies. Josian angled his way behind me, cutting Brace off.

Without going into crazy detail, I'll just say the food was out-of-this-world amazing. The variety was something I was sure I'd never get used to. Cold-cut selections and a variety of meats, along with an array of seafood. Lallielle particularly loved a strange orange bug thing. She continued to wave it at me to try. By the end I'd sampled everything.

All the meat varieties. Crackers topped with rich, creamy cheeses. Piles of pre-cut fresh fruit in every color of the rainbow.

I barely found pause to breathe I was so busy eating. I also had a little love affair going on with the sweet pink juice made from *quant* fruit. Like that meant anything to me. Other than a green-tinged meat, which was disgusting, I loved everything. Although I was starting to feel slightly queasy from having stuffed myself. I wasn't used to the richness or variety of the food.

By this time, through the large front windows, the sun was setting over the ocean.

Knowing we would soon be heading back to Earth, I was ready to rid myself of one responsibility that had been weighing on me uneasily. Pushing aside my empty plate, I looked around for my backpack. I had no idea where Brace had dropped it. They were all involved in a quiet discussion, so, without disturbing anyone, I set off to search for my bag. I found both packs resting against the entrance hall.

Retrieving the stone, I walked back into the room. Everyone looked up.

"I need to give this back to you. I don't want to be responsible for losing it again."

I held the blue stone in front of me and for the first time noticed that it looked slightly different on First World. There were definite flashes through the blue and it was no longer one solid color. It looked as if it was transitioning through stages of blues.

Josian stood so quickly there was almost no shift from sitting to standing. He took the stone from me. At that first contact, I jumped backwards. Blue sparks lit the room.

He laughed. "Oh, I've missed that little jolt. I know all First Worlders think this is one of the royal stones, but in actual fact it's not really a stone. They're small living worlds which have their own energy and ecosystem. We call them *lalunas*. They were discovered by the original seven, who believed they were what collided with *moonstale* to create our race. Only fourteen separate lalunas were discovered."

Lallielle and Brace looked astonished. I was wondering how I'd known there was something more when I first touched it. Was it my Walker side connecting?

"To keep them safe, the fourteen were gifted by Walkers to First World and each of its younglings."

I watched nervously as he tossed it from hand to hand.

Lallielle's eyes were wide. "Josian, you've never told me that before."

He shrugged. "Sorry, my love, it just never crossed my mind. I have so many years of stories and legends." He turned to Brace and I. "And it is a secret. The worlds cannot know of them."

Lallielle smiled at me, just a gentle curve of full lips. "You don't have to give it back, the stone, laluna..." She threw a sideways glance at Josian. "Whichever one, it is yours, Aribella. You're the first baby of the new millennium, born under a blood moon – you're the empress." She smiled like that was the greatest honor.

She was clearly crazy, and I was hoping it wasn't hereditary.

Josian cleared his throat. "Uh, now don't get upset, Lalli dear, but the laluna simply recognizes Aribella because it recognizes Walker power. I know we've argued about this before, but we must not just assume."

I was highly amused to see him tip-toe around his wife.

"We don't argue, Josian, we discuss," Lallielle admonished.

Brace interrupted from the across the room. "If Abby's not the chosen empress, why has there never been another born?" He didn't make any attempt to move closer. "Lucas needs his empress more than ever."

I glared at him. *What the eff?*

Brace was all ready to marry me off to Lucas like a prize cow won at auction.

Josian snorted. I looked up and he shrugged. "Sorry. You have a unique way of looking at things."

I needed to figure out how to end the mind-reading thing.

Josian distracted me by answering Brace. "And to answer you, Brace, Aribella's not the empress. Why another hasn't been born, I don't know. Keep in mind she isn't even a full First Worlder ... she is Walker, which is even more potent and dominant."

I waited for him to elaborate. I totally love it when people talk about me like I'm not in the room.

"The world crisis stems from a larger and more universal issue. In the last twenty years many Walkers who were in sleep stasis are waking – ahead of time. The imbalance in the universe is disturbing them."

His tone changed.

"This tells me that this all has something to do with Walkers. Not a First World or royal family issue. They're just collateral damage.

"Remember Aribella's the only 'half' in existence, and maybe if I give you a small insight to our origins..."

Worry creased his defined brow. "Legends tell that our race was created from an explosion of energy – moonstale and laluna – in an empty universe. Seven Walkers emerged, pure and powerful. They were uniquely linked and created a complete supremacy."

That was the second time he had mentioned moonstale. I wondered what it was.

Josian was powering along with his explanation. "I've been hearing whispers that this is about the Seventine. They are the universal balance to Walkers, although we do not acknowledge them as Walkers. They're made from the anti-matter to ours.

"Allegedly the last great act of the seven, before they disappeared from all knowledge, was to banish the Seventine to a barren wasteland. Its location, one of our greatest secrets, has never been discovered."

His voiced lowered. Unconsciously, I shifted close. "It's said that the Seventine's evil will never die, and if all of them escape their combined negative energy will consume the essence of every living entity. It will end the worlds."

"Shut. The. Door." I jumped to my feet, horror

and panic consuming me. "That's what you think is causing the chaos? How the hell are we supposed to fix that?"

He looked baffled for a heartbeat, but recovered. "No, I am not saying that's what's happening, I personally don't believe it. But even if it were true we can't fix it. Only the original seven have the knowledge and power."

I crossed my arms. "If you can't die, they're out there somewhere. And this is their problem."

Josian shook his head. "In a manner, we can choose to 'die'. The essence of our power can be given freely, rendering our skins useless."

Say what? "Are you telling me that our bodies are just the ... coating we wear?"

He gave me a slight wink. Was that a yes?

"Beside a few weapons which can disable us, we can also choose to free our powers to the universe. The weary will free themselves to be reborn and start the cycle again."

Lallielle chimed in. "On First World we also do not age. Cell regeneration's an integral part of our world. At birth we're infused with an activation substrate that prompts the continual regeneration of cells. This kicks in after the age of maturity."

"I guess that explains why no one has looked over thirty here... well, except Quarn." He had an aged grimness.

Lallielle looked troubled. "I'm not sure why that would be. We still die from injuries and illness – there are some terrible diseases. Plus, there are always those who have lived through too many circles of First World. They will choose to release their energies."

I stared. "If I'm correctly interpreting your words, I'm going to live forever – providing I don't suicide or get stabbed in the heart."

I shook my head, wondering why that news didn't fill me with joy. "What the hell does a person do for an eternity?"

Josian laughed. "You're thinking like an Earthling, with their finite lives. Always trying to fit everything in, never knowing when it will all be over." He winked at Lalli. "All you have to do is find your other half and live happily for eternity, arguing, traveling – and something mmmmm."

His raised his eyebrows suggestively. Lallielle elbowed him.

I laughed in derision. "Surely you're kidding? You and Lallielle possibly have a special relationship, but for how long? Even before this negative energy destroyed our limited mental capacity, people on Earth were still lucky to be together five years."

Brace shook his head, his perfect lips rising in another of his little half-smiles. I wondered when

I'd become less mesmerized by his particular brand of masculine beauty, when this crazy chemistry wouldn't keep knocking me around with its intensity.

"We've evolved past that. Our emotions are strong; our capacity for love is much greater than Earthlings. Of which you are not, Red. Whilst we're a logical species, when it comes to our mates, it's for life." He shrugged. "Although true pairs are much rarer than they used to be."

I tried to imagine that world. I knew there would still be fights and pain, but apparently no one would be sneaking around with the neighbor to relieve this week's boredom. Yeah, right. It wasn't in my nature to believe in perfection.

Brace was still speaking. "If we die, either by choice or accident, that energy's transferred to a new life, and is the only way to have a child on First World. When you find your true mate, if you wish for a child, you must add your name to the free-energy list. You can also gift or steal energy."

Lallielle cleared her throat before speaking. "That's how I fell pregnant with Samuel. The man killed his sister. She bled to death in front of me."

My expression was a little horrified. I definitely understood her 'born of drama' comment. And, considering my current mini-obsession with Brace, I wondered...

"Say I fell madly in love with someone and they didn't return the feelings. I'll never let that go? I'll never love another?"

Lallielle cast a soft glance at Josian. "Don't worry, Aribella. We exist in pairs, in balance. For every individual's energy there is another that's the perfect match. Anything else is infatuation, not love. You will learn the difference with time. But please don't misunderstand; most of the couples on First World are not true matches. They will continue to seek, but it's a lonely life, so many settle for companionship."

Josian added. "There're a few who let infatuation turn them crazy, and then we have the situation Lallielle was in."

Josian swung her close, her waist-length hair flying behind. "Walkers carry darkness inside. Millennia alone is more than most can accept. That is why they choose to sleep or release. We rarely find our mate. Until recently we didn't know we could mate outside our people. But Lallielle and I prove there's more connecting our two races – and you, my girl, are the most convincing evidence."

"Who had to die so I could be born?" I understood the concept of the great circle of life but ... gross.

For the first time, Josian grasped my hand. It was warm and comforting. "No one had to die. I can create my own energy. I can bring life." He said it so arrogantly.

But simple little Earthlings can create their own life as well. Maybe that was the exchange for having no magic and short 'finite' lives.

"So where's my Walker mark you mentioned earlier?" I was positive there wasn't another mark, spot, or mole on my body, and that at any time they would realize they were mistaken and there was nothing exceptional about me.

Josian smiled. "Wait here." He zoomed out of the room, Lallielle right behind him.

By the time I'd sunk into the white sofa, Lallielle was back. She carried a floor-length mirror. Brace moved to help, but she waved him away.

She placed the large white mirror, with a kickstand support, in front of me. I stared at my reflection. I saw tired green eyes surrounded by dark circles, long red hair tousled again, many strands escaping my braid.

Brace sat next to me. "You doing okay with all of this, Red?"

I sighed, resisting the urge to grasp his shirt front and pull him closer. I intertwined my hands instead.

"Honestly, it'd all be awesome. Except ... Lucy's missing." Tears pricked at my eyes again. I blinked them away.

He leaned back closer to me, our shoulders

almost touching. "Don't panic yet. We'll find her. The men are still looking – the town was put into shut-down almost immediately, even though Josian is pretty sure she's not here. If that's the case, I'm with you all the way to Earth."

I nodded. Why Brace would want to accompany us, I didn't know, but I'd welcome any help. A guy of his size was perfect intimidation against gangers.

"Do ... do you think she's okay?" I whispered, some of my anguish leaking out in my voice.

Reaching over, Brace hesitated a moment before he picked up my left hand. He laced his fingers through mine and the world slowed. My heart skipped a beat and heat flooded my body. Forcing myself to breathe and my ears to listen, I focused on him. That delicious male scent, so uniquely his, and his features ... so unnaturally perfect.

"I made a promise to myself that I would get you and Lucy here safely and I failed. I will not rest until I make this right, Abby."

I blinked at his formality, although in the First-World accent, it sounded perfect.

Josian appeared behind the mirror. The laluna had been replaced by an object covered with a dark gray cloth.

Brace stood abruptly, jolting me on the couch. "One of the men needs my assistance. I'll be right back."

My gaze followed his broad shoulders as he exited the room.

Josian's eyes were glued to me.

Did he not notice that strange behavior? And how the hell did Brace get out the door?

Probably Josian didn't harbor the same mini-obsession I held for Brace.

"Are you ready?" The red-haired Walker's anticipation and excitement drew my attention. "This mark is for identification. Every Walker clan has a unique design. It can only be viewed under the light of a moonstale crystal – remember, they're part of the original colliding energies that created the Walkers."

Ahhhh, that's what moonstale *was.*

I nodded. *Let's get this show on the road.*

He removed the cloth to reveal a small dark-gray crystal. I squinted, trying to get a clear image. Shimmery sections glittered, casting illusions and emitting a yellow light.

I gasped, staring at my reflection covered in its glow.

Josian exclaimed loudly, his expression that of a stereotypical proud father, "You look beautiful, Aribella, my girl."

I was Walker.

From the creamy white of my skin, the mark emerged. It started along my forehead, moving around my left eye and down my face, continuing to the edge of my shirt and down my left arm, like a dense network of lace, dark red to match my hair. It wasn't solid, like a tattoo. It pulsed. I looked up into Josian's joy-filled face. He'd never looked more god-like than with his own red mark pulsing along his right side.

Lallielle stood to the side, hands on her slender hips and a tearful smile across her face.

"Why is yours on the right?" It was amazing and mesmerizing. I couldn't stop staring.

"Men's are on the right, women's the opposite." He grinned. "The marks were passed from the original Walkers. There are seven distinct clans descended from each."

I was trying to understand. "How is that possible? Uh, surely you need two Walkers to make baby Walkers?"

I blushed slightly – it was a delicate subject to be discussing with your father – and he chortled loudly at my pink cheeks. "The seven had a unique energy. They could create more Walkers without the need of humanoids' complex reproductive systems."

It never seemed that complex to me, but what the hell did I know.

After many minutes, Josian covered the crystal. My mark lingered for a moment before fading away beneath my skin.

With the moonstale in one hand, he used the other to hoist the mirror, before leaving the room. I was pretty sure he grinned the entire way.

Suddenly I found myself alone with Lallielle. She looked at me and I turned away. It was probably unfair to lay the majority of blame for my tough upbringing on her.

Okay, definitely unfair.

She'd been forced to make some tough decisions which might have screwed up my life. And she didn't have hindsight. But right now I couldn't forgive her. Well, I guess technically I could, but I really didn't want to.

Ignoring my reticence, she sat next to me. Continuing to disregard her, I simply enjoyed the opulence of the couch, sinking into its luxurious depths.

Lallielle was rigid, twisting her hands over and over. Eventually, when I couldn't stand the uncomfortable atmosphere any longer, I faced her.

"So how does the mind-reading and telepathy work?" I asked, needing more information to figure out how to block my thoughts.

She smiled hesitantly. "I can't read your thoughts. You have a strong natural mind-block, same as your father. Sometime during our evolution, we learned to communicate over distance and mind to mind. How it works is beyond me.

From our age of power maturity, we're mainly taught how to control the powers, not about their origin.

"We keep constant mind-blocks in place, but if someone wants to communicate with me there is a nudge in my head, as if someone is scratching lightly. When that happens I can open my mind enough to talk – like a one-way door. Or I can open a window and allow a back-and-forth flow of information. Each nudge is unique. You'll sense who's trying to communicate – if they're familiar to you."

"Can I see memories?"

Lallielle opened her hands, palms out. "If the person allows you full access." She shrugged. "And maybe even if they don't. We're not sure of your powers. They won't enlighten until your eighteenth birthday."

It was all useful and interesting information, although my tired brain was starting to ache. Despite this I wanted to try something. Taking a deep breath, feeling a tad stupid, I squinted and pictured entering Lallielle's skull.

The strain must have shown on my face.

She laughed. "Are you trying to read my mind?"

I shook my head, but I was fooling no one.

"I'll help you," she said, "but you have to relax. Close your eyes."

Sighing, I obeyed, allowing a small trust and letting her voice guide me.

"Now you need to find the energy inside. It will be a deep place that you know and feel but have never examined too closely."

As her words washed over me, I started an internal exploration. It wasn't difficult. I knew the spot she referred to. Even on Earth I had felt the warm, pulsing depth. It *was* familiar to me so I had never questioned its existence.

"Have you found it?" At my nod, she continued. "Now draw on the energy, take a small strand and pull."

I attempted to mentally follow her directions. The substance felt like sticky taffy as a coil started to remove from the center.

"Now direct the energy toward my mind. Create an entrance. I'll stay blocked. See if you can disable my wall."

The strand continued to unravel. Taking a deep breath, I gathered as much as I could and threw it toward Lallielle. I pictured it slamming into her mind and creating a huge hole.

My eyes flew open at her loud wheeze. She was clutching her head.

"Are you okay?" I grasped her arm. "I'm so sorry. I didn't mean to hurt you."

She shook her head. "No ... no, it's fine. Just a

slight shock." Looking up, she smiled in a reassuring manner. "You don't need to blast quite so hard. Try for subtle."

Sucking in a deep breath, I closed my eyes. I was nervous to try again, but my determination to learn outweighed this. I repeated the process, but this time understated, allowing the energy to seep through small cracks in her wall.

And just like that I was inside.

I don't know how to explain the sensation of being in another person's mind. Probably how a schizophrenic feels: your own thoughts and then a completely separate entity's as well. Images ... random words, like watching snippets from lots of different movies.

There was something else. Lallielle had been hiding it well, but she was in agony. Every time I treated her indifferently I was killing her. The strength added to my guilt. Brace hadn't been kidding when he said they felt emotions intensely.

I waded through the pain. Pushing it aside for a moment, I tried not to be overwhelmed by the plethora of memories.

Suddenly a scene appeared before me – Lallielle was outside – in the street. A young baby was safely tucked into a pram behind her. I squinted. No one was touching the little cart, but it drove along unassisted behind Lallielle. Some of this world was wicked advanced.

Lallielle smiled as the baby girl waved fat little hands in the air. I knew immediately that the chubby child with rosy cheeks, short red curls and huge green eyes was me. I noticed Quarn, a few steps behind, looking much younger and carefree. Lallielle paused in front of a small store with dark-blue walls. She hesitated a moment before opening the faded and patched door-hanging and stepping through. The carriage and Quarn followed.

The room was small, dark and smoky. I couldn't interact with the scene, but I imagined a musky smell.

Without hesitation, Lallielle moved toward the back right corner. Cushions formed a semicircle, and sitting against a wall was a woman. She had long white hair, not gray or silver, pure white. But she was not old, her face young and unlined. Her eyes were closed and she made no movement. She didn't speak as Lallielle sank down onto one of the large colorful cushions.

But then her eyes flew open.

I gasped, before trying to stifle it. Stupid, of course. This was a memory and no one could hear me.

Her eyes were the same white as her hair, no iris, no pupil. Was she blind?

"Daughter of emperors and empresses. Why

have you called on me today?"

She twirled an odd round glass object in her hands, but her scary eyes never wavered from Lallielle.

Lallielle spoke, her voice tinged with desperation and what sounded like familiarity. "I need a reading, Frannie. I need to know the future for Aribella."

Leaving the glass on the table, the woman turned. Extending her hand, tipped with long talon nails, she reached into my carriage. Quarn made a movement toward me, but Lallielle waved him away.

She touched her index finger to my forehead. Her eyes closed.

Lallielle froze, her desperation apparent, perspiration beading her forehead.

The woman's eyes flew open, filling the room with a white light. She started to chant.

Children of Gods, born unknown and alone,
the seven are needed to eliminate. Take heed,
for baby will not live till four and one year
unless removed from the world here.
The youngest and strongest to collect.
Lost and alone, a god-man is the key.
Gather the Halflings, stone and fear.
The end of days is written in mineral.

The words filled the room as light shone from her sightless eyes. Lallielle gasped, before reaching out a hand and pulling the baby carriage closer. The white woman collapsed onto the cushions, grief racking her features. The scene was rushing away from me. I tried to stay in the room. I wanted to know what was about to happen, but everything blurred.

Then I was back in my own head, staring around the room in confusion. Lallielle was on the couch, watching me closely.

"Don't worry. You'll get used to the sensation, and eventually be able to stay aware of your surroundings." Her eyes were slightly downcast. "When you entered my mind, you left a rift and I could see some of your life."

She took a deep breath. "I'm sorry – it was a hard life I left you in – I need you to know I'm so proud. You're strong, beautiful and brave. I could not have asked for more."

She smiled. "And Lucy. We'd better find her soon, because I can't wait to meet her. She's quite the character."

I nodded, my throat tight with unshed tears. The memories, losing Lucy, it was emotionally overwhelming. I cleared my throat. "Do you know the memories I saw?" I asked her.

She nodded. "Yes, but once you learn how to

block your thoughts I won't sense anything."

Well, that was interesting.

"So, the white-haired woman, what happened to her? What does that poem mean?"

Lallielle shook her head. "She disappeared. I didn't realize at first because I was in panic mode – that's when I sent you away. By the time I went back to question her she was gone. The rest of the poem is a mystery to me, though Josian and I have theories."

"So how do I block my thoughts?"

She looked at me closely. "Take your energy and wrap it tightly around your mind. Encasing it will protect your thoughts. It will be hard at first, but just keep practicing. Eventually it will be second nature."

I reached toward my inner spot again. Pulling at the taffy substance, I imagined it winding round and round my thoughts. It was difficult. The moment I stopped concentrating, the energy would slip back and again I'd feel the less guarded nature of my mind. It was definitely going to take practice.

I glanced up again toward the doorway. It had been some time since Josian and Brace had left. Where were they? I was ready to go to Earth.

I faced Lallielle again. "How do the Walkers travel between the worlds?" I asked for curiosity's sake and to fill in time.

A mild fear crossed her face. "It's a guarded secret, Aribella. The only reason I know is because of your father."

That increased my interest.

At that point Josian walked back in. In the time he'd been gone I'd forgotten how tall and impressive he was. His presence filled the room again, and I couldn't believe I was related to this extraordinary creature. If I hadn't seen the Walker mark, I would be seriously questioning that. And the extraordinary continued as Brace followed. His otherworldly beauty, controlled power – maybe that was the attraction. I was half-Walker, a race of beings that valued power.

"The men are done for the day. They offered to come back tomorrow, but I told them we would handle it ourselves."

Brace stood in the entrance. I jumped up. Finally the lockdown was over.

Josian's expressive features lifted in a half-smile. "Let's head to Earth now, find Quarn and see if we can figure out what happened."

Lallielle stood. "Yes, let's get my son and other daughter..." She smiled at me. "Lucy back."

Finally we were moving, but first I wanted to warn them. "Earth is very chaotic. I have no idea what we're going to walk into. But since I know New York, let's start there."

Josian straightened. "Whenever you're ready, I'll open the doorway. Should we take anything with us, Aribella?"

I wasn't sure at what stage I'd just accepted the name Aribella. In reality, it had never seemed odd to me.

"It's violent and dangerous. Do you have any weapons? And food? You never know where your next meal is."

Lallielle clapped her hands, part of her gentle mannerisms. "I'll have some packs done immediately."

Josian turned to me. "We don't use active weapons on First World, except for our powers. We're just going to have to wing it."

I sighed. "We may have some weapons at the compound. If the security access hasn't changed, I might be able to find something."

Brace crossed his arms. "Worst case scenario, Josian, you open a doorway and get us back to First World."

Josian agreed. "Let's not forget they can follow us through the doorway."

Brace laughed, and not in a nice way. "They would regret that decision."

Lallielle straightened, breaking the mood. "I'll gather the food. And I have a little something for Aribella."

She left the room.

I stared up at my hypnotic father. "They can follow us through the doorway?"

His memories were the ones I wanted to examine. I couldn't even imagine the things he had seen.

Josian nodded. "Every time I access the energy stream, I leave a rift behind. It's temporary. The universe corrects it. But for a few days it's basically a black hole – anyone can fall through."

Interesting.

I turned to Brace. He'd made no move to enter the large room. Sometimes his face was such a distraction. I tried not to stare at it any more than courtesy demanded.

"You don't have to come, Brace. You've done more than enough."

His broad shoulders shifted, he straightened. "Don't you worry about me, Red. It's my duty to help, and I'm curious about this planet you grew up on."

Lallielle distracted me as she walked back into the room. In her hand she carried a small white box tied with a purple ribbon. She held it out to me.

"Just a little gift we had made ... to keep you safe. You'll always have a small piece of your people."

My eyes widened – my first real present. Hesitantly, I reached out. My hand trembled as I took the light package. I untied the ribbon and it fell free. Lifting the lid off, I gasped at the gorgeous necklace nestled inside. A globe locket, two-tone in color and medium-sized. It was the perfect replica of a miniature world. Looking closer, I didn't recognize any of the land masses, but they looked larger, with less water than Earth.

"It's First World," Lallielle said, smiling brightly. "Open it, there's something special inside."

I lifted it free. The long silver chain trailed behind. I spun the locket to find a small clasp. When I pressed the raised area, it popped open – a perfect half-sphere on either side, connected by a small hinge.

Yellow light washed over my face. Nestled in both spheres were moonstale crystals.

I felt a strange inner relief. I'd always have the identification crystal on me now. I could see my mark anytime I wanted.

Closing the locket, I slipped the large chain over my head. It fell to rest between my breasts, forming a perfect representation of my heritage.

Having had no experience with accepting gifts, I had no idea what to say. I faced Lallielle and Josian. Letting my joyful expression speak for itself, I kept it short.

"Thank you. I love it."

For the first time since returning, Brace stepped into the room. His expression was full of an unexplained emotion. "Your Walker mark is amazing. So detailed and ... beautiful." He looked away for a minute and then his normal smile was back.

"Thanks. I think it's amazing too." I smiled wistfully. "I kind of wish it was always there."

His cocky grin was back. "Then your name would be Red Lace."

I rolled my eyes at him. I still hadn't found the perfect nickname to reciprocate.

Josian lifted his right hand. "I feel much better knowing you have some moonstale now." Wiggling his pointing finger, he showcased a large flat ring. "This ring encases my crystal. Traditionally, Walkers are given a gift of moonstale from the elders."

"Everyone is given one?" Brace asked, his brows furrowed.

Josian threw his hands about in his usual grand gesturing. "The crystal is our essence. It's part of who we are. Without an actual world to be tied to, these energies are our anchors."

As he spoke, the sun made its final descent and sank below the horizon. All of a sudden the room was awash in light from various sources. Lamps, candles, strange speckles of ascending lights imbedded in the walls. I hadn't seen anyone touch a switch. They just automatically came alight at sunset.

Another arrival distracted me. A small cart entered the room under its own power, in a similar manner to the baby carriage in Lallielle's memory. Four large black bags sat in its caged center.

Lallielle moved forward. "Excellent. Our packs are done. The supplies will be evenly spread, so just grab one each."

I lifted one free. It was really light. I could strap it to the top of my other pack, no problem at all.

"Are you sure you packed enough? My bag is really light." I bounced it in one hand.

Lallielle smiled. "They're full. They only feel light because this design of bag is energy-touched. The carbon in the air helps to take the burden of the weight."

I smiled. "That's great here, but we're going to Earth. I don't think your energy thing is going to work there."

Josian, moving faster than fast, expelled the bags from our hands. "You're unmanning me. I must show brute strength and carry all packs," he joked as he threw both into this crazy extra-large pack, custom-made for a nearly seven-foot man.

Lallielle blew him a kiss before turning to me. "I know you are going to say no immediately,

Aribella, but I think you should consider freshening up before we leave."

Looking left and right, I attempted to subtly sniff my armpits. *Did I smell that bad?*

"I just think it might be a while before you have the chance again, and you've already been on the road for a couple of days."

Since I'd just gagged a little at the smell of my shirt, she made a good point.

"Great idea, Lalli love. Brace and I will discuss some tactics while you show Aribella to her room." They both dropped their bags and sank onto the couch.

Now that I'd noticed, the smell seemed extra bad. No way was I sneaking up on anyone right now. Lallielle was waiting patiently for me.

"I have a room?"

"Of course you do. I change it from time to time. But essentially it's the same as when you were born."

She waved me through the arched doorway. At this point I realized that front living area was the only room I'd seen in this massive house. I was about get a first-hand view of what I had missed out on.

Chapter 10

Lallielle led me quickly through her sumptuous house. I wanted time to explore each and every amazing room, but that would have to wait for another occasion.

From the small glimpses I was getting, the house was stunning. Clean and uncluttered, it still had that homely feel to it. We moved along a hallway. The walls were light and covered in elaborate paintings. On top of that, every corner, crevice and spare indent held a bright sculpture. Colors I couldn't even describe, but Lucy would be in her element – color chart in hand.

"I love the artwork. It's so bright." Each piece further captured my attention. "The artist is amazingly talented. They have a real eye for color."

Lallielle laughed in delight. "Why, thank you. Josian does love to display my work throughout the house. And I've been lucky enough for others to love my art as well. I had a thriving gallery; people would come from all over for my sculptures and paintings." Her smile dimmed a little. "But lately I haven't been able to reach my same levels of creativity. Everything feels substandard."

Well, I was shocked again. Lallielle was the artist? I would never have expected such passionate, vibrant pieces from a woman who was so proper and contained. There was true passion and joy in this work and it opened up a side of Lallielle I hadn't even realized was there.

I was jealous – as a child I'd struggled with paint-by-numbers and color-in-the-lines. I couldn't draw a straight line and my people were stick figures at best.

Lallielle was still talking as we walked. "This wing is yours and Sammy's, along with your childhood playroom. There's also a theatre room."

I bounced a little, well ... on the inside. When I found Lucy we were spending an entire day watching movies. Of course, I didn't have a clue what type of programs were here, but I was going to find out.

"There's a games room with all the interactive tech devices. They're probably a little outdated now. Sammy loves gaming. He kept us up to date." Her hands flew, pointing out different doorways as we walked. "The library – both electronic and old-fashioned books. I know it's not trendy to clutter your house, but I just love books, something about the sight and smell of a roomful."

I agreed wholeheartedly, except I had no idea what an electronic library was.

"When you have more time you can explore the entire house. Josian and I have the wing on the floor above. There is nothing off limits, so don't hesitate to snoop."

"It's no fun snooping when you have permission."

Lallielle laughed. "Even as a child you were a troublemaker. That's your father's influence."

She stopped at a rose-pink door. The word 'Aribella' was etched deep into the material; the name glowed for a moment.

"Touch the door, Aribella. Connect." She smiled. "You'll be able to control the energy once you connect."

During our walk, I'd continued my attempts to pull energy to surround my mind. It was becoming a little easier to leave it there for a minute and still perform other tasks.

Letting that go, I took a breath and hesitantly pressed my hand to the door. My name flared, and a vibration traversed my arm. The material was smooth, nothing under my hand to give texture.

Then that spot, my coiled energy, started a low vibrating hum. I felt a response within the door, a similar hum. It took no effort to connect. My strand flew out and intertwined. After that I knew instinctively what to do.

The door slid open.

I clapped my hands. Finally I'd figured out these crazy doors. "Will I be able to open any door that way?"

Lallielle seemed to shake her head and nod at the same time. "It really depends on where you are and the security they have. At night, I set the outside perimeter and you will not be able to open any doors or remove the iso field unless you either have a pre-approved energy pattern or you know the combination."

"Deralick mentioned iso shields when he captured us."

She flicked an odd look in my direction, before smiling. "They are simply energy shields to add a little more security. Most people don't bother with them."

It would take me another eighteen years to learn the inner workings of this world.

Unwilling to waste another moment, I stepped into my room. The creamy white carpet was soft under my boots. I sank into the luxuriously fluffy depths.

I took a moment to look around. The pale pink walls were covered in painted art, but instead of abstracts they were portraits. Lallielle had painted a timeline mural. I recognized myself as the chubby-cheeked baby, and there was also a dark-haired young boy and a few images of my parents.

I could trace the days, weeks and months I'd been on First World.

"I painted this once you were gone. I needed something to hold on to until we got you back."

Her presence was strong in the room. She had spent a lot of time here over the years.

A large balcony ran along the front of the huge room, with three sets of double doors ready to be flung open. The center of the room was dominated by a massive bed with four large white posts, over which was draped filmy white netting.

There were mountains of pillows and cushions in lilac and pinks. Basically, this room was any girl's fantasy room. I wanted to take my time to explore the many shelves of photo frames, toys, stuffed animals, little trinkets. But Lucy was my priority. Lallielle, sensing my urgency, moved toward two side-by-side doors.

"This is your bathing room." The first door slid open. "And here is your dressing room." The second door opened. "Every few years I donate the old clothes and procure a new wardrobe." She paused.

"It's probably not to your taste, but I hope you'll find something suitable."

Considering I'd left my other pack downstairs, I wasn't going to have much choice. The only use for my current clothes was as kindling for a fire, if anyone was brave enough to touch them.

"I'm sure I'll find something."

Lallielle smiled. "Off you go, Aribella. We'll wait for you downstairs." She left.

Wasting no time, I entered the room. As I looked around, I gasped in pleasure.

It was spectacular and massive, with white and aqua tiles checkered throughout. A mirror framed the back wall, starting halfway and ascending to the ceiling. Just beneath the mirror were two large sinks about two feet apart. They were opaque and shaped like glass bowls perched on a marble shelf. The corner held a tall set of built-in shelves. A glass front protected the contents.

This was mine?

I approached for a closer look and, with almost no effort, used my energy to open the glass door. Inside were shelves of beauty products. The compound hadn't been much for luxuries. We had basic toiletries, but besides Lucy's pirated mascara, which I never bothered with, nothing else. But this was a mini beauty store. Once I rescued Lucy, she was going to go nuts over this world. And in order to rescue her, I needed to get back downstairs, like yesterday.

My clothes were stiff with grime. Eager beyond words, I shed them quickly and kicked them into the corner of the room. Once I was naked I noticed my necklace hanging low. There was one thing I had to do before I showered. I pushed the clasp, allowing the necklace to fall open. The yellow light reflected around the room, and I was again covered in my birthmark.

This time, though, I could see every detail. The mark covered the top curve of my breast, down my ribs before curving back to meet the detail on my arm. The pulsing red lace-style network was hypnotizing. It was thicker in some places, and in others just the finest little detail.

I froze as I continued to observe the pattern. It seemed as if the faintest voices were echoing in my mind. Shaking off the feeling, I closed my locket.

Time to figure out the shower.

There was a bathtub in one corner, and adjacent to it a square stall with patterned stained glass separating it from the room. I opened the door and stepped inside, closing it after me.

I looked around – no taps or nozzles to be found. When I touched the wall I could feel the energy stream running through the stall.

Water.

Droplets sprang from the ceiling, raining on my face. I squinted up, attempting to see where it came from. Shaking my head, I gave up, excited just to be clean. I sighed, soaking up every soothing drop. I don't know how it was possible, but the water here actually felt softer.

Once I was completely soaked through and I'd freed my long hair from its braid, I looked around for soaps and other cleaning tools. I should have known. At this thought, the water changed, turning soapy and emitting a fragrant berry aroma. A panel in the wall slid open to reveal an aqua poof. I'd figured out this world far quicker than anticipated. I finished washing as quickly as possible.

Scrubbed clean, I shut off the water and the glass slid open. I stepped out onto the tiles into the warm room and looked around for a towel. Nothing. Naked and wet, I hopped on the spot for a minute before a gentle breeze wafted through the room.

I looked around in alarm, searching for the breach of my area. But I was alone. The breeze continued and, as the puddle under my feet disappeared, I realized what was happening. Within seconds I was dry. Even my hair was wavy and frizz-free. That breeze had sucked up any excess moisture in the room. Once again I was struck by the strangeness of my life. But, for some reason, it just didn't feel that extraordinary to me. I probably should book in some time later for a major breakdown.

Alright, time to find some clothes and get out of here.

I had no robe but I figured my room would be empty. I was wrong. Smashing into something solid, I let out a painful yelp. Immediately recognizing the dark hair that flew in my face, I mentally cringed. My face felt burning hot as mortification suffocated me.

Brace spun at the last minute, so I landed on top of him. Butt-ass naked? Holy mother of... *Why do these things happen to me?*

He jumped to his feet, trying to dislodge me. But for some reason my instincts had decided, the tighter I held on, the less of my naked body he could see. In my own innocence, I wasn't really thinking about the fact my naked body was plastered to his.

"This is a little awkward, Red."

He'd stopped trying to dislodge me and was now pointedly staring at the ceiling. "Do you think maybe you could let me go now? It's getting a little warm over here."

I burst into laughter. My body shook so hard that Brace managed to pry himself free. Eyes still averted, he sucked in a deep breath, although the smallest smile played on his lips. "As difficult as this is right now, I'm going to go. Before Josian kills me and then reincarnates me to kill me again."

That was an interesting thought. I wondered if he could really do that. Brace smoothly set me aside. He made it as far as the door before I saw his eyes flick back in my direction. Shaking his head, he quickly turned away again and exited the room.

What was he doing in my room?

I looked down at my nakedness – laughter burst from me again. I was literally gasping for breath. Lucy would die when she heard this. Shaking off the mirth and shame, I entered my dressing room.

"Oh, hell yeah!"

It was brightly lit, a large chandelier, the center piece, casting soft shadows. Built-in wardrobes lined the walls, and clothes hung everywhere. Walking deeper into the room, I paused – the entire back wall was dedicated to shoes – each displayed in its own little cubby. I stopped counting at fifty pairs. It took effort, although not as massive as Lucy's would be, but I dragged myself from the shoes and continued toward the back where there were floor-to-ceiling drawers and little nooks.

I opened the first drawer. Panties, in every color and style. I picked up a scrap of lace that seemed to be missing most of the back part. Luckily there were plenty of other styles. I grabbed a pair of lacy 'boy-leg' panties in a bright turquoise green. I found a matching bra in the next drawer. Everything was my size. How Lallielle knew that was beyond me. With underwear taken care of, I now had to find something to wear amongst the thousands of clothes. I needed comfortable, easy to run in.

Moving with determination, I perused the imposing row of clothes. The first section was long formal dresses, the next shorter cocktail dresses. Who in the world would need this many evening dresses? You'd have to attend an event once a week.

Further along I paused at a large section of jeans. Flicking through, I grabbed a gorgeous pair, dark denim with numerous ripped sections covered in a purple lace. The material was softer than I expected. It didn't feel like denim. Pulling them on and zipping them up, I found they fitted perfectly. Dream-weaving wasn't Lallielle's only skill. I found a pair of to-die-for, tight, over-the-knee boots. They were soft black leather and worlds away from my old pair in the bathroom. They had a couple of silver buckles running up the side.

Now to find a shirt.

I moved to the casual clothes and pulled a royal purple top off a hanger. A tank top in simple cotton – ribbed and baby soft. Whatever material they made clothes from, or what they washed them in, was amazing. Dressed now, and semi-ready to marry my wardrobe, I noticed a row of coats just before exiting. If it was still December, New York would be freezing, maybe even snowing. I grabbed a mid-thigh trench coat. Thick and black, with a zippable lining, it would be plenty warm.

I left without another glance. For once I let my red curls hang heavy down my back. I'd tie it back later. I ran down the hallway, focused now. Time to find Lucy.

Chapter 11

They were already standing with their packs on. Lallielle turned at my entrance, and a dazzling smile lit her face.

"My goodness, Aribella, you look stunning." She took Josian's hand. "Your hair is amazing. It's as if you took both of our coloring."

Considering I hadn't checked the mirror before leaving, I wasn't sure what I looked like. But my hair felt silky and smooth. It was working for me today. With curls you never knew what you were going to wake up to.

Josian disengaged from Lallielle and moved forward. Before I could react, he engulfed me in a hug. There was nothing tight or overpowering about it, despite his size. It was comforting, gentle and warm. The world disappeared for a moment. I could have used this hug millions of times over the years.

Shaking my head, I pulled away.

His eyes were narrowed and his brow creased as he stepped back. "Sorry, Aribella, I couldn't help myself. Walkers are demonstrative people, and right now you look so grown up. Just the perfect mix of Lallielle and myself."

Lallielle stayed back, her expression neutral. Remembering the pain she encased in her mind, I felt a strange need to offer her a token. Taking a deep breath, I stepped around Josian and walked toward her.

"Josian had his chance; it's only fair that you have one too." I held my arms open. I was going for sainthood or something.

Without hesitation, she threw her arms around me. Unlike Josian, she held me tightly. I might have heard one or two soft sobs. Another set of arms encased both of us. Josian again.

"You had your chance. Don't be a hug-hog," I mumbled into my mother's shoulder.

He laughed, the comforting rumble surrounding me. Eventually I managed to extract myself.

Brace stood near the back door, watching me. As our eyes met, I blushed, warmth rushing to my cheeks as I was reminded of the naked incident from upstairs.

His returning smile was full of heat, but the slight nod spoke volumes of his approval, like I needed it.

Josian moved next to me. "Okay, time to go to Earth. Picture a safe place for us to go. I'll find a doorway close by."

Right. Somewhere safe in New York. Not an easy task. The alley was at least a small area that we could try and defend ourselves in. I dropped the energy encasing my mind and let images of the alley linger.

"There aren't many places in New York one would consider safe, but this alley is generally deserted. And we might find Quarn there."

Josian closed his eyes. As a little experiment I threw some energy at his mind, trying to read his thoughts. I really wanted to know how they traveled between the worlds. I slammed up against a hardness the consistency of diamond. No way was I tunneling through that. Josian opened one eye to grin at me, before he spoke to everyone.

"Okay, link hands."

I waited for the shimmer, but as Josian stepped back there was something very different there.

It was freaking scary.

A swirling vortex, a deep purple. It reminded me of the night sky with no stars to break the endless depth of the black. Like a dark tunnel and at the end I could see the New York alley. But it was contorted, as if there were millions of miles to traverse between where I was standing and where we would end up.

"What the hell is that?" I took a step back. No way was I walking into that death trap. I prefer shimmer and sparkles, thanks.

Josian looked up in surprise.

He gestured. "It's a doorway between the worlds, part of the energy wormholes that connect all seven worlds. This is what the doorways look like. How did you get here, Aribella, if it wasn't through one of these?"

I clenched my hands into tight fists to stop the shaking. "It was nothing like this, just a shimmery wall I stepped through from Earth into First World."

Josian locked gazes with Lallielle. I'd guess they were communicating. Noticing my interest, Josian smiled.

"This is part of what makes Walkers so dangerous. We have the innate ability to open doorways to any part of any star system that we want. As long as we can picture where we want to end up, a doorway will open. We then traverse that distance at the speed of light, and we can take others with us."

While I was interested in learning about Walkers, it hadn't escaped my attention how deftly he'd changed the subject from Quarn's unusual doorway. I let it slide for now.

Brace stepped up then and grasped my left hand.

Lallielle linked hands with Josian, and offered me her other. Taking it cautiously, I waited with apprehension.

Josian stepped into the doorway, pulling us along.

The force sucked me through fast.

Whilst Quarn's style was a simple and gentle transition, the trip back was a little different.

I was being drawn through a black slide. There was no pain; I didn't bump into anything, but every particle in my body was traveling too fast.

I wanted to climb off. My claustrophobia was starting to rear its head as the darkness encased me. I couldn't breathe.

Ripping my hands free, I wrapped them around myself and tried to slow my racing heart.

I felt arms encase me as Brace held me against him. I heard words. I'm not sure if they were out loud or in my head.

"Breathe for me, Red ... breathe."

His closeness and soothing accent were the perfect distractions. I buried my head into his rather enjoyably muscular chest, and waited for the sensation to be over. Walkers everywhere would be hanging their heads in shame. I was a disgrace.

There was no other noise in the tunnel. It was a vacuum. I didn't even know if noise could exist there, like in space there was nothing. But I knew instantly when we were about to arrive. My cells stopped jumping around, I could breathe freely again. The sensation was unmistakable and I wouldn't be forgetting it any time soon.

Without a jolt, we exited. I'd expected the worm hole to spit us out in a great jumble. Instead we were all standing, unscathed, in the alley. Brace was across from me, my hands encased in his. He let go abruptly, before rubbing his head a few times and walking away. I hugged my arms close again, before zipping up my coat. Small ice particles floated past my face.

"Don't worry. You'll get used to it. Walking the worlds is in your blood." Josian placed a comforting hand on my back. His breath came out in puffs of condensed air.

I looked around. There was trash everywhere, and despite the cold the dumpsters were in fine stinking form. It felt like I was home.

Smiling, I glanced along the empty alley. It was early morning. Light filtered throughout the dimly lit area. Lallielle looked around as well, her elegant nose wrinkled.

Josian paced. "I hate the sensation of being on Earth. I feel like I'm functioning with half my senses. Blind, deaf, and dumb." He growled.

I laughed. "Well, personally, I love that no one can rummage through my head. Plus everything has rules, and works the way it's supposed to. Buildings don't have energy I can manipulate."

Three set of wide-eyes and slack jaws alighted on me. Yep, they thought I was insane.

Josian took Lallielle's hand and pulled her close. For some reason I found it reassuring to see their constant contact, like watching a fairy tale, all the way to its happy ending.

Brace continued to rub his temples. "You're just not used to the convenience of things on First World. Once you figure it out you'll wonder how you ever did without them." He shook his head in a jerky manner.

Josian cleared his throat. "That won't help, Brace. The more energy you have on First World, the harder it is to adjust to Earth. You'll get used to the sensation soon."

Brace didn't seem convinced.

Josian looked at me. "Once your powers are enlightened, Aribella, you will hate being without them. They will be comforting, your favorite warm blanket to keep you safe." He shrugged. "And with the combination of your mother's and my powers, we have no idea of your capabilities."

Lallielle's derisive laughter trickled through the alley. "When I fell pregnant with you, some First Worlders and apparently a few Walkers thought we should destroy the unknown power. You're unique, one of a kind."

Josian stroked Lallielle's face. "Your mother didn't even realize at the time the extent of your enemies. She almost definitely saved your life."

"Come on ... why would anyone even care?" I couldn't comprehend the fact I had 'enemies'. Important people, and bad people, had enemies. I was neither.

Lallielle shrugged. "I guess to them you should not have existed: Walkers cannot breed with any but Walkers."

Josian placed a hand on Lallielle's elbow. "Can we walk and talk. I don't like our lack of movement." He ushered us to the entrance of the alley.

I stepped out onto the sidewalk and indicated that they should follow me. We needed to check out the compound first. If we ended up in a battle, weapons were important.

Josian's voice wasn't even breathless as we hurried along. "We were always warned against having relationships with any beside Walkers, but I thought that was simply a Walker superiority."

"How many Walkers are there exactly?" At first I'd had the impression there weren't many, but I was starting to think I was wrong.

A calculated look crossed Josian's face. "Why do you ask, Aribella?"

I shrugged, watching the puffs of condensed air exit my mouth.

Josian kept pace beside me. "I can't be too sure. I know our clan numbers in the tens of thousands. And there are seven clans."

He let me do the general maths. They were far less in numbers than the population on either of our planets. But with their power, that probably didn't matter.

As I led them through the streets, I thought of how helpless First Worlders, and Josian probably, would feel here. People so reliant on their magic and energy. On Earth, technology was the only 'magic'.

I spoke my thoughts aloud. "You know, if you're trying to take down First World, and in turn all the younglings, hiding out on Earth seems like the perfect solution."

Josian nodded. "I have a feeling some entity is taking advantage of the anomaly that is the dead zone of Earth."

Brace jogged up to be next to me, and for the first time I noticed the form-fitted dark clothes he was wearing. And just like that I was very distracted.

I hadn't been paying attention before, but everyone looked to be in new clothes, close-fitted, dark and perfect for running.

The streets appeared a little more derelict than when I had left. I couldn't believe it was only three days before. It felt like lifetimes had passed. There were new burnt-out vehicles, more buildings reduced to ruins.

As I approached the compound, I slowed and then came to a stop to one side of the gate. Moving the vines, I stepped closer to the security panel. I reached out a hand, fingers hovering just above the pad.

Something was wrong. The light to indicate activation was no longer lit. I turned toward the gate. It was already slightly ajar. I gave it a shove. It swung open.

Peering around the edge, I couldn't see anything untoward in the outer gardens. Stepping through, I ran to the front door with everyone following. There was a real feeling of neglect surrounding the compound now. I tried the front door – it was unlocked. Josian stopped me from entering first. I rolled my eyes as he pushed me behind him and stepped through the doorway.

As we moved into the front hallway, a familiar voice echoed throughout.

"Well, it is about time you got back here, Aribella. I've been waiting for a week."

Josian spun around defensively as a familiar figure stepped out from the small side classroom.

Pushing my protective giant aside, I ran forward and threw my arms around Quarn in a tight hug. He looked exactly the same and I was so relieved. He stepped back, holding me at arm's length. It was hard to tell through his usual stoic expression, but I think he was happy to see me.

"What happened, Quarn? Where is everyone?"

Before answering, he stepped over to Lallielle and took her hand. He gave her a gentle kiss on the cheek. Josian was at Lallielle's side so fast he blurred.

"I've missed you, old friend," Lallielle said as she shooed the deliberately towering over them Josian.

But Quarn stepped back quickly enough. At no point did he acknowledge Brace or Josian's presence.

I cleared my throat. He smiled. "I see you have not learned patience in your time on First World." He stepped closer. "When you and Lucy left me in the alley, I was ambushed moments later. The same men, but with fifteen of their closest friends. I was all for having a shot, but I realized even for me that wasn't the best odds. I managed to get out of the alley and they gave chase."

He had enjoyed that, which in my brief experience of his behavior, seemed to be typical.

"I made it as far as this compound. When I noticed the gate was open, I ducked inside. Being so far ahead, no one noticed or followed me. I moved closer to check out the house, and it was a warzone. Girls were everywhere. Your compound leader was in the middle of a girl-rebellion. But then something unusual happened."

He looked troubled.

"Somehow she subdued the girls. They turned into ... zombies before, quite literally, disappearing from the compound."

"How could she have subdued all of the girls? Even if she used some type of drug, she couldn't get them all at once." I looked around the messy hallway. "Where did she take them?"

"I don't know how she got there, but I followed one of the men she left behind." He looked directly at me. "Are you missing something, Aribella?"

I was confused for a minute, before understanding kicked in. "She has Lucy?"

He nodded. "I staked out her hideout for a few days, and in that time Lucy was one of the many herded inside. That's why I returned here to wait. I knew it wouldn't be long before you came looking for her."

"They only took Lucy like six hours ago, Quarn. It couldn't have been a week."

Lallielle interrupted us. "I'm so sorry, Aribella. Josian and I should have mentioned: it takes time to move through the wormholes. I'm not sure of the exact ratio, but a week could definitely pass on

Earth. Even though we move at the speed of light, our planets are very far away, inhabiting their own star systems."

Josian gave a succinct nod. He was proud of Lallielle's Walker knowledge.

I blinked a few times. "I guess that explains my exhaustion. I'm jetlagged, apparently. One day to one week is quite a time-zone jump."

Quarn spoke again. "Since that day, no one has come back to the compound."

Josian stepped forward again, but this time, instead of ignoring him, Quarn's expressive features narrowed in hostility.

"What are you doing here, Josian? I trusted you with Lallielle and you left her alone and pregnant. My Hallow was killed coming to Earth and there's no one to blame but you."

Lallielle gasped then. Moving forward, she stopped in front of Quarn. "No ... Qua... tell me it isn't true. Hallow can't be gone." Her pain was palpable as she gulped back tears, although a few overflowed. "My choices cost so many people."

Quarn shook his head. "No, Lalli, it was not your choices, and it wasn't Josian's either. I just have seventeen years of anger, and since he's an arrogant piece of ... well, let's just say I was content to focus my ire on him."

Josian's face twitched and he ran his hands

through his red mane. Generally he didn't seem to possess the same nervous twitches as the rest of us. Mostly he seemed upset by how close Lallielle and Quarn were standing.

"Hallow was killed as we arrived on Earth. We landed in the midst of a gang shootout. I did the best I could with Aribella, but without Hallow I couldn't look after her. I left her in a rebel's compound and stayed around to protect her." He glared at me. "Which wasn't always easy. The girl has a slight problem with staying put."

I shrugged. "It's not my fault. I obviously have some crazy-ass genetics. I was looking for home and freedom."

I wondered if all those 'lucky' close calls I had on the streets were mainly due to Quarn's vigilance in keeping me alive.

I smiled at him. "Thanks for being an awesome protector."

His return expression told me two things: he loved me and he loved my mother. I just hoped Josian wouldn't notice and decide to kill him.

I focused again on our mission, starting to pace back and forth.

"I thought Lucy was missing for only six hours. Now I find out it's been a week." My voice rose a little as the potential images flooded my mind. "We have to hurry."

"The only reason for them to take Lucy from First World is as a trap for you, Red. Someone knew about your relationship, because Lucy has no significance to either world."

My head flew up; we locked eyes.

"Olden knew. She's our compound leader. But how would she know about First World?" I started pacing again, musing as I went. "Olden had an awful lot of cash in her room. Maybe it was bigger than just working for the gangs."

"If it's a trap, Aribella can't just stroll up there and hand herself over. I won't let her." Lallielle's black hair was practically bristling around her, hands firmly planted on her hips.

I shrugged. "I'll be going no matter what. Lucy would do the same for me and I've left her long enough."

Josian was also exuding annoying levels of concern. "They'll expect you to have that very attitude."

I opened my mouth to argue, but he cut me off.

"All Walkers have a slight problem with impatience, so I understand. I'm not saying don't go, I'm saying be smart about it. Running in there blind, without a plan, is just stupid."

I sighed, conceding to them for the moment. "Okay, we need some type of plan. But first let's see what weapons we can be packing on our way."

I turned to Quarn. "Give me a quick rundown on where they're being held."

A blind moron could tell Quarn was military trained. His reply was quick and succinct.

"Large warehouse in the Upper East Side. Surrounded by deserted industrial zones. Isolated but close enough to the compounds to get any supplies they could need. I observed two entrances: one in front and the other on the left side. The rest of the building is locked down very tightly. Each entrance is guarded by two men. They're armed, dangerous, and highly trained.

"An armored hummer arrived each day at fourteen hundred hours. A cloaked person would exit with four armed guards. They entered the building, and stayed around forty-five minutes each time. The guard shift changes at seven hundred and nineteen hundred. The rotation of guards is the same each day."

This was good information, but we needed weapons. There was no doubt the guards would have them.

"The building is huge, with two stories, but I couldn't get inside to check out the layout."

I took a deep breath. "They're going to vastly outnumber us. And, despite the shortage on the streets, I'm sure they'll have guns in that type of setup."

Lallielle shook her head. "What's a gun?"

I closed my eyes briefly. This lack of knowledge was going to get someone killed.

Opening them again, I quickly explained. "It's a weapon that ejects a piece of metal at a rapid trajectory, faster than the eye can track. They are deadly, easily able to blow a large hole in a person."

Quarn's face was grim. "A gun was what ... took Hallow when we first arrived. I'd never seen a weapon like it and we weren't prepared. Depending where the projectile hits, the damage can be too great for our cells to repair." He looked around, throwing his hands to emphasize his words. "But even in the deadzone, with our abilities limited, we're still fast enough to track the bullets. Don't lose focus. If they start shooting, expand your senses."

I shuddered at the thought. "Okay, let's leave that as a last resort. Ideally, we should get in and out without anyone really noticing. We don't want a shoot-out. Innocent people will get killed."

Lucy didn't have any super speed and a stray bullet would end her life.

"So, I'm going to the training room now, to see if anything useful has been left."

"We'll all go with you. Now's not the time to split up," Brace said, his tone serious.

I tried to get a read on him, but right now he was

locked down tight. Was his lack of power making him nervous?

The group were waiting on me. I stepped away from my biggest distraction, Brace, to gather my focus. It was battle time. Lucy was depending on me to save her.

Well, she probably wasn't. She'd be trying to save herself and irritating everyone to death in the process. I just hoped she wouldn't get hurt through sheer bloody-minded stubbornness.

The solar power was still working, so the stairs were lit enough for us to traverse them. They were narrow and rickety, and in the low light I almost lost it down the last three steps.

Nothing looked disturbed on the lower level, but there was a strange feeling in the damp air. I stepped across the cement floor.

"Aribella – stop!" I froze at Josian's order.

He was looking around, his face frozen in confused worry. "A doorway has been opened here ... recently. The rift is still open."

That must be the heaviness I could feel in the air. "Why does it seem so ... angry?"

His eyes were still darting around. "It is unusually strong, the resonating energy left behind. But as long as we don't step too close, we should be fine."

I could feel his unease spreading through our

group.

"I don't feel anything." Quarn looked around. "Where is it?"

Josian pointed to the far corner. "It's in the space over there, although there seems to be a trailing of power I don't like."

I was feeling a little nauseated. Like a cloak of heaviness was pressing down on my stomach, threatening to expel all the delicious food I'd eaten earlier.

Lallielle moved closer to Josian. He draped one of his massive long arms around her protectively.

I stepped around them, staying as far from that corner as possible. Moving across the cold room, I made my way to the built-in shelves lining the back wall. Nauseating shivers continued to rack my body.

Shoving a few of the blue workout mats to the side, I wrinkled my nose as the smell of old sweat assaulted me, bringing back a few memories. I sighed, reminded of how much I loved fight class. Skills I was sure to be utilizing in the very near future.

I had to crouch down to check the bottom lockers first. After some rummaging through old clothes and ratty bits of screwed-up paper, I did manage to find a familiar small blue box – compound-issued lock-picking kit.

Bending from his lofty heights, Brace peered over my shoulder. "I doubt that is much of a weapon, Red."

Quarn laughed derisively. "I'm constantly amazed at the weapons they utilize on Earth. Sometimes they're much smaller than you'd expect."

Brace looked more interested now.

I shook my head. "Sorry to disappoint. This is just a lock-pick kit."

I stood quickly, forgetting Brace was right above me. I smacked hard into his chest, and I'm pretty sure I saw stars as I fell to the floor again.

Reaching down, he helped me back to my feet. His hand lingered just longer than necessary on my own, the sparks between us alive and well, even in the dead zone.

I shook my head and stepped around the group. The tall locker was the storage vessel for this compound's training weapons. And also the reason I needed the pick kit.

Josian reached out to grab my arm. "That's where the rift is."

I shrugged off my over-protective father. "I know, but I need to get into that cabinet. I'll be careful," I assured him.

Josian turned back to the group. "You all stay here."

Quarn and Brace's expressions were a mirror of annoyance, but they didn't comment.

I took the four steps across the room. Josian was on my butt the entire way. I resisted the urge to roll my eyes. Go from having no parents to hovering worried ones in a matter of hours.

Okay, I kind of liked it.

When I reached the cabinet, the energy was so strong I almost gagged. Swallowing loudly around the lump in my throat, I flipped open the blue box and withdrew the two-piece tool. This locking mechanism was slightly more technical than the ones we generally practiced on, so it took a few minutes of twisting. The quiet in the room made the job easier. Finally, as the last of the grooves clicked into place, the bolt released.

Yanking the door open, I peered inside.

"Anything we can use?" Josian peered over my head, riffling through the higher shelves.

Damn these giants.

Focusing on the contents, I smiled, one of my first true ones since Lucy's disappearance. We were going in armed.

Reaching forward, I grabbed a handful of palm-sized grenades. Dark gray in color, they had small red tags attached to their detonator pins. Smoke and gas grenades, we used them in simulation practices, but they were real. Apparently that was the only way to really understand their debilitating nature. More like the only way Olden could torture us and receive payment for it.

They weren't lethal, but you'd damn well find yourself dizzy and disoriented.

Josian opened his pack.

I placed them inside with care. "These grenades will be perfect for our initial infiltration," I said as I went back to the cabinet. "And the goggles help with night vision." I threw a pair to everyone. "Keep them on you until we get there."

I went back to the hidden gold mine in the cabinet.

"Pepper spray." I held it up for all to see. "Spray straight into their eyes." I moved on to the next gem. "Tasers – hold and press." They were high voltage, knock an elephant down.

I pressed the button. Brace looked impressed as the visible electricity arced across the prongs.

Near the back, I found the gun lock-box. Dragging the heavy container toward me, I dropped it to the floor. It rattled loudly. I crossed my fingers that it still contained the training weapons.

I picked the bolt-lock. Within thirty seconds I was inside staring at three revolvers.

I pulled out the first gun.

"This is a Colt 911, a semi-automatic weapon." I checked the clip. "It has seven rounds, so you need to make the shots count."

I turned to Quarn. "Do you have any experience handling guns?"

He was my best chance. Despite guns' rarity on the streets, they weren't non-existent.

Quarn nodded. "Besides chasing you around York, my other aim in life was to remove every gun from the gangers. Which was hard to achieve without handling them on more than one occasion."

The second gun was the same. I handed that to Josian, after pointing out the basics. "That's the safety. Click it off before you shoot."

He dropped the gun into his deep side pocket.

The third gun was useless, just a prop for beginners.

"So the guns are just as useful as a threaten-scare tactic. They will fear the weapons. With some luck we won't need to use them," I explained to the men.

At some point everyone had moved nearer and we were pushing uncomfortably close to the corner of the room.

Most of the gear went into Josian's bag, although the tasers and pepper spray were shared around.

Josian reached up to the top shelves. He pulled out a sheaf of rolled material, which he handed to me. I recognized it immediately.

A wicked smile crossed my face. This was my weapon.

I untied the leather string that held it together. I felt a slow motion flood of anticipation as the roll unraveled.

Quarn, smiling broadly, let out an exclamation. "A throwing-knife set. Are you going to use that?"

He leaned forward eagerly, his blue eyes alight. He wanted his sword, a gun and the throwing knives. Someone had a problem sharing ... weapons hog.

I nodded. "Oh, yes. This was one of my specialized advanced classes. I've been waiting to get my hands on this set for a long time."

I lovingly stroked the shiny pearl handle of one of the eight knives. Lifting it free, I laid it flat on my hand, inspecting the high quality and perfect balance.

Reluctantly, I re-sheathed the weapon and tucked the leather into the deep pockets of my coat.

"Let's go kick some ass."

"Aribella," Lallielle protested half-heartedly.

My swearing had eventually breached her maximum mother capacity.

Josian laughed. "You're definitely my daughter. Your mother is going to have her work cut out."

He ducked down to kiss her cheek. She chuckled, accepting his attempt to appease her.

Looking away, I found myself caught in Brace's stare. Something was up with him. His aloof coldness was growing the longer we were on Earth.

I didn't have time – but something was there and I would figure it out. I shook my head. Well, I probably wouldn't. Brace was awfully good with the secrets.

I moved aside then as Quarn took the lead.

As I was moving forward to follow them, I felt a strong shove from the right that sent me reeling. I had no chance to recover my balance, so I simply closed my eyes, prepared to hit the ground.

But I never did.

I was back in the vacuum. I'd fallen straight into the rift.

Chapter 12

I screamed silently in the pressing darkness. My energized cells bounced around my body as I moved at the speed of light. I hadn't realized the last time how much Brace's presence and embrace had calmed me. It was quicker this time for the rift to expel me violently. Suffice to say I wouldn't be sitting easy for a week.

The room was dark and I couldn't find anything to anchor myself in it. I stayed still and quiet, trying to sense what dangers were lurking around me.

I could be anywhere in the entire universe. A jostling on my arm reminded me I still had my night-vision goggles.

Hmmm, Abby, they may be useful right now.

Pulling the rubber strap back, I slid them over my head, groaning as I poked myself repeatedly in the eye. Finally they settled over my face and images jumped at me. The darkness turned to a landscape of green and gray.

It took a few minutes for me to focus. The strange color plateaus from the night vision were disorientating. Eventually, the room came into focus. It was small and empty. There was a door on the far wall. An empty room whose only purpose could be receiving from the compound.

I walked a few steps forward, moving toward the door. I wondered why no one had followed me through the rift. Did it close behind me?

I refused to stand around waiting to be rescued. There was only one way to figure out where I was.

I dropped my hand onto the handle. Taking a deep breath, I pushed down and the door clicked open. I gave a gentle shove.

The next room was dark as well; I took my time before stepping through into what looked like a huge single-level room. I was puzzled by what I saw through the goggles. The room looked like a dungeon – like those from the fifteenth century, similar to those I'd seen in books about the medieval period.

I moved forward two steps. The straw on the floor crunched under my boots. Yes, I said straw. The room appeared to consist of a long row of cells, with large and heavy bars along them.

Crap, could you time-travel using the doorways?

I couldn't tell if there were people in the cells. Although, as I moved further along, my nose wrinkled in distaste. There was a distinctive smell of sweat, fear, and other disgusting-ness lingering in the air. If that aroma was any indication, humans had been held here and it hadn't been that long ago.

A noise from behind had me swinging around. The door was opening.

Awesome.

What was coming through there now?

I crouched down to present a smaller target. I was just fumbling for my throwing knives when a massively tall person stepped through.

Okay, how many people could be that tall? I hesitated for a moment, just in case I was wrong.

"Baby girl?"

Relief flooded through me. I recognized that whispered and deep baritone.

Trembling, I scrambled to my feet and took off at a flat-out run, before diving into Josian's arms.

"What the hell. Where have you been?" I whispered into his shirt front.

He was clutching me close, my feet hanging off the ground.

"Sorry, baby girl. It takes a few minutes before anyone can use a doorway again."

Lallielle was at our side. I could smell her unique flowery scent. "Thank the gods we found you. I could not get through that rift fast enough."

Josian laughed as he lowered me back to the ground. "She was definitely a riled-up mama bear. I was a little scared for my life."

"Yes, my love. Lucky you got us here in time or things could have gotten very dangerous for you." She sounded only half-serious.

Josian kissed the top of her head.

"I would never let our baby go again, Lalli. You know that."

"Where are we, Aribella?" I smiled as Quarn interrupted them, probably deliberately.

"No idea. I didn't make it far before you arrived." I tried to keep my voice low, but someone had to have heard this racket.

It appeared that everyone had better eyesight then me. None of them were using their goggles. I turned back to look around the room again.

"Can we go back in time using the Walker doors, Josian?"

I felt him shift next to me. "There are no Walkers that have that type of power anymore. One of the powers we've lost."

I shook my head. "It's just strange. This looks medieval." I pointed toward the barred cells. "Fifteenth to sixteenth century."

Brace's voice came from the darkness. "We're definitely still on Earth. My energy power isn't swirling around as it usually does."

Now just to figure out where on Earth.

A loud clang sounded from behind us. Josian pushed me and Lallielle aside and he stepped forward, hands raised. The door at the far end was opening. We fell silent, waiting as keys clanked and a whistling man stepped inside.

"Time to wake, you disgusting wastes of good quality air."

I felt a small relief that he had the distinctive clipped tones of Brooklyn. We might still be near New York.

Suddenly the room lit up. One by one, each cell came alight.

We remained crouched in the darkness near the back of the room. As each cell was illuminated, the inhabitants began to move behind the bars, as if they had been in stasis until that moment.

I shoved my glasses up to rest on top of my head and squinted into the brightness for a moment. Finally the scene before me came into focus.

Noise was suddenly everywhere, sobs and groans echoing throughout the stone walls. There were about twenty cells, ten lining each wall.

The occupants had moved forward to grasp at the bars of their cages.

For the first time I could see every one of them.

A hand covered my mouth just as I was about to

scream out loud. I looked up. Brace was beside me, and it was his hand preventing my shriek of outrage.

The girls from the compound filled many of the cells. But that wasn't all. Lucy was there, and she looked terrible, thin and pale. Her hair was limp and dirty, hanging in swirls around her face.

I tried to wriggle out of Brace's grasp, but he tightened his hold. I had to get to Lucy. Her expression was blank, as if she had seen it all and nothing affected her anymore. Something inside of me crushed, seeing her so broken.

I bit down into the fleshy pad of Brace's hand.

"Naughty, Red, don't make me spank you," he whispered into my ear.

I spun around to glare at him. At the same time my elbow flew back into his abdomen. He released me slightly.

"In your dreams, douchewad." I muttered.

"I know this is probably beyond your capabilities, Abigail, but try and exercise a small level of patience. We need to assess this threat before we act." His tantalizing voice was still low in my ear, sending shivers along my spine.

I was way too hot-blooded to assess anything before acting. I was 'action first, consequences later', thank you very much.

Lallielle's gasp had me spinning back around, searching for the source of her concern.

"Sammy?" Brace murmured.

What? My brother was here as well? I craned my neck trying to see into all of the cages. A tall, dark-haired man, who looked eerily like Lallielle, but without her green eyes, moved forward into the light. He was in the cell next to Lucy's.

He'd just reached through the bars to squeeze Lucy's hand. He was hovering over her protectively, glaring at the man jauntily making his way through the cells.

The whistling intruder was easy to see now. He was short, with a large stomach protruding over his dirty pants, and a filthy white shirt, buttons missing so that his fat rolls hung prominently on display.

Brace's silky hair tickled my ear as he leaned in close to murmur, "That's a quality packaging that man has."

"Don't be jealous," I whispered back. "You're bound to be that attractive one day."

He exhaled loudly. I ignored him, continuing my observations of the man. He was around fifty years old, his face dominated by a beaky nose and small angry eyes. He was walking in our direction, pausing at each cell and throwing a brown paper bag through the bars.

The occupants snatched at the bags before scurrying back into their cells.

No one had noticed us standing there, but I was

over waiting. We could take out this one little rat-man.

As if she'd read my thoughts, Lallielle bolted into the light. Josian's attempt to stop her was useless. He was close behind but she got to rat-man first.

She hit him hard. He was turning at the sound of her steps when she right-hooked him straight in the jaw. His eyes rolled up in his head before he crashed to the floor.

To be honest: I was impressed.

Josian laughed out loud. "Taught her that."

"Mom! How are...? Where did you come from?"

Samuel had their beautiful accent; his was just rougher ... husky, as if something had damaged his vocal cords. Lallielle headed toward him. I was distracted by Lucy.

"Abby. Oh gods. I can't believe you're here." The dead expression she'd been wearing wavered and suddenly she was crying, tears pouring down her face.

She pulled her hands free of Samuel and held them out. I ran into her arms, hitting the bars hard.

She winced as I pulled her close. I loosened my hold a little.

"Are you okay?"

She smiled, with a fraction of her old joy. "I'll be much better when you get me out of here."

Lallielle was hugging Samuel through the bars to his cell. Brace and Josian were right behind, huge grins on their faces. Quarn was crouched over rat-man on the floor.

I searched the cell front to find the lock. There was nothing on the smooth bars.

"We have to get out of here. There seems to be a permanent delivery door between the warehouse and the compound." I was thankful my calm voice didn't express the cold trickles of fear inside.

Josian's brow wrinkled in worry. "That's not possible. It can't be done."

Brace was clipped and short. "All the more reason to get out of here."

"Quarn, does rat-man have any keys or remote locking devices on him?"

I tried to turn, but Lucy clung to my hand.

Quarn smiled. "Rat man." He shook his head, screwing up his nose. "That's appropriate, actually."

Most of the occupants of the other cells had moved toward their bars.

"Abby?" I turned to see Chrissie and Chandra, plus a few of the other girls together in one cell. I smiled, but couldn't help notice the vacancy in their stares, the motley nature of their skin and general air of neglect they were all rocking today.

"Hang tight, girls, I'll get you out of here." My

words barely registered with them.

"He doesn't have keys. There's only one person who ever accessed these cells." Lucy drew my attention. With her free hand she pointed toward the entrance. "Try that little box next to the door. I think that's some type of control panel."

Quarn moved away from the group to inspect the small black box which was attached to the wall.

"Sammy baby." Lallielle held both of his hands. "This is Aribella, your sister."

Lucy and Samuel both nodded.

Lucy answered. "After I explained the situation, Sam and I kind of figured that Abby must be his sister."

Josian stood near Lallielle, staring at Lucy. His expression was ... odd. I reminded myself to ask him about that later.

A creak was the first indication the cell doors were opening. Quarn shut the box again and nodded: success.

Lucy squeezed herself through the small gap. The center of the room filled, as one by one Samuel and the girls managed to escape.

Lallielle swept Samuel into a proper hug. Lucy's smile was shaky, her eyes crinkled up in worry as she watched them. Samuel held back, stiff and unresponsive, but eventually he reached around and gave Lallielle a half-hearted hug.

"I've missed you, Mom." His voice broke a little on the last word. "I thought I'd die here and no one would ever know."

"I've missed you so much, Sammy." Lallielle sobbed out both her sorrow and relief.

Josian untangled Lallielle from her uncomfortable son. Samuel had an air of fragility, like one wrong word could break him into a million pieces. By the looks of it, his year in this dungeon had almost been the end of him. No wonder Lucy's expression was going all protective-kitten toward him.

Samuel turned then and walked toward me.

I didn't know what to do. Looking left and right, I backed up a few steps.

Only it wasn't me he was coming to. He stopped before Lucy, staring down into her face for a moment. The height difference between them was ridiculous, well over a foot. I looked at the floor, trying hard to stifle my laughter. Brace caught my eye. His expression just made it worse. *Ass-hat*.

Samuel reached out and captured Lucy's face in his hand. Then without hesitation he swept her off her feet ... literally. He then proceeded to kiss the hell out of her.

Throughout the room, clearing throats and mutters sounded, along with a random whoop. It was a tad awkward ... and lovely ... and a lot romantic.

I ignored the fact my brother was currently kissing my sister. The mood was affecting everyone. Josian pulled Lallielle closer, placing gentle kisses on her face.

Come on. Where was I supposed to look now?

I was drawn to Brace. *Oh, yeah. Much better.*

I expected to see him staring at the happy couple, like the rest of the room, but he was staring at me.

The heat of his gaze held me immobile. My head started to spin; I hadn't taken one breath since we locked eyes. He turned away, releasing me.

Breathe, Abby.

Inner voice or whispered words? Once again, I couldn't tell. The room broke into scattered applause as Samuel and Lucy pulled apart.

I wouldn't admit it – maybe under torture – but I was kind of annoyed. I'd just gotten Lucy back; I wasn't ready to share her.

She snapped out of her kiss-haze. As if she could read my thoughts, she stepped away from Samuel and toward me, although they continued to exchange intense looks.

"So, Josian. Can you open a Walker door for this many people to leave at once?" Brace was pacing, looking toward the far doorway.

"No problem..."

I sighed in relief.

But then he said, "Except something is blocking me here."

I looked at him in disbelief. "What do you mean?"

He shook his head, his voice deepening. "There's something here I cannot explain. They have this building locked down, and a permanent Walker doorway."

Samuel spoke then, the slight rasp in his voice even more prominent. "That's why we're held here. They siphon our energy."

I looked around at the huddled groups of girls. I recognized many of them. While a few had taken the chance – well-deserved, I'm sure – to kick ratman in the ribs, the rest were sitting around, faces blank. Where was the running? Hysterical screaming? Escape attempts? They were as Quarn described: zombies.

"How are you still alive?" Lallielle's voice broke as the true horror of Samuel's situation dawned on her. "They've been siphoning you for a year."

Samuel shrugged, but his eyes were flat, emotionless. "I have no idea. I'm much stronger than Earthlings. They only last a few months."

As Lucy took his hand, a smile crossed his features.

"We average a few deaths a week." He pointed toward the scattered people. "This is a new group."

"How do they have such extensive knowledge of the ways of the Walkers?" Josian asked furious. His red hair swirled around him. "They're dealing with myth and legend, no longer obtainable abilities."

I wondered if everyone was thinking what I was. Then Lucy nailed it.

"We're screwed."

Chrissie limped over. She was much thinner than the last time I saw her and she wrapped her arms tightly around herself, as if she was afraid she would fall apart at any moment.

"So what's the escape plan, Abby?" Her anger flowed around me. "And can I be the one to rip Olden's head from her shoulders?" No zombie behavior from her.

Lucy pushed forward. "Get in line, Chris," she said darkly.

I looked from one to the other, wondering what had happened here.

Quarn, with his military training, scanned the room. "Our best chance is to exit together. Go out as a group and confuse them."

A groan sounded from the floor as rat-man started to shift. I looked at Lucy for a minute. She nodded once. It was information-gathering time.

I crouched next to him. By the time he opened his beady eyes, he was surrounded on all sides. Glares rained down on him.

He was confused. For about a minute. And then he laughed.

I watched him. His actions were ... unexpected. It wasn't a small I-just-got-a-concussion chuckle. No, this was a full-throated belly laugh. His fat rolls jiggled all over the place.

It was irritating, grating on my last nerve. I lunged for his face. My closed fist crunched against his nose.

Wow, that was satisfying.

Brace had dived after me. I'm not sure if it was to stop me, or to hit him too. Blood poured from rat-man's nose, and with a coughing splutter he grabbed my shirt, and with unforeseen strength attempted to bring my face close to his.

Brace reached out a huge hand and cupped the man around the throat.

"I'd let her go now. Unless, of course, you don't want the privilege of breathing any longer."

Pulling myself free, I stood up. As Brace released him, the dirty-man attempted to roll away. I halted this by stomping my foot onto his fragile ribs. I noted the red marks marring the folds under his chin. Brace had had quite the grip on him.

"I got this, Chuck. You can back off now." I nodded at Brace. He was still Chuck until a better name presented itself.

His lips curved slightly, but he stepped back.

"Okay, rodent, I'm going to ask you a few very simple questions. Even you should be able to understand them. And I would like nice timely responses."

He winced as I dug my foot in a little more.

"I don't want to ask twice."

Lucy snickered under her breath. I heard it, though, and I could almost read her thoughts. I'd gone a little mad with power.

As he looked up, pain was apparent, but there was no fear.

If anything, his confidence was pissing me off. "How many people are in the building?"

"It doesn't matter, girl." His accent was even more nasally as he attempted to breathe through the blood flowing from his nose. "Master has been waiting for you and now you're exactly where he wants you."

His ribs were flexing under the strain.

"What does he want me for?"

He laughed breathlessly, using the small amounts of air I was allowing.

"We've been watching you for a while. He was so angry when they took the wrong girl from First World. But Patty assured him you would come for your friend."

Patty? Did he mean Olden?

I closed my eyes. *Don't kill him, Abby. He's not*

worth it.

Opening my eyes, I spun around and stepped away. I couldn't trust myself right then not to hit him again. Josian took my place.

He didn't touch him. He just lowered from his impressive height to gaze eye to eye.

For the first time, rat-man's cocky smile faltered. He started slithering backwards, but the kicking feet kept him in the same spot.

"You – you can't be here – all others are barred from this hall," rat-man stuttered.

Josian continued to stare. After a few more rants, rat-man fell silent, trance-like.

A sheen of sweat was developing on both of their faces. *What type of battle of wills is this?*

"If I push any harder I'm going to break his mind. He has strong blocks. Someone powerful trained him," Josian thundered, looking around as if he would find the culprit in this room.

Lallielle pushed Josian closer. "You have to continue. We don't have a choice. We need to get out of here safely and for some reason you can't open a doorway."

He searched her face for a second before finding whatever acceptance he was seeking.

Reaching down, he wrapped his huge hands around rat-man's head, who then began to struggle, emitting small whimpers.

"What's he doing?" I wondered out loud, wincing at the painful sounds.

Lucy, Chrissie and the others had no such qualms. They watched with expressions of satisfaction. There was not a lot of love for old rat-man in the room that day.

Brace answered, his gaze also locked on the pair. "Josian has the stronger mind. He can hack through the blocks to access information."

The jiggle of fat rolls slowed, until the rodent's struggles ceased. His eyes rolled back into his head and a puddle of drool emerged from the corner of his mouth. It had taken Josian thirty seconds.

"With anything destructive, there's always damage to fundamental connections in their mind," Josian said as he stood, disgust across his features. "He didn't know much of importance. He's never met his master, only received orders. He is the bottom of their food chain here. There was one main person who issued his orders, a scrawny black-haired woman ... Patty?"

"Olden!" Lucy and half the compound girls screeched together.

Josian looked at us. I answered for the group. "She was our compound leader. That has to be why that Walker doorway was in our manor."

"That evil bitch," Lucy fumed. Samuel held her back from storming straight out the door. "I'm going to kill her."

Josian nodded. "Oh yes. She's on my list to be eliminated. But I'm worried about this power accumulation. Until we know more, we cannot confront them head on."

I was standing close enough now that I could hear him mutter, "Need to talk to my brothers."

I wondered, just for a brief moment, if he meant actual family brothers. Or if that was more 'Walkers in the hood' – buddies – bros.

Lallielle looked around. "Did he have any information that might help us escape?"

Josian nodded again. "There weren't many people inside the warehouse when he entered this room. If we take off as a large group, we must run forward about fifty yards, and then take a sharp right, between the two large pallet stacks. That's the exit."

He issued his command. "No heroes today. Let's get out in one piece." He turned back to our more intimate group. "Once we are outside these walls I'll be able to access the doorways again and get us back home."

I took the grenades from Josian's pack and handed them around the room. The girls knew what to do with them.

Pulling the rolled material from my pocket, I opened it to palm two throwing knives. I slid them under the sleeve of my jacket as a makeshift wrist sheath. I flexed my hands – not perfect, but would do the job. I handed Lucy and Chrissie two knives each, leaving the last as backup.

We gathered the girls together.

Josian had no problem capturing the attention of the room. "Alright, everyone listen closely. We're going to escape now. We'll exit as one group. I'll lead and I expect you all to follow."

I bit back my 'sir, yes, sir' which sprung immediately to mind. A sense of energy and life was filtering through the group.

"Wait a few minutes for the grenades to do their jobs," I reminded them.

Josian hit the lights, throwing the room into darkness. He stepped up and opened the door. Those holding grenades stepped forward, and as soon as they'd been tossed out I slammed the door closed again. We couldn't run out into that yet.

I gave us as much leeway as I could, but eventually we had to bail.

We bolted from the room, through dispersing clouds of smoke. Josian charged ahead. I was close to his heels, with Lucy beside me. The room was huge, a well-lit warehouse. And it looked like it was currently being used to store thousands of stacked box pallets. Whether from the 'nades', or something else, we had a clear path in front of us.

But not for long.

Black-clad security guards began to run in from everywhere. None of them had their guns out yet, so we still had a chance. Plus their hesitation spoke of their wariness in being stampeded by our mob.

I had a glimmer of hope that we were going to make it out unscathed. Then Olden stepped into the end of our pathway, a large machine gun in her hands.

"Machine gun! Take cover!" I screamed before diving off the passageway as the first of the bullets echoed around the cavernous room.

I'd managed to grab Lucy's hand and take her with me, but I couldn't see anyone else. Olden continued to fire. Bullets rained relentlessly.

Breathing in a harsh, jagged manner, I attempted to push my panic aside – I couldn't help anyone if I was having a heart attack – before moving further behind the table.

I barely breathed until there was a lull in the fire. It would take her sixty seconds to reload, just enough time to assess the situation. I peeked around the corner. My heart hammered as I saw the scattered bodies in the pathway. I gagged at the sight of masses of blood.

Olden's gun had carved a destructive path through the group. She was in the same spot, right at the junction of our lane, wearing her usual overconfident self-satisfied expression. There was a large male guard on each side of her.

Smiling broadly, she rested the gun over her shoulder.

I couldn't tell who was down. There were too many body parts scattered, although I frantically continued to survey the destruction. Breathing in heavy pants, I pulled back behind the table.

"Abigail, nice to see you again," Olden's voice echoed around the room. "How terrible, a few of your friends didn't make it."

She chuckled after that, like this was the most fun she'd had all year. Freak.

"What do you want, Olden?" I yelled over my shoulder.

As we waited for a reply, Lucy and I moved back against the table, sliding down lower.

Looking at the ground, I picked up one of my knives. I'd lost it as I dived away. The other was still strapped into my jacket cuff. I was lucky I hadn't cut my hand off.

"I'll run through the tables and draw her fire," Lucy whispered. "You take Olden out."

I shook my head fervently. No way ... hell, no.

"You know I'm right. You're awesome with the knives, but even you can't dodge bullets and aim." Fire burned in her blue eyes.

"Wait a minute. My father's like a superman

dude or something. Maybe bullets do just bounce off me?"

Our murmured conversation was interrupted. "Sorry, baby girl, we're not bulletproof. Weapons can injure and incapacitate us. We just have the ability to heal from almost anything."

I jumped about a foot in the air. Lucy pretty much ended up in my lap.

I hadn't even seen Josian arrive. Bloody sneaky superman.

"So I think I'll be the distraction. You girls do what you need to take your leader out."

I looked into the burnt amber of his eyes and nodded. This was a plan I could work with.

He smiled. "On the count of three."

Between us we had six knives. Time to make them count.

I tightened my hold on the handle, breathing in and out to calm my nerves.

Olden's mocking voice rang out. "I never took you for a coward, Abigail ... if that's even your name."

I ignored her. I had people to save. The fact Josian wasn't going mental and killing everyone meant Lallielle was still alive, but I didn't know about the rest.

"One ... two ... three ... go."

He dived into the center of the path. By the time

I stood, knives-ready, Josian was already dodging in and out along the path, moving almost too quickly for me to track him. He seemed to be throwing small balls of light in Olden's direction. It was utter confusion.

Olden definitely hadn't been expecting that. In the few moments it took her to raise her weapon back to firing position, I dived sideways from my table into the path. I palmed off the first knife, mid-flight. Crouching, I took an extra heartbeat to breathe and calm before releasing my second.

The first flew a little wide. It embedded in the crate behind Olden's head. But the second was a direct hit. Unfortunately her guard was good at his job. He sprung forth, and by the time I looked again the knife was hilt-deep in his throat. Lucy had followed suit and her knife took out the other guard. I didn't have time to comprehend that I'd probably just ended a life. Something for therapy at a later date. I needed to help my father.

Josian was almost at the end of the path. Pulling out my remaining knives, I followed him. I dodged and dived, waiting for shots to rain on me. I couldn't see Olden through the confusion – people had started moving. I jumped a few of the bodies lying in the path. Some familiar faces with lifeless eyes. My chest was tight with anger, the panic ebbing on and off along with high doses of nausea.

"Where's Olden?" I puffed to Lucy, who was right behind me.

"I have no idea. I can't see her anymore."

We reached the junction of the path. Josian had the lifeless body of the second guard clutched in his hand. I couldn't see any damage, except for Lucy's knife protruding from the man's biceps. But he was dead.

"Broken neck," Josian said shortly.

"There's a blood trail here. Did Olden get hit?" Lucy pointed out a path of drops that became heavier the further they went.

She was distracted as Samuel reached her side, sweeping her into a hug. "Lucy, are you okay? I couldn't find you." The stress was apparent in his voice.

She gave him a squeeze. "I was with Abbs. We're all good. Sorry I scared you." Her voice lowered then. "I understand your fears, but you know over-protective crap just pisses me off, Sammy."

His eyes met mine over her shoulder. The smallest grin graced his lips. Despite my own small petty jealousy, it made me happy to see he enjoyed Lucy's smart mouth for more than just kissing the heck out of her.

I couldn't see Brace anywhere as I anxiously scanned the room. I refused to think anything had happened to him. After so many years of dream meetings and then this recent time, I wasn't sure I could imagine a world he wasn't part of. Turning away, I followed the bloody path for a short distance. Chrissie appeared at my side – scaring the crap out of me – her face tear-streaked.

"Chandra's dead." She said it without emotion.

I gasped, trying to breathe through the shock and pain. Although we'd never had much to do with each other, I liked Chandra. Chrissie's best friend, with her golden-brown hair and stunning chocolate eyes, had been the outgoing center of attention. Funny and charming.

The weight of her loss wore heavy on Chrissie's downturned face. She pointed a finger at me, her black hair lying in limp scraggly strands, her brows drawn together in sorrow.

"I know you didn't directly do this, Abby. But it feels like all of this happened because of you ... Chandra ... the torture. Because you came to our compound. Because Olden wanted you." She sobbed once before composing herself. "Just stay away from me; I don't want to see you again. You can only be a reminder of everything I've lost."

I swallowed and opened my mouth to ... I don't know ... apologize or something. But the look on her face said she didn't want to hear it. My breathing was harsh and ragged as I stared at Chrissie. Seeing no forgiveness there, I just nodded. Chrissie wiped roughly at her tears before turning and walking away without a backwards glance.

Ouch! I clutched at my throat as her words resonated deep. She was right. Indirectly, I was the reason for many lives lost.

I knew I'd made myself an enemy from someone I'd once counted as a friend. A few of my own tears escaped, their saltiness gathering on my lips. I batted them away angrily.

My heart was heavy as I turned to make my way back to the people gathering at the junction of the path.

A man dove at me from behind a large pile of boxes. Instinct and training kicked in. Hitting the floor hard, I already had my knife in my hand, ready for the attack.

He came at me quickly, darting in with his own switch-blade held aloft. I managed to dodge two attacks, and I nicked him twice in the process. He was fast, flicking droplets of blood as he stabbed toward me. Changing tactics, I threw out a progression of roundhouse kicks and elbows. There was a distinct groan as I connected with his mid-section. I darted away again. My speed, as always, was my greatest asset.

As I went to take him down, I looked around and realized he had been herding me toward a back section. I was now in a secluded space, separated from my group.

Stupid me. I'd been so busy fighting I hadn't noticed.

Another man came at me from the side.

I held both hands in front, my right clutching my best chance: the throwing knife. With a flick of my wrist I nailed the first man in the right side of his chest, high up. Not fatal – if he found help. The other charged me. I used his momentum and body weight to throw him clean over my head and into a pile of boxes.

Olden appeared at my right side.

"Hello, Abigail," she said as she lunged at me. Her thin physique hid strength I had no idea she possessed.

I attempted to dodge the second attack, but something tangled at my feet and brought me down. I landed next to the man, who still had my knife in his chest. He'd somehow dragged himself over, leaving large trailing puddles of gore, to wrap his arms around my legs. I ordered my stomach not to react to the pungent aroma of the congealing blood.

Olden straddled me. "The master wants you, Abigail. But he didn't say in what condition."

She laughed. Her eyes were bright, feverish, her pupils dilated and moving rapidly. I'd seen cracked-out gangers before. Olden was off-her-face.

I wriggled and kicked, but with the man's dead weight on my legs I was stuck.

"Get off me! I don't have time to deal with your particular brand of crazy today," I yelled into her face. Gods I hated her.

She moved and a sharp burning pain was my first indication. Looking down, I shook my head. I knew I was in shock. Nothing was registering.

With my free right hand, I reached out and grasped the handle of the large knife that had just been plunged into my chest.

Olden leaned close to hiss at me. "I wouldn't move so much. You wouldn't want that blade to twitch any closer to your heart."

The pain was nauseating, the world flashing at me in black, then color. My vision wavered. Squeezing my eyes closed, I grasped the knife, attempting to yank it free.

An ear-piercing scream echoed. I realized it was from me. Hoarse little gasps bubbled from my lips. I waited to die. I wanted to die – or black out at least.

From the shadows, Brace appeared behind Olden. Even through the flashing world and blinding pain, relief flooded over me. He was alive.

He lifted her off me, his expression dark and deadly. With a cold and clinical ability, he broke her neck. Without effort. So quick she hadn't even had a chance to turn her head.

Throwing her aside, he moved my way, but was intercepted by two black-clad men. Brace's half-smile glower was terrifying. If I had been facing him I would have run for my life. Adrenalin flooded through me, which forced my heart to pump faster, and the blood to gush out around the knife wound. I was afraid for Brace – and it only took frantic seconds for me to realize I didn't have to be.

Lucy might have joked that we were ninjas, but Brace actually was. He'd picked up a long, broad, sword from somewhere and was moving between the two men with the grace and skill of a trained assassin. They didn't stand a chance. I must have blacked out for a second. The world fluttered as reality came back. I could see that Brace had dispatched one – he was down in a pool of blood – and the other followed swiftly. Dropping the blood-drenched sword, Brace dived toward me.

He pitched the semi-conscious man that was still resting on my legs into a pile of boxes and dropped down beside me. I continued to gasp, my hand on the knife. Sounds seemed both loud and soft, and I couldn't concentrate on his words.

"Red ... Red. You are going to be okay. Do you hear me? Just ... don't you leave me."

"I don't want to leave ... Brace, it hurts."

He leaned closer, his lips grazing my cheek. My tears fell unchecked.

"I know it hurts." His voice caressed me, soothing as it always did. "I'll fix this, I promise, Red."

Faces appeared behind him. Lucy dropped to my other side.

"Abbs, no ... no. This can't be happening." Tears poured from her wide blue eyes. She clutched my hand tightly. Her distraught expression pleaded with me. "Don't you dare die, Abigail," she spluttered through her tears.

"Help her," Brace, on my other side, roared at Josian. "Do something."

Lallielle's face was white as death beside him.

Power crackled around Brace. I thought I could see lightning arcing. His velvety eyes, normally a deep rich brown, were black. I thought it must be hallucinations before death. Brace leaned in, pulling my hand from the knife handle. I gasped, then my screams echoed through the warehouse.

Chapter 13

The days that followed were both restful and frustrating.

Lallielle and Josian were yet to let me far from their sight. Apparently that little incident was too close for comfort, even for a Walker. I have little recollection of my trip back, and thankfully I was completely out for the knife removal.

With some help from Josian's energy, my recovery was progressing. The puckered pink scar on my chest ached on and off, but I was alive.

I awoke from my afternoon nap to find Lucy perched on the side of my bed.

"You know, Abbs, I could live in your wardrobe." She lay back, sighing wistfully. "And the blue stone is back again."

Rubbing my eyes, I sat up, working through the stiff pain that shot through my chest. Lucy was dressed in an ankle-length, floaty white dress. It was perfect for the balmy weather of First World. She'd already been making up for all our years without a massive walk-in wardrobe and had taken to wearing at least two different sets of clothes a day. The dress, generally thigh-high, looked gorgeous on her blond beauty.

Glancing to my left I could see the laluna nestled in the pillow next to mine. The blue pulsed, and I could feel the warmth it created. No matter how many times Josian took it away, it just kept reappearing. The little Walker world had claimed me.

Shifting it to my side table, I looked around the room. "Where has everyone disappeared to?" I hadn't seen anyone all day. Odd for my overprotective parents.

Lucy laughed. "I have no idea. Sam took off with your parents earlier, something about having to meet an old acquaintance." She shrugged.

"How are things going with Samuel?" I asked her.

Since my revival from the dead, I hadn't spent any quality time with my brother. He appeared to be avoiding me and, not wanting the emotional drama,

I hadn't bothered to care. I'd had enough of my own emotional breakdowns.

At least the last few nights I hadn't being dragged awake by my own screams. I continued to dream of my own grisly death, sometimes stabbed again; in others it was a broken neck, and Olden was always the murderer. Thankfully, the image of the dead guard, my knife in his throat, was fading. Though my last confrontation with Chrissie never seemed to disappear. Lucy thought all of the girls from the compound had scattered from the warehouse. By the time they got me into a doorway to First World, none had been around.

Lucy again distracted me from my dark thoughts, her lovely smile spreading across her face. It'd been absent too long. I missed my usual snarky friend, but she was getting her groove back.

"Honestly, he's wonderful ... awesome ... and too sexy for his own good. I would never have made it through my kidnapping without him."

The scars crisscrossing Lucy's back had not faded much. She wouldn't talk about it, but I knew she'd been tortured for information, on more than one occasion.

Then she surprised me. "You know whenever Olden took me away, Sam would fight through his bars to stop her. And then when I came back into the room, worse for wear, he talked to me for hours.

His voice, his stories, they allowed me to escape for a time."

I hated it when her blue eyes held that empty horror.

"I'm pretty sure his stories and lovely husky accent got us all through the day."

One of the few things Lucy had confided was the reason for Samuel's unique husky tones. His vocal cords had been damaged during his year of imprisonment and torture.

"I still can't believe I dreamed of those cells and then ended up there, Abbs. Sometimes I'm afraid to fall asleep, afraid I'll dream a new catastrophe."

I laid a hand on her arm for comfort, but I couldn't contain my own worry. I'd had my own weird dreams that night, and really wasn't keen for them to come to life. I knew it was to punish us that Olden deliberately targeted Lucy for the worst of the treatment. A familiar white flash of anger threaded through me. Olden was dead, and a person could only be killed once, but sometimes I wished that wasn't the case.

"Luce, there is no doubt a true bond exists between you and Samuel."

The type of unbreakable bond forged in battle.

She smiled, the sheen of happy memories in her eyes. I pushed down my brief flashes of jealousy.

I hadn't seen Quarn or Brace since arriving back on First World. Quarn had gone back to his home. He wanted some time with Hallow's things – which Lallielle had stored for him – and to mourn properly. I'd given up questioning Brace's absence. There had been no word from him since we'd returned. Sometimes the ache in my chest was from more than a big-ass knife wound.

I had a sudden thought. "Did I tell you Brace has seen me naked?"

We both needed some light-hearted relief. My blunt statement had its desired effect. Lucy whipped her head around so fast that she fell off the bed.

Climbing back up, her face was a mask of disbelief. "You and Brace ... what? Had sex?" Her mouth parted in shock.

I laughed, one hand holding my chest to ease the pain.

"Of course not. What type of girl do you think I am?"

Lucy shrugged. "One that takes advantage of all the hotness that is Brace."

I shook my head, and before she could create any other elaborate scenarios, I explained what had happened that day. As expected, she got a good laugh out of the entire scenario.

Lucy changed the subject as she rolled back onto the bed. "You know, Lalli's finished my room. She let me pick the wall color."

I rolled my eyes. "Bet she regretted that decision."

Her laughter sprang forth. "It's amazing. Turquoise with chocolate brown accessories. Just how I always pictured my first room."

Tired again, I rested against my pillows, ignoring the familiar need to escape.

Leaning down, I sniffed a few times. I really needed a shower; when the smell starts to bother your own nose, you know it's time.

"Lalli said, when you're up to it, I can go clothes shopping."

I nodded, closing my eyes. "Sounds great, Luce. You know how much I love to shop."

Despite my sarcasm, I was happy she was there and loving everything. It went a long way to soften the memories of her time with Olden.

She'd gushed to me for hours about how gorgeous the house was, and her room and Samuel. She was happy.

My door opened. Lallielle and Josian crowded into the room.

I smiled at my parents. My relationship with Josian was wonderful. He was huge and intimidating and passionate, but I already loved him. Maybe it was genetic, but I didn't care.

After the stabbing, he'd been crazy protective, barely allowing anyone except Lallielle near me, which might have had something to do with Brace's abrupt departure. Even Lallielle and I were ... better. I was growing up, accepting her tough decisions. And she was giving me the space to come to terms with it.

"Hi, where have you been today?" I looked between the two of them as they dropped into armchairs on the other side of my bed.

Lallielle leaned forward, excitement across her nobly gorgeous face, green eyes alight.

"We had to speak with the town chair about possibly throwing an event for your birthday."

I shook my head as I sat up again. "No ... seriously. No way. I don't want to be the center of attention." I looked toward Josian in desperation. "I'd rather be stabbed again."

Lallielle shook her head. "Don't even joke about that, Aribella."

Josian chuckled. "Sorry, baby girl." He'd taken to calling me that constantly. "I've been outvoted by your mother."

Rolling my eyes, I groaned. "There's no way for me to get out of this, is there?"

Lallielle shook her head. "No, Aribella. You need to be revealed to First World. And ... it'll be fun."

I stared at the ceiling. "I heard that hesitation. What are you not telling me?"

She smiled brightly. "Nothing. I just want to show you off."

I gritted my teeth. Lucy was practically bouncing next to me she was so excited. "Next week, we're getting new dresses," she said.

Lallielle clapped her hands together as she stood. "I'll start prepping the ballroom immediately." She walked off, muttering about how much she had to do.

I turned panicked eyes on Josian. "Reel her in, Dad, or I won't be responsible for my actions."

Leaning over, he kissed me on the forehead. "I'll see what I can do. Don't lose it yet."

With a wink, he took off. I groaned. This event was all I'd hear about from Lucy and Lallielle until my birthday.

Later that week, after managing to shower and change, I was downstairs in the living room, sprawled back on plush couches so soft that I sank into their depths. Lucy was on the floor, stuffing her face with popcorn.

"Your newfound love of junk food is astounding."

She couldn't answer; her mouth was too full. Any attempts to speak simply spluttered bits of kernel from her mouth.

We were watching a movie. Apparently First World didn't have an entertainment industry, so everything we had was pirated from some network connection to Earth. Don't ask me how it worked. Samuel was the Flecho here, dominating all things technological and manmade. They were the same movies we used to have back home. I smiled as an animated ogre argued with a donkey. This was one of my old favorites. Now this world made perfect sense to me.

Samuel appeared in the doorway. I averted my eyes as he swept Lucy up off the floor for a kiss. For some reason, the pair couldn't go more than ten minutes without touching. Lucy was the calm to all the broken that was Samuel. She didn't seem to mind, but I worried that he might be damaged beyond repair.

Lucy was breathless and flushed. She smiled into his face. "What's up, my sexy Sam? Everything okay?" She seemed to like teasing him more when I was around.

His hard features gentled. The only time I ever saw his mask fall was around Lucy. "Yes, I just wanted to see you."

He looked over his shoulder toward me. I stared resolutely at the screen. "Mom wants you, Aribella. Something to do with color sashes."

I groaned. It never ended. What center piece? Help with the seating charts for people I had no idea about. And there was no point avoiding it. She was tenacious.

The pain was minimal now, so without much distress I strode out of the room, relieved to be escaping their distinctive murmurs and soft laughter. I was halfway down the hall when I realized I'd left my necklace on the couch. I'd taken it off earlier that day to show Lucy both the moonstale and my marks. Clutching at the neckline of my shirt, I suddenly felt naked.

Turning, I made my way back to the room. But at the sound of conversation I paused outside the slightly open doorway. Lucy and Samuel were in the midst of a discussion, their tones somber.

Lucy's soft voice drifted out to me. "I'm just worried about her, Sammy. She's not sleeping well, despite what she thinks. And I hate that no one knows her future."

Awesome. She was discussing me with my idiot brother. I couldn't wait to hear his reply, considering my serious doubts about his intelligence.

"From what I have seen of Aribella, she's a strong person. I have no uncertainty that anything thrown her way she'll deal with."

Hmmm, maybe he was smarter than he looked. I was shocked to hear that almost positive-character-trait observation from Samuel.

"When I was locked in the cage, all I could think about was getting to Abbs. And then watching that bitch Olden stab her, thinking she was lost to me again, forever this time ... it changed me fundamentally. I can't live in a world that Abby isn't in."

I was hearting Lucy so much right now.

"I understand. Abby, in a manner, is your soul mate."

"Hell, yeah! She's my BFF, soul mate, coolest chick I know."

Samuel laughed. I took a staggered step back. I hadn't heard happiness from him before. For a moment I had a brief glimpse of the light-hearted friend Brace had lost.

"But before you make any crazy plans, I need you to remember I can't live in a world you're not in, Luce. The darkness I existed in – until they opened that door and led you to the cell next to mine – it was an all-consuming darkness. I was a changed person, I was destroyed, no longer Samuel. But now, you're my light."

There was silence for a few minutes. I was not even going to imagine what they were doing.

Lucy's voice sounded teary. "Abby worries the kidnapping was too much for me to handle. But it was actually the best thing to happen." She cleared her throat. "You are also my soul mate, Sammy. I feel it in the ache of my heart, in the urge to be by your side for eternity."

"It does feel strong, and maybe it is even unnatural the way this has happened, Luce. But I can promise you will never regret choosing me. I'll be that man for you, the one who wipes your tears, kills your spiders, chases away the fears, fights the darkness, and never ever leaves you."

Okay, now I was kind of hearting Samuel as well. And I really didn't even like the big douchewad.

Silence descended over the room again, maybe a few murmurs but I couldn't make out any more words. They were going to be here forever, but I really wanted my necklace.

I walked back ten steps before moving forward again. But this time I was loud and whistling as I moved closer to the door. I knocked once before strolling right in.

They were snuggled on the couch. Lucy looked a little dazed as she smiled at me.

"Hey, Abbs, that was fast. What did Lalli want?"

I shook my head. "Nah, I was almost there when I realized I'd forgotten my necklace. You know I hate being without it now."

Lucy jumped up immediately. "Where did you leave it? On the couch after you showed me your un-freaking-believable Walker marks?"

I nodded once, a small smile turning up the corners of my lips. I loved my marks too.

Lucy scrabbled around in the corner chaise before emerging triumphant. I'd been studiously ignoring Samuel, but he caught my eye as I turned. There was something buried in his light-brown depths. And for once it didn't seem to be animosity, maybe more curiosity.

I took the necklace from Lucy, and blew her a kiss before I left the room again to find Lallielle. My thoughts were troubled, worried about everything that had happened, but mostly that which was still to come.

Lallielle was in the entrance room. The white and burnt-orange couches had been pushed aside to make room for a massive table, which groaned under paper, material samples and other crap.

I slouched into the orange single-seater. Lallielle hadn't even noticed my arrival. She was engrossed in a book of material samples.

"Alright, Lalli, hit me with these sash choices," I finally said.

She didn't flinch. My arrival hadn't been as unnoticeable as I'd thought. She couldn't have picked up my thoughts. My shield was solid. Josian had worked with me until my head ached, but I was shielded.

Lallielle didn't answer immediately, busy finishing up something, so my perturbed thoughts went back to yesterday's training session. I'd eventually asked Josian about his strange expression when he'd first met Lucy. Generally, I felt as if I could read him pretty well. Highly emotional, his feelings were out there for all. But the moment I asked, his expression shut down. He'd said she reminded him of someone, which was totally not the whole story. But that was all the information I could get before he kicked my butt back to training.

Shaking off my worries, I waited patiently. Eventually Lallielle finished what she was doing and spun around, book clutched in her hand. As she opened her mouth to speak, we were interrupted.

Crystaline, the head housekeeper, had appeared in the doorway. "You have a visitor, Madam."

Without preamble, a woman stepped into the room. Lallielle gasped, the book falling to the carpeted floor. I sat upright in my chair as I recognized her: the woman from Lallielle's memory.

Her waist-length white hair was braided off her face, a few strands framing her pale skin and white eyes. Those eyes were creepy as creep, and to complete the creepiness she was covered from head to foot in a white cloak.

"Francesca?" Lallielle moved closer, disbelief in her voice. "Where have you been?"

The woman reached out a hand, sorrow in her expression. "Lalli, I'm so sorry. Sister – please forgive me."

I attempted to pick my jaw up off the floor. This was my aunt. Why had no one ever mentioned that to me?

Lallielle clutched the outstretched hand. "Why did you leave then, Frannie? I needed you. Aribella needed you. I thought you were dead." Her voice shook. "I never even told Aribella that you were her aunt. I believed it to be easier since she was never going to meet you."

Lallielle and I were going to have words soon about this protecting me for my own good thing. It was annoying.

Pulling her arm free, Francesca crossed the room and sank into a chair. She looked exhausted.

"I've traveled non-stop for two days to reach you, Lalli. Just give me a chance to explain."

Taking a calming breath, Lallielle sat next to her.

"I know how angry and hurt you are. I just need you to wait for the end of my story before you berate and question me."

I found it disturbing to try to track eyes without color, iris or pigmentation. Pure white. As I had that thought, she faced me. I decided it was safe to stare somewhere in the middle of her face.

"Aribella. I knew this would be the moment we met officially. How I wished things would be different for us all." She tugged nervously on the long strands of free hair. "From the moment I touched you as a baby, three different paths for your future opened up to me. I've spent the rest of these years hoping I made the right choice, and watching the future shift and change."

Lallielle shook her head. "I don't understand. You told me the poem thing. You never mentioned different outcomes."

"Always the same, little sister: impatient. Let me tell my story. That poem appears to be technically correct, but I only gave you half the information."

Lallielle sat straighter, emotions ready to burst forth. But she held her tongue, simply glaring at her white-haired sister.

Francesca was looking at me again. "This is about the Walkers. More importantly, the original Walkers."

Josian walked into the room. With his hearing and general sneakiness, he'd probably been listening the entire time. For some reason the man was everywhere and knew everything. He leaned against the far wall but didn't interrupt.

"The worlds are dying. The negative energy from First World is moving into the ether of the six youngling planets. Which of course we already know. But I've figured out why." She looked toward Josian. "Someone's freeing the Seventine."

He grew even more rigid as something passed between them.

I looked around the room. "Is this the same Seventine you mentioned earlier?"

Josian shook his head. "That's just a theory. This is pure legend at this point, Frannie."

She glared. "You of all people should know that everything legend has a basis in truth, has an origin and a history."

"Don't you tell me what I shou–"

"Two are free."

Josian shook his head. "That's impossible. There are none left with the knowledge to find them."

"Someone has figured it out," Francesca said, before turning to me. "They must be stopped. I have seen that you're important, although you cannot do it alone."

I didn't know what to say.

A sigh drew Francesca's attention. She reached over to separate Lallielle's tightly clenched fists and hold both hands.

"I have a confession to make."

I couldn't be sure, but the white of her eyes looked pleading.

"When you brought Aribella to me, I didn't see her early demise. I *saw* that she had to grow up on Earth. I couldn't tell you the truth, Lalli, for you loved Aribella too much and would never have parted with her for anything less than her death."

A single tear trailed down her cheek. "It pained my heart to hurt you, but there was so much more at stake than you even realized. It's literally the fate of the entire universe."

The room erupted then. Pretty much everyone started yelling at once. Except for me. I just sat there feeling bemused.

"How could you not tell me the truth, Frannie? And why did Aribella need to be on Earth? What's this great reason you ripped our family apart?" Lallielle's loud voice wasn't the only one.

Josian boomed: "How do you know of the Walkers and Seventine? These are private stories. Who have you spoken with?"

"I told you, Sam. Didn't I tell you something was happening here?" Lucy had somehow made her way downstairs to hear the last part, Samuel right behind her.

"Yes, Luce, you told me," he replied in his typical dry manner.

She looked at me. "And let's put a little more pressure on Abby. Save the world, Abby. Oh, no. Wait. If you're not too busy – save the universe."

"Aunty Frannie?" Samuel looked shocked. "I haven't seen you since I was a child. Where have you been?"

Ignoring the loudness echoing around the room, Lallielle was now muttering in another language, something she tended to do when upset.

I leaned forward in my chair. "What else did you see?" I don't know why I asked but at least the room quietened again as Francesca spoke.

"I disappeared because if I didn't go into hiding I'd have been captured and forced to reveal my visions for the future – altering everything. I foresaw my return, at this exact date and time."

Lallielle smiled, just slightly at this. "Frannie is one of the only natural-born soothsayers. It's among the rarest talent. Her skills have always been in demand, although she's equally admired and feared."

"So the hair ... eyes ... part of the package?" Lucy leaned forward. She was now sitting on the floor with Samuel.

Lallielle nodded and Francesca continued. "I stayed hidden, waiting, watching events unfold. But now I've returned to reveal the information that could spell the difference between survival and annihilation." She shook her head in frustration. "I don't see everything, just glimpses and they keep changing."

"Why does it change?" Lucy took the words out of my mouth.

Lallielle laughed derisively. "Because free will exists. Frannie sees a path, but people change their minds, make other choices, and everything shifts."

"Yes. I saw one future for Aribella at first. But the moment Lallielle sent her away an entirely new path opened."

I rubbed a hand over my face, and up to the tension forming in my temples. "So what am I supposed to do now?" Since apparently it was outside my control.

Francesca shook her head. "You need to stay here until you turn eighteen. As I told your mother long ago, this is the enlightening of your Walker powers."

I shook my head. But she continued anyway.

"But after this you have to find the other half-Walkers girls."

"Excuse me? Half-Walkers." Josian snorted out his disbelief. "Aribella's the only one."

Francesca shook her head. "No, she's not. There has been one woman of power on each planet to carry a half-Walker female to term."

"So you're telling me I need to travel to other planets, which are vastly different to any world I've ever seen and what … just stumble across these girls?"

Francesca's eerie smile crossed her face. "Exactly ... you catch on quickly, Aribella."

I looked around the room in puzzlement. "And if I don't do this, the world will end?"

She nodded again.

Excellent.

"I'll check my schedule and get back to you." I stood to leave the room, needing some air. As I walked out the front, I could still hear them arguing through the open window.

"I'm going with her," Josian said loudly.

"You cannot go, Josian. You need to start rallying your people. I see an epic battle. We already have the smaller chance. There are too many outcomes for a clear future. But we need all the Walkers."

Lallielle sounded angry. "I just got Aribella back. She was stabbed in the chest and now you expect me to send her off alone, to strange planets."

"No, Lalli. I see a few of her friends along for the journey."

Lucy's voice came from behind me. "You're not going without me, Abbs."

She'd joined me on the front porch. I was sitting on the railing, my feet dangling, so she leaned in next to me.

Josian's voice rose again. "I can't even sense Aribella. How will I find her or know if she needs me?"

"The half-Walkers are cloaked to Walker powers. It's a safeguard. You can't sense her, but neither can any other Walkers. The only reason you've ever caught any of her thoughts was through close proximity and a paternal relationship."

Josian continued to roar: "She's too precious to risk in this endeavor." He really was like a red-maned lion at times.

Lallielle's voice was calmer. "If Aribella wants to do this, we'll let her go. She's strong. She survived Earth for years without us. This is probably why I had to send her away: to make her strong enough for this challenge."

There was silence for a minute, before Josian spoke again, quiet and deadly. "Know this, soothsayer, if anything happens to my Aribella, if she doesn't return to me safe and sound, you will not need to worry about the Seventine. My rage will destroy the worlds."

Sighing, I took Lucy's hand. We walked back inside to face the angry and concerned room.

I glanced between everyone. "I want to say hell no and eff this. But since we're talking the end of the worlds, it's looking like I have no choice but to find these half-Walkers."

No doubt that was going to much harder than it sounded, seriously.

Lucy glared around. "I'm going with Abby, though, and no one better stop me."

Samuel stood then. "Over my dead body. If Aribella chooses to leave, well that's her prerogative, but ... Lucy cannot be risked." For once he was stepping away from his reserved personality.

Over his dead body? "That can be arranged, ass-hat," I muttered.

He glared before turning back to Lucy. She simply raised her eyebrows. Samuel took a moment before reaching up to massage his temples. He pushed his dark hair back.

"I'll be accompanying the girls," he said unhappily.

I laughed out loud. Samuel glared his hatred. I shrugged. *What?* It was funny.

I turned to Francesca. "So where do we go first?" Besides Earth, I had no idea about the other youngling planets.

"The day after your enlightening, you need to leave. You'll head to Spurn."

"Spurn? What's that supposed to be?"

Samuel spoke up then. "A planet that's ninety-five percent water. I've heard their inhabitants are hybrid fish."

"Uh, Luce and I aren't exactly strong swimmers," I said, as I worried at my bottom lip.

Lucy fidgeted next to me.

Lallielle looked concerned. "What do you mean?"

I shrugged. "We'd drown in a bathtub – if it was too deep."

Samuel added more. "There's a section of land. It's small, housing their materials for construction. No one resides there, but we can use that as our base. The air content is the same as here and Earth, so we'll be able to breathe."

"How do you know so much?" Lucy asked him.

He shrugged. "We're taught of First World's younglings during our years in the learning centers."

Francesca spoke again. "For some reason you have to face Spurn first. But it should be an easy initial task. The order of the planets is clear, but not the reasons for that order. The one warning I do have: don't spend too long in the waters of Spurn. I sense an unusual darkness."

Got to love unhelpful crazy talk from soothsayers.

"You're seeing Aribella's future very clearly, Frannie," Lallielle said, narrowing her brows.

"I've had almost seventeen years to piece together the facts, Lalli. Plus you know I see family better than I see others."

Lallielle shook her head. "Sometimes I wonder why it's always my family that has to 'save the world'."

Francesca took her hand. "With power comes responsibility. We've always known that."

Later that night, sleep eluded me. As I rolled over for the fiftieth time to stare at the ceiling, I contemplated how out of control my life was. Needing to escape, I hopped out of bed and stepped through my balcony doors onto the large deck off my room. As I stood at the railings, the cool clean air washed the sheen of restless sweat from my body.

My room was on the side of the house that faced the ocean. In the light of First World's bright moon, I watched the cresting waves. I was becoming accustomed to the salty tang of the air. Although at first it had caused my curls to go haywire, after using this spray from Lallielle, I'd almost no frizz. It was magic in a bottle.

Yesterday I'd discovered swimming wasn't quite as easy as I'd anticipated. I'd managed a short paddle. My slightly pink shoulders were a warm reminder.

I squinted into the darkness. There appeared to be a shadow beneath the overhanging cliffs. I watched for a few moments, but saw nothing more. I could have sworn a person was standing there, watching me. Shaking off my unease, I turned to make my way back inside.

I wasn't surprised to see Lucy in my bed. She snuck in whenever the nightmares were bad. And we were so used to sleeping close to each other, we struggled with the distance.

She yawned loudly. "Couldn't sleep either, Abbs?"

While the restless nights really affected her, I seemed to be able to go longer without sleep.

"Not really." I climbed in beside her. "I enjoy listening to the waves. It's calming."

"Then you must be excited beyond belief that we're heading to water-world," she muttered, snuggling into the pillow.

No, not really.

Closing my eyes, finally tired, I drifted off. I hadn't dreamed of First World since we'd been at Deralick's house. In fact, once the nightmares of killing the guard waned, my nights had been surprisingly dream-free.

But not tonight. I was tormented with dreams of thrashing in endless water for hours, while boats filled with blank-faced people drifted past me. Shadowy figures rose from the depths, tormenting me with fear, but never fully revealing themselves.

Chapter 14

I kept my eyes closed.

"Come on, Abby. It's not that bad. Open your eyes."

I shook my head. "No, I'm fine. I don't need to see."

For the past hour Lucy had had me glued to a chair in my bedroom. She and Lallielle had been flittering around me, primping my hair, fixing my make-up.

Tonight was my birthday party. I wasn't officially eighteen until the next day, and so far there hadn't been any weird changes in powers or abilities. I hoped to skip all of that.

"Aribella, open your eyes." Lallielle was smiling. Even through closed eyes I could tell.

With a sigh, my eyelashes fluttered open. Immediately, I was yanked to my feet by an excited Lucy.

Lallielle hugged me. "Okay, I'm going to head down now. You both look stunning."

She was worried about being late. It had taken them longer than expected to tackle me into the chair. She was already dressed in a flowing floor-length green gown. She looked amazing and exotic, like a Grecian goddess in her one-shouldered dress. Blowing me a final kiss, she left the room.

"Luce," I exclaimed, seeing her for the first time. "You look gorgeous."

At some point during my torture, she'd found time to get ready. Her wavy hair had been straightened. She was wearing a strapless blue dress which matched the color of her eyes. They looked even bluer than normal. As she moved, the chiffon lace sheath swished around her legs.

"How have you had time to get ready and help me?"

She rolled her eyes. "Making you look beautiful is not exactly a difficult thing."

I groaned. It had certainly felt difficult.

We made it into my wardrobe. Lucy grabbed my dress from the hanger. I had chosen a simple black silk. Hand-tailored to fit me, it was all kinds of stunning. Stepping into the tightly fitted sheath and adjusting the bodice, I slipped the halter over my neck. For the first time I had cleavage and I was a bit proud of it. It even covered the pink scar on my chest.

Lucy zipped me up before handing me a pair of killer black heels. And killer was right. After two minutes in these five-inch stilettos, I'll probably have broken my neck.

Sighing, I took them. I'd put them on downstairs.

"Are you going to check out our hard work before we head down?" She had no problem stomping around in her own heels.

Screwing up my nose, I shook my head. I wasn't ready to face a mirror. I wasn't ready to turn eighteen. I just needed everything to slow down. I could see the backpack, ready for our adventure the next day. Code name: save the world.

"No, I trust you and we're already late." I needed air and to wash my face. But if I did that Lucy would knock me out for sure. We left my room and headed down the hall.

"So, do you think Brace is going to be here tonight?"

Most of the time I managed to avoid talking about him. Now if I could just stop thinking about him, I'd be set. I kept reliving his expression as he broke Olden's neck, the panic I read in his eyes as he dropped beside me. His soft words in my ears … gah.

Lucy walked smoothly, despite her own six-inch heels. "Sam mentioned that Deralick and Quarn should be here tonight, but I'm not sure of Brace."

"He's just so different from my dream, Luce. I never thought it would be this complicated."

She smiled knowingly. "Of course he's different. You had a one-dimensional view of a fictional character. I know you enjoyed the mystery and even a little the pain as he was wrenched away from you each night, but this is real life. He's flesh and blood, with emotions and issues of his own. You need to take the time to get to know him."

Her insight was a refreshing change from her usual suggestive comments.

"You're different since your kidnapping."

Her eyes twinkled. "It's not just the time on Earth. It's Sam."

I came to a grinding halt at her suggestive tone. "Are you saying – you and Sam – like did the deed? Went the whole hog?"

She laughed. "Seriously? The whole hog. One would think we were farm animals. How am I supposed to use those mental pictures the next time I'm with all the hotness that's Sammy?"

"I want to scrub my eyes, ears and mouth out. Brother, remember?"

Continuing to chuckle, she dragged me along the hall again. "Speaking of sexy, have I told you how much I'm 'in love hearting' your marks?"

She hadn't stopped gushing about them since I'd revealed them to her the other day. She'd already known the basics about the Walkers from Samuel. But seeing the real thing had impressed her.

"They're just gorgeous. It's like a frame was made to showcase your unfairly advantageous beauty."

I laughed. As she took my arm, her expression was calculated. We paused at the landing outside the ballroom.

"You ready, Abbs?"

I attempted to pat my hair, which appeared to be piled on my head in an elaborate up-do, and Lucy snatched at my hand.

"Starting to regret not checking the mirror before you left?"

Oh, that was just evil. I grabbed at her arm as she stepped away, stalling my inevitable entrance into the ballroom.

"I'm scared to see him, Luce." I shared the unshakable fears I held deep in my heart. "He just doesn't feel the connection." My heart was heavy with a multitude of regret and despair.

"Who? Dumb-ass, hot-ass?" She raised her eyebrows, her nose wrinkled. "Abbs, come on.

Don't you see the way Brace looks at you?"

My eyes swung around to stare at her. She'd never mentioned this to me before.

"Like you're the last piece of forbidden fruit in the bowl." A slow grin ensued. "He wants you, to pick you, taste you, eat–"

"I get your point, Lucy." I interrupted her drily. I stood there contemplating her words.

She leaned in closer. "He feels it. Something holds him back, Abbs, but he definitely feels it."

She left me there then, stepping through the doorway. The announcement of her arrival was loud, even through the closed door. Lallielle had decided I needed to make a sole appearance or some such crap. I shook off Lucy's words and attempted to focus on my entrance.

I'd had all of this procedure explained already. I probably should have paid closer attention. Burying my head in the sand had not prevented Lallielle's crazy party planning. I slipped on my shoes, wobbling slightly before finding my balance.

Deep breath, Abby. You got this.

I stepped through the double doors to the top of a massive curving staircase.

"Announcing the arrival of Aribella, Contessa Frayre." My new name and title.

The announcer dude had the perfect First World accent. Deep and rich, it echoed throughout the room without the aid of a microphone. I stopped breathing as the entire room fell silent and faced me. I wasn't a shy or introverted person, but after so much of my life spent alone or with Lucy, I mostly hated crowds.

Two seconds from hyperventilating, I was turning to exit the way I'd just come, when I found myself tangled with a man.

"Oh, my apologies. I thought you'd already entered," he said. His masculine voice wrapping around me.

Putting some space between us, I did a double-take. He was massive, typical of the advanced evolution of First Worlders. His features were blond, but his skin was an unusual golden brown. He had an icy cold beauty, almost inhuman. But he was definitely beautiful. Not in the same way as Brace, whose perfection encased a dark warmth that drove me crazy. Blondie was the opposite: a chiseled cold iciness.

"Announcing the arrival of Lucas Questialia, to-be Crown Emperor."

I guess it was time for me to finally meet Lucas.

Reaching forward, he grasped my hand before bringing it to his lips. A jolt of something shocked my arm. It flowed between us. At that moment, a slight smile crossed Lucas's face.

"It's a pleasure to meet you, Aribella. I've been

waiting a long time."

His expression was unemotional, but there was something there that made me uncomfortable. As I pulled my hand free, the tendrils between our grips unraveled and his icy blue eyes flashed. With a slight nod, I turned away and moved forward to walk the massive staircase. He was another complication I didn't need that night. I stumbled at the first step and almost made my birthday debut by tumbling to my death.

With a tight grip on the railing and my eyes focused on my feet, somehow I made the torturous journey down those stairs.

I stepped onto the ballroom floor and was immediately swamped by the crowd. Apparently, when there hasn't been a celebration for years, First Worlders really let their hair down. I smiled at each introduction, but could guarantee I wouldn't remember any of them by morning.

Except maybe Lucas. It was hard to forget an emperor.

He was standing near me, being fawned over by heaps of ass-kissers, although I noticed how easy it was for him to brush them off and move on to the next group. He paused a little longer with a strikingly tall blond woman whose red dress plunged to her navel. She had a husky laugh that floated through the throngs of people. Her red-tipped nails rested easily on Lucas's jacket.

I was distracted from my observations as Josian reached my side. He had created a path so easily through the crowd.

"How are you going, baby girl?" He enveloped me in one of his amazing hugs. He was so huge it was like being engulfed. "You look so beautiful, just like your mother."

"Honestly, Dad … this sucks. I want to escape. My eyelashes weigh two tons, my face is stiff from this make-up, and I swear these heels are communing with Olden's ghost and trying to kill me."

He caught me as I stumbled for about the tenth time in as many minutes.

"Well, you're the right height for a Walker now." He smiled down from his still much more impressive height. "Did you see the presents table, though? Good haul."

I looked over at the large table running along the back wall. It was packed with gorgeous wrapped packages.

This was becoming absurd. "I don't have to open those in front of everyone, right?" Pretending to love gifts from strangers was beyond my meagre acting skills.

Josian was distracted from answering by Lallielle waving us over. She was a little away, chatting to a large group of people. I could see Quarn standing to one side. I waved and he acknowledged me with a nod and mimed a noose around his neck. I laughed. He'd be hating this.

"You go, baby girl. I'll take one for the team." Josian shooed me off in the opposite direction before he moved toward Lallielle.

I walked away as fast as the ridiculous heels allowed and managed to grab a glass of *quant* juice. Looking around, I noticed a nice quiet corner where I could kick off my death-trap heels, and made my way there.

Sinking into a chair, I closed my eyes.

"What're you doing hiding in the corner at your own party, Red?"

I jumped at the smooth voice. When I opened my eyes, I found Brace standing in front of me. He stared for an immeasurable moment, his eyes heated and his expression unreadable.

"There are not words to describe how you look tonight," he said finally before looking away. He let out a strangled breath as he turned back. "I want to say breathtaking, and breathtaking is correct, but it's not enough."

I drowned in the heat of his eyes for a moment, and then I took in the full picture.

Speaking of breathtaking! My heart stuttered. Before that moment I'd never seen him in anything but casual clothes. Tonight his height was emphasized in a perfect fitted black tuxedo. His broad shoulders filled out the jacket. He was huge, solidly built, falling just short of being bulky. He looked dark and dangerous. The silky strands of his stylishly tousled, inky black hair fell along his forehead.

I stood then, torn between throwing myself into his arms, pride be damned, or punching him in his perfect nose.

Angry words erupted before I could stop them. "Where have you been, Brace? Why did you bother to come at all?"

Okay, I was even more pissed off than I'd thought.

Before he could answer, I turned and walked away. The punching in the face option was definitely starting to win.

As I stormed off, I realized I'd left my shoes under the chair. Shrugging, I decided to retrieve them later, hoping no one would notice.

A hand caught my arm. Only at the last second I stopped myself from flipping the person over my shoulder. Old habits. I turned, expecting to see Brace, but it was someone else.

Lucas stood before me. "Would you like to dance, Aribella?"

I should have known. Although the jolt wasn't as

obvious, there was still some type of mild electric connection between us.

I looked to the corner where I'd left Brace. He was gone. I turned back and, with a sigh, nodded.

"As long as you call me Abby."

I placed my hand into the crook of his outstretched arm. He smiled broadly. "Abby it is then." He spun me out onto the floor.

I swayed awkwardly a few times, uncomfortably, but at least I was more coordinated barefoot.

"Sorry, I have no idea how to dance."

Lucas smiled. "Oh, really? I couldn't tell. You do such a perfect sway."

Flushing a little, I returned his smile. "You should see me do the chicken dance. I was compound champion."

Laughing, he leaned closer, the standard First Worlders' perfect white teeth flashing, the cold iciness of his blond beauty softening as he smiled.

"I have no idea what a chicken dance is." He looked down. "Do you realize you aren't wearing shoes?"

I followed his gaze down at my bare toes. At least my toenails looked wicked. They were painted a shimmery black to match my dress.

"Yeah, they're over in the corner somewhere." I sighed. "They were killing my feet."

Lucas threw back his head, laughing out loud. "You're definitely not what I expected."

He wasn't exactly my expectation of the spoilt future emperor either. But there was still something about him that made me feel edgy.

I turned at a low deep growl. There was no one around us. I couldn't tell where the rumble came from. Suddenly a hand appeared on Lucas's arm. Brace appeared from nowhere to stand before us, serious and beautiful. And, as usual, those damn eyes called to me, tantalizing me.

"Do you mind if I steal Abby away for a minute?"

I could hear the restrained anger in his voice. *What was his problem?*

Lucas looked down at me before facing Brace. He had to look up a little to meet his eyes, but eventually he nodded and stepped away.

I noticed Brace had my shiny black heels hooked over his right hand.

"Did you lose something, Red?"

Shaking my head, I snatched the heels from him.

"Now, now, snatching isn't nice, Abby."

Screwing up my nose, I stuck my tongue out at him.

With great difficulty, I managed to finagle my shoes on. Brace stood back, grinning at me.

"Abbs, everything okay over here?"

Lucy and Samuel were swaying next to us. We were in the center of the dance floor.

I nodded once, and before she could question me further, Samuel swept her off. As I watched them, Samuel laughed into her upturned glaring face, before leaning in closer to whisper in her ear. She turned back toward me, looking curious. I shifted my attention before she returned to rescue me again.

Brace held out a hand. "So, how about that dance?"

I glared at him. At least with those stupid heels we were much closer in height.

"How about 'no'?" I turned to leave.

He caught my hand, and hauled me back against his body. "Come on, you don't want to create a scene at your own party," he whispered into my ear.

I couldn't move or answer. Electricity zoomed through our closely pressed bodies. I stopped struggling and just breathed. The connection between us was as strong as ever.

"I'm sorry I haven't been around to visit you."

We were swaying closely. The entire world disappeared.

"I just had a few things to take care of. But Sammy told me about Spurn. I've decided you need me, so I'm coming along."

I pulled back, spluttering a little. "What makes you think we need you?"

What was Brace up to now?

Shaking his head, he pulled me back into his arms. "I said you need me and, more importantly, Sam doesn't want to be the only guy on the trip."

I continued to glare. But there was something I'd been wanting to say, and since this was the first time I'd seen him since Earth, now was it.

I took a deep breath. "Thank you for ... uh ... killing Olden ... saving me." I stuttered over my words. I didn't really know how to express my gratitude.

His light-hearted expression sobered. "I was too slow. There were too many distractions, but ... you should never have been hurt."

I shook my head, but before I could satisfy my need to reassure him, his mood lifted and, grinning, he swirled me away, out of the main dance floor. We moved closer to the large balconies. The doors were thrown wide open and huge fire torches were scattered around. Along one wall were massive antique mirrors with ornate gilded framing.

I caught the first glimpse of my reflection. I looked again, just to make sure that was really me. I looked tall and slim. My full glossy red lips were parted in surprise. The long black dress fitted flawlessly, contrasting with masses of dark red and black hair, which was piled up in messy curls, a few falling to frame my face.

Lallielle and Lucy had outdone themselves with my makeup. My skin was always clear, but tonight it glowed. And my eyes looked even larger and more cat-like than usual; the black kohl lining them enhanced the emerald green.

"I told you. You really have a beauty that is otherworldly," Brace said, observing my stunned expression. "You have the beauty of a Walker."

I turned away. Maybe for the first time I actually did have the otherworldly look of Josian. But that didn't mean I wanted to be the world savior. Or that I even could be.

I turned at the sound of Brace's name. A group of suit-clad men, his friends I assumed, were calling him over. With a regretful glance, he left me there, making his way to them.

I followed him across the room, where he was cajoled into a dance with 'boobs', my nickname for 'vulture woman in the red dress'. Clenching my nails into my wrist, I turned away, attempting to calm my murderous thoughts. I was pretty close to ripping every strand of blond hair from her head. I stepped out onto the balcony, allowing the cool breeze and sounds of the ocean to soothe the ragged edges Brace always left me with.

Later that night, after numerous awkward dances, and countless introductions, the party was over.

Lallielle was off ushering the last of the revelers out the door. Lucy and I were lying on the ballroom floor, staring up at the massive ceiling.

"So, could you have ever imagined this would be your eighteenth birthday?"

Turning my head to the side, I smiled. "I was just hoping we wouldn't be in some type of people-smuggling rape ring for my birthday."

Lucy shoved me. "There's still time, Abbs, twenty minutes till midnight." She looked thoughtful. "What was with you and blondie in the red dress?"

Lucy was referring to the incident that had taken place ten minutes earlier, when 'boobs' had been leaving with her parents. They'd stopped to thank Lallielle. I was standing there as well. As our parents started chatting, she'd leaned in close to me.

"Don't even think you can have First World's most eligible bachelors, Aribella. I don't care what anyone else believes, I know you're not the empress." That wasn't the first time tonight I'd caught murmurs of that. She continued to sneer at me. "I was here first and I'll be long after you're done and gone."

I didn't even flinch at the snarling venom in her low voice. I smiled sweetly as I lowered my own voice. "Seriously, boobs, you don't scare me. I grew up in New York and ran in the ganglands. Hormonal women are the least of my worries. If you don't get your bitchy ass out of my house, I'm going to break your nose."

Lucy erupted into laughter as I explained what had happened. "You called her 'boobs'?"

At my nod, she snorted louder.

While we were relaxing, the boys were off playing some game on a huge felt-covered table. They'd tried to explain the rules, but it was beyond me. Some type of cross between pool and chess, with large colored balls and stone statue people that had to be moved around in a pattern.

I changed the subject from 'boobs'.

"Thanks for the earrings too, Luce, I love them." I reached up to touch the beautiful emerald-colored stone studs. That and my necklace were the only jewelry I had on.

She shrugged. "I did have a vintage tee stashed back home. But these will do."

I laughed.

"So give me a quick rundown on the tales of Abby, First Worlder and Walker." Lucy's side profile looked both worried and intrigued.

I tilted my head back further, staring into the massive and ornate ceiling. In each corner someone had painted an angel warrior. They all held a weapon pointed toward the center of the room. It was spectacular and unusual all at the same time.

"Well, first there is the whole 'half-Walker shouldn't exist' theory. I'm apparently the one to destabilize ... no demoralize ... no that's not right either. Oh, right, I think it was *destroy* them." I rolled my eyes as I mocked the over-dramatics of Walkers.

"Maybe it was 'delight them with your duck-face'?" Lucy offered helpfully. "Maybe that's the 'd' word you're looking for?"

"Duck-face?"

She shrugged. "I got caught up in the alliteration."

Laughing, I continued again, my eyes still locked on the entrancing angels.

"The next one is where I might be the Empress of First World. Apparently my husband-to-be Lucas is a top dude."

Lucy lost it then. She laughed until she was breathless. I'd have laughed too, but unfortunately this was actually my life.

"And lastly, I'm setting out to find some half-Walkers – that don't exist apparently – and prevent an apocalyptic universal battle of mother-effing proportions." I threw my arm over my eyes. "You know, because I'm just that awesome."

"And lucky," Lucy tacked on. "Don't forget lucky."

I snorted at the mere thought.

Lallielle interrupted us, appearing above our heads. "I've organized a little after-dinner in the sitting room downstairs." She smiled. "That way we can all be there when Aribella officially turns eighteen."

As I looked down the long length of my tight black dress, I realized I had no idea how I was getting up off the floor. At least my shoes were off again, and nothing was making me put them back on. For the fiftieth time I flexed my pained toes.

"Lalli, you could have included a huge slit up the side of this dress," I complained. "I can't get my butt up off the floor."

Josian appeared out of nowhere and hauled Lucy and me up together. He threw us each over a shoulder.

I gasped as he dashed from the room. His super speed was breath-stealing.

We ended up dropped together into one of the big soft couches downstairs.

"Superman at your service." Josian got a total kick out of our descriptions of superheroes. He was sure many of them were based on Walkers.

Lucy giggled as she tried to sit up. Josian left us and we were there for at least ten minutes before the others made it to the room.

Quarn looked happier now the crowds were gone. He walked arm-in-arm with Francesca.

I guessed no one had told him that it was her false predictions that had sent us all to Earth. I still hadn't really warmed to the soothsayer. She was unnerving, knowing things the way she did. Plus her eyes had never become any less creepy.

Brace, Samuel and Lallielle were the last to arrive.

Josian stepped back into the room. In his arms he carried a massive bouquet of pink and purple roses.

Struggling out of the couch, I bounced over to him. "They're gorgeous."

"Happy birthday, baby girl." He kissed my cheek. "These are *menorial* roses. If you put them into water, they won't die."

I was relieved to hear that. Much as I loved beautiful flowers, I hated that they died so quickly.

Lallielle organized a huge vase to be delivered, half full of water. I placed my roses one at a time. Their floral and deep musky scent filled the room. Once I was done, I took a seat again.

Samuel shifted in his spot next to Lucy. "Lucas? What are you still doing here?"

Lucas had just walked into the room unannounced. His jacket was off and draped over his shoulder. It was clear no one had known he was still there.

Lallielle spoke fiercely, marching to my side. "You cannot have her, Lucas. She's not the empress." Never mind that last week she'd been sure that I was.

"I'm not here to take Abby," he said, as if I were a piece of furniture he needed delivered. Without expression, he continued, pushing back his blond hair. "Brace explained the mission you're to undertake. I want to assist."

God, these men gossiped worse than Earth women.

Josian leaned casually against the wall. "Why would you want to do that?" I knew him well enough now: that was his suspicious voice.

Lucas shrugged. "This seems to be the way to repair First World." He looked directly at me. "I'd think that was my job more than anyone's."

I hated to say it – the unease was still there – but I couldn't shake the slight curiosity. But that didn't mean I wanted him along on the journey. I was interrupted as I opened my mouth to object.

"Are we getting this party started or what?" Francesca's light-hearted words broke the tension. Surprisingly, she had a wicked sense of humor. She'd be enjoying the strain in the room.

"You knew this was going to happen, didn't you, Frannie?" Lallielle glared at her. "So Aribella goes with Lucy, Samuel, Brace and Lucas? Is there anyone else about to join the group?"

Francesca shook her head, her mouth apparently

too full of cake to speak.

When I looked out the window, the large glowing numbers in the sky told me it was eight minutes to midnight. Eight more minutes before I stopped being Abigail, Earthling, and my destiny as Aribella, First Worlder and Walker, kicked in.

Leaving the arguing group, I stepped outside. I needed a few minutes to walk, so I scooped up the train of my long dress and strode out onto the sand.

No one knew what to expect when I reached my power enlightenment. Josian had told me that full Walkers were born with their powers; they just developed further as they aged. First Worlders' powers kicked in at maturity, twenty-eight. Francesca told them I'd fall between this.

"You shouldn't wander off by yourself, Red." Brace appeared at my side. He was as sneaky as Josian sometimes.

I was standing on the edge of the water line, allowing the cool water to wash over my aching feet. I mentally made plans to burn those heels the next day.

He too was barefoot, with just dress pants and his white shirt, the top two buttons free. "What are you thinking about?"

I glared at him. "You can't actually expect me to share my thoughts with you, disappearing Chuck."

He sighed, staring out into the horizon. "Actually, I'm almost hoping you don't share too many of them. You already drive me crazy with your words. Thoughts are sure to be much worse."

Did I really want to know what that was about?

Once again I found myself turning to leave the crazy tension he created. I'd never think of myself as a coward, but something about Brace scared me to death.

It didn't matter, though. Brace captured my hand, preventing me from escaping.

I'd had enough. Using his bulk, I brought myself in close, lowering my shoulder, and flipped him cleanly over my back. I was lucky enough to have taken him by surprise. Yanking my dress up, I went to pin him down, but he was too fast. Within seconds he reversed our positions. I found myself on my back in the sand, staring up at him. He used his bulk to hold me down before bringing his face close to mine.

"You're important, Abby." He was serious. "These events are much bigger than you and me." His velvet brown eyes softened. "Despite the fact you constantly irritate me." He leaned closer. "But I would take on anyone to keep you safe, by my side, where you belong."

The last part was barely a whisper. I wasn't sure if I would hear any more over the beating of my heart.

I sucked in a ragged breath. His lips were inches from mine.

He shook his head. "Why did it have to be you, Abigail ... all this time?" His thick sooty lashes framing those captivating eyes, his expression and body against mine was driving me insane.

And then he kissed me.

His full firm lips pressed into mine and I forgot everything.

His strange behavior.

The long absence.

My lips opened as the kiss deepened. He kept the bulk of his weight off me, as if he knew I'd hate the loss of independence. All that touched were our lips. I could escape at any point – not that I wanted to.

He did bring one hand down to cup my face. Fireworks exploded behind my closed eyes. A fire burned through me.

Brace groaned against my lips.

And in that moment the time clicked over to midnight. A surge of energy arched me under Brace. The pain was suddenly everywhere, sharp and intense. I looked down to see if knives were filleting my bones from my body.

"Red, what is it? What's happening?"

Pain arched my back again. Brace held me as he tried to figure out what was attacking. With a bloodcurdling scream, my body succumbed to the pain and I writhed on the ground for a few endless moments. My sole aim: just keep breathing.

Chapter 15

Clarity returned in an instant. All pain ceased.

I was still in the sand. But I was alone.

Sitting up, I looked around. I was overwhelmed by the crashing influx of sensory information. In rapid movements my eyes darted left and right. Damn, my eyesight was so much clearer. Even in the dark I could make out certain landmarks I'd never have seen before. My hearing was also improved. I could hear Josian yelling from inside the house. Within moments, he was at my side.

"Baby girl, Brace said something happened to you."

I must have been down only seconds. Josian's shock was apparent as he helped me to my feet. The rest of the group were making their way along the beach to where we stood.

Josian kept staring at me.

"Dad, I'm fine." I grimaced at him. "But you could have told me about the pain. That was brutal."

I rubbed my face. The ache of dicing knives hadn't quite left me yet.

Josian shook his head. "There shouldn't have been pain."

I looked at him closely. Disbelief laced his tone.

I looked around for the problem. "What's wrong?"

The rest of the group reached us. Their faces were as shocked as Josian's.

I looked at Lucy. "Is my skin green? Do I actually look like an alien now?" I patted my face again, disturbing large chunks of sand residing in my hair.

"Your marks, Abbs ... we can all see your marks," she said in a kind of stuttering awe.

In surprise I looked down to see if my necklace had fallen open. It was resting in its usual spot, closed up tight. But, pulsing in the moonlight, my marks ran down my arm into the black of my dress.

Without thought, I raced back up the beach, pounding across the deck and inside to the nearest mirror: the downstairs powder room.

I used the energy stream to turn on the lights and open the door. I stared at my reflection.

The marks were fainter than under the moonstale crystal, but they were there. And my knife wound had disappeared. The pink puckered scar, which had been hidden under my dress strap, was gone. In fact my skin looked perfect, not one spot, scar or blemish. Besides my Walker marks pulsing away at me.

Josian crowded in behind me. I turned my shocked eyes in his direction. "Why has this happened?"

He shook his head. "I don't know, baby girl. I've never seen this happen to any Walker before. But you are the first half-Walker that I've seen reach power enlightenment."

He paused for a moment. Everyone else had crowded into the room behind us. I found myself pressed right against the sink that sat below the mirror.

Lallielle's panicked voice came from the back of the group. "You told me the original Walkers had their marks on display, Jos."

Josian sighed. "Yes, but this has to be something different. Aribella's only half-Walker. I don't know if this has something to do with the combination of First-World and Walker powers or something else entirely."

I glared at my reflection. "This is probably why people wanted to kill me as a baby. No one likes the unknown."

Lallielle forged her way to us. "Josian, we need

to figure this out. We cannot send Aribella out to the youngling planets with Walker marks on display."

"The average person doesn't know about our marks," was his helpful reply.

"Don't worry yourselves," Francesca chimed in from the back of the room. "This is meant to be for Aribella to complete her task. There's nothing more that can be done."

"Thank you, Frannie, succinct and crazy as usual." Lallielle was becoming much too adept at sarcasm.

"No need to be a witch, Lallielle. I was just imparting my wisdom."

Clearly sisters are the same no matter what planet or age. I ran a hand along the pulsing pattern on my arm. I now had the world's biggest ice breaker. Something this out-there was sure to be useful when trying to make friends on other planets.

"We should think up a cover story for your marks," Lucy said as Samuel lifted her up for a better look. "Although, you look gorgeous. They really suit you."

"Thanks, Luce, that makes me feel so much better."

She shrugged. "Who cares how you feel? Haven't I always taught you it's how you look that counts?"

I stuck my tongue out at her.

I started shoving people back so I could leave the powder room. Brace halted me with a hand on my arm. His expression appeared to be light-hearted, but his eyes were a smoldering cauldron of emotion.

"Lucy's right, Red. You do look gorgeous. But please, if you value my sanity, no more screams of pain." He leaned in closer, talking so low I almost missed the words. "I know my kisses are potent, but that was more of a reaction than even I expected."

Flushing, I elbowed him in the ribs as I moved past. His kiss had been potent, and hot, and...

Focus, Abby.

Taking a breath, I finally made it out of the room and back into the hall. Lallielle, who had followed me, took one look at my expression before turning to the group.

"Alright, everyone, to bed now. You're leaving in the morning and you all need as much rest as possible."

Thank God she'd seen that I'd had enough for tonight.

Josian reinforced her. "I want to speak with Aribella before she goes, but, the rest of you, we meet back here at 0800 hours."

I pointedly ignored the worried glances thrown my way. One by one they filed out of the room, taking off to finalize their lives.

Lallielle stopped Lucas with a hand on his arm.

"If you're leaving with them tomorrow, would you like to stay here tonight?"

He nodded. "That'd probably be the easiest. I'll have my assistant drop off a bag."

Lallielle nodded before gesturing for Lucas to follow the rest. He saluted us politely and walked off down the hallway. The edgy feelings disappeared with him.

Francesca stopped in front of me. "I don't know everything. For some reason I'm getting less information than usual." She laughed in her odd way. "But I do know that this has happened to you, Aribella, because you were born to stand out. You're important. You're needed. And one day I hope my visions all come together and make sense to me." She shook her head.

Smiling in a calm manner, I patted her on the shoulder. Her insanity would never make sense to anyone, but it had to be annoying to just get snippets of an ever-changing future. And then be expected to make correctly interpreted predictions.

Lallielle watched her walk away and then kissed my cheek. "I know this is very stressful and confusing, but try and get some sleep tonight. You'll need to be at your best for this journey."

Despite her words, she hadn't completely erased the worry from her eyes. My gaze followed her along the hallway.

Once the space was clear, Josian had my sole attention.

"Okay, before you leave, I need to make sure you can access basic Walker powers. Have you noticed a change since you awoke?"

I nodded. "Yes, my senses are all heightened."

Josian looked happy with that. "Excellent. Your powers will continue to change and grow as you age and as you practice using them."

"So they might just burst out of me randomly?" I asked in horror.

He shook his head. "It should be a slow growth. But then I never expected the marks, so what do I know?"

I could see Josian wasn't used to being unsure. I grabbed his hand and squeezed it. He clutched me a little closer.

"I need to make sure you can access the energy wormholes and open doorways to other worlds. I will not be letting you leave, no matter what *Frannie* says, if you don't have the ability to escape."

He took a deep breath. "I'm going to show you a crude way of creating a doorway. Once you're more in tune with your abilities you'll no longer need to resort to this type of energy manipulation."

I nodded once, running my tongue nervously over my lips.

"Okay, as we've practiced, take some of your energy."

I closed my eyes and reached into my inner spot. It was still there, in the same place. Only this time it was different. Now there was a bottomless pit of pulsing energy, alive and electric, with the same burning warmth I'd felt during my enlightenment. But thankfully muted.

"Draw from the energy, continue pulling it like string. Send it outside yourself, looping into a continuous circle. But do not let go of the end yet."

The substance was still like sticky taffy, but there was a tensile strength now that it had lacked before.

"Visualize the completed circle, but hold on to the end of the string. In the inner space of the circle project an image of your bedroom upstairs."

I followed Josian's words, picturing my gorgeous king-sized bed.

"Open your eyes," Josian directed. "And let go of the string."

I obeyed again, and as my lashes flicked up I gasped.

In front of me, shining brightly, was the dark night of a Walker doorway. Not as large or clear as the one we had taken to Earth. But it was there. And I could see my bed, not too far in the distance.

Without warning, Josian took my hand and pulled me in. I was encased by the familiar sucking sensation. But it was different this time. Instead of an over-abundance of energized cells, moving at the speed of light, I simply drifted with the currents. It was a much shorter trip and at the end we exited onto my bed. No drama.

"That was amazing."

Josian, demonstrative as always, pulled me into a tight hug. "When all of this is over, I'll show you the right way to open a doorway and walk between the worlds.

"And remember, if you need to transport more than one or two people, you have to make sure your doorway is strong enough. At least two rounds of energy per person."

I nodded as I pulled back. "Thanks. And I'll be careful, I promise."

He smiled and moved to exit my room. "See you in the morning, baby girl."

My power hummed as I walked into my wardrobe to finally take off the dress, leaving it bunched on the floor. Everything I left on the floor here was washed and back in my wardrobe the next day. Magic – or housekeepers.

I showered and climbed into bed. I couldn't be bothered with pajamas, so I just wore fresh underwear. My marks continued to pulse at me. I raised a hand above my head so I could see them more clearly.

The enlightenment hadn't gone to plan, but I needed to get some sleep before tomorrow. I closed my eyes, only to find that strange new depthless pit of energy tugging at my attention, like an itch that wouldn't go away. It wanted me to explore, coaxing me closer. Shaking my head, I slammed a heavy roof onto it for now. I was scared to traverse those depths, to know what was there, deep down.

The next morning my eyes flew open. My newfound internal alarm clock had just woken me. It was early in the morning. I had quite a few hours until it was time to leave. As I sprang out of bed, I found my energy was boundless. I dashed into my dressing room. I felt stronger, faster, and I knew exactly where I wanted to be.

Ten minutes later, I quietly walked out the front door and down to the water. The sun was mid-rise, its golden hue highlighted in the now familiar indigo sky. I dropped my drying sheet – the material they used to dry off from the ocean – onto the sand before stepping into the cool water. I'd left my hair loose and wore a simple black two-piece swimsuit. It was skimpier than I would usually wear, but I wasn't expecting company.

I stopped before the calm water reached my waist. I still wasn't a strong swimmer. Palms down on the water, I crested with each small wave, enjoying the fresh air and rays of the rising sun. All too soon, I had to leave. It was time to prepare for the next adventure. I froze as heat traversed my spine to settle at the base of my skull. It was the heat of a stare, and I recognized the signature warmth. I turned away from the horizon, and was not surprised to find Brace standing on the beach, watching me. He looked as if he had been going for a morning run, and with my newfound senses I could see the sweat beading on his sun-kissed skin. By the time I made it out of the water he was gone.

My skin felt flushed and too tight over my entire body. That kiss last night had set off fireworks. I couldn't help but wonder if that chemistry had anything to do with the marks now permanently visible on my skin.

Back in my room, I stood in the bathroom and stared in the mirror for a few minutes. My skin was gleaming. The luminosity was fainter than Josian's but there was a definite glow. My hair was more vibrant, especially against the red marks pulsing back at me. My lips were even naturally redder. Everything I had been before was further enhanced.

I showered quickly before dressing. Ready to leave, pack on back, I made my way downstairs. Lucy and I had coordinated our outfits. We were going with 'bad-ass explorer' – faded blue jeans, stylishly torn, black combat calf-high boots, a white t-shirt, and a black combat vest – the kind that had pockets everywhere. Coats and other essentials were packed.

As I walked along, I could hear everyone in the kitchen long before I reached them. These new senses were going to take some getting used to.

I dumped my pack with the group near the door and walked into the room. I took a plate and filled it before sitting down. The food was so amazing. Lallielle's staff, local women from Angelisian, should all receive awards daily. I was not looking forward to being on the road again, although I was likely to start gaining unwelcome weight if I continued to eat this way. I glanced at Josian. Or maybe not. The way he ate, it appeared as if Walkers had an over-active metabolism.

Lucy raised her head for a moment and waved her hand in my general direction before going back to stuffing her face. For a tiny person, she was a champion eater.

Brace and Lucas were in deep discussion at the end of the table. Lucas gave me a half-smile acknowledgement, but Brace was focused on his plate, his expression troubled.

Got to love men. Kissed the hell out of me yesterday, swim-stalked me on the beach this morning, and now couldn't even look up when I entered the room.

"Morning, baby girl. How did you sleep?" Josian was glowing away at the end of the table, his red hair smoothed down, golden skin luminous, a large stack of flat round pastry pieces in front of him.

These delicious little miracles were shaped like pancakes but filled with a buttery golden syrup. True magic, if you asked me.

"Had some weird waking dreams. Figured out how to open Walker doorways. Got a permanent tattoo and no one knows why. And about to head to another planet." I shrugged. "Can't really complain."

I'd started eating as I talked. A few small pieces of food flew out of my mouth onto the crisp white table cloth.

Josian boomed his laughter. Francesca shook her head. "I don't see too many obstacles in your path." She shrugged. "At least not today."

I shook my head. "I'd feel much better about that if you didn't have your face all wrinkled up with worry."

She smiled, although that was a generous description. More of a grimace.

I laughed. "Very reassuring, thank you. Don't quit your day job, Frannie."

She looked affronted. "But this is my day job." She winked at me.

Brace was still ignoring me. Jerk. Should leave him here with Samuel. Also a jerk.

Look at me making friends everywhere I go.

Josian stood suddenly. "I don't want her to go, Lalli. I don't have a good feeling about this." Worry lined his permanently young features.

She stood as well, reaching out to grip his arms. "I don't want either of my children to take off on their own to some unknown planet, but if it's that or the end of the world then I don't think we have much choice."

He scoffed. "End of this world, maybe. I'll find us another one. A better one."

I laughed. Josian took arrogance to a completely new level. "Can you transport the billions of people on all seven planets?"

With a resigned sigh, he shook his head in my direction. To Josian, those that weren't family didn't factor into his plan.

Brace joined the standees. "I'll keep them safe, Lalli and Josian. Don't worry, we'll be back before you know it."

Josian pointed his finger at Brace. "I'm feeling a decided lack of trust in you at the moment, Brace. I see how you look at my daughter."

For the first time Brace's eyes swung in my direction, before he looked back at Josian. Flushing a little, I stared at my half-eaten food.

"I promise I have no ulterior motives, other than adventure and keeping my friends safe."

Brace was lying. He said that without an ounce of emotion, as if repeating a rehearsed line.

Josian turned his gaze toward me. I nodded at him. I wouldn't be letting my guard down around Brace. Well, I'd try really hard not to, but if he looked at me I was a goner.

Francesca interrupted us. "It's time now. Josian, you go, gather your family. You're going to struggle to find them all. Some have made it their mission to remain hidden indefinitely. Start at the junction between the four quadrants of this universe. And you must hurry or you will miss something important."

Josian frowned at her. "You're getting on my last nerve, Frannie." He marched to the end of the table, muttering about crazy sisters-in-law. Reaching down, he pulled me from my chair for one last hug.

"Stay safe, Aribella. Trust your instincts and make me proud. If you need me, I'll find you, no matter the consequences."

I reached up high to pat his shoulder, offering whatever small comfort I could. "Luce and I are used to looking after ourselves. We'll be fine." He nodded once. "I love you, Dad." I wanted to say it, just in case.

He placed one hand on his heart, before raising it to his lips, kissing it and then touching it to my lips.

"May your journey away from me be short, but your experiences life-changing. Love you too, *Miqueriona*."

I really should find out what that meant.

He moved toward Lallielle then. He touched her face before lowering himself close to press his lips to hers. It was short and ever so sweet.

Lallielle turned away as Josian opened a doorway in an unused corner. I caught a glimpse of fire and night in the far distance, and then with one last kiss blown in my direction, he was gone. The room felt empty. The absence of his presence was huge. Lallielle, looking lost, hugged her arms around her body tightly, but then she pulled herself together.

"Okay, it's time for the rest of you to go as well. Grab your packs and trust no one but each other. These planets are unique and their inhabitants even more so. They will not think the way you expect."

Samuel stepped forward first, hugging her for an extra moment. "Love you, Mother. Don't worry too much. We'll be back soon. Plus Josian and Aribella are pretty much indestructible."

She laughed. "I wouldn't be letting them leave my side if that wasn't the case. The only reason you are going is I know I can't stop you. You're too old to send to your room now."

Francesca ushered us out into the main hall. "Everyone, get your bags. Aribella will open a doorway. Don't worry about Lalli. I will stay here with her."

"That's very reassuring, Frannie, since it's your predictions that have put us all in this position. And most of the time no one has a clue what you're talking about."

"Shut up, Lalli. We aren't too old that I can't hurt you."

Lallielle laughed. "Actually, sister, you're much too old."

Lallielle and Francesca had conveyed that they were well over a hundred years old, despite the fact they looked young enough to be twenty-five. Although neither of them would tell me their exact age.

Reaching down, I grabbed my pack. During breakfast, some food and other items had been added. The pack was light, but probably wouldn't be on Spurn.

We gathered as a group in the main entranceway. Francesca handed me a photo. "This is the place on Spurn you want to picture."

I glanced down to an island paradise. Pink-colored sky and weak-sunlight glinting off the sandy white beaches. Nice.

Lallielle stood before me. "Stay safe, Aribella, my daughter. I love you."

Taking a deep breath, I threw my arms around her. "Thank you, Mom. I love you too."

At some point her kindness had chipped away at the hard shell surrounding my heart. And if there was ever a time to use 'Mom', it was now.

Needing to concentrate, I closed my eyes and blocked everything out. I lifted the lid on my energy spot. It surged in protest of last night's containment. Ignoring this, I started to pull, taking my time, weaving a large and strong circle. Two cycles per person, and large enough for everyone to step through. Once I was finished, I held the end of the string and pictured the island in the center. Then I released it.

Lucy gasped as I opened my eyes. "Damn, Abby, it actually worked."

I laughed. "Thanks for the faith."

She shrugged. "What can I say? I may have smiled and nodded, but deep down I didn't think you had a chance."

I snorted with laughter. *Typical Lucy.*

"Okay, are we ready to go now?" Samuel took Lucy's hand, gesturing that we all should follow.

Brace moved in to take mine; he gave it a gentle squeeze. In that split second our eyes linked. I forced myself to ignore him and focus on the doorway. Taking a deep breath, I stepped through, pulling them with me. I rode the waves, moving at super speed without any issue and doing my best to keep everyone from collapsing around me. The journey was longer than expected, and there was a strange turbulence in the quiet expanse of the wormhole.

As we were expelled, the light was so bright I was blinded in those first few moments. Hands were wrenched from my grasp as everyone tumbled to the ground. I jumped to my feet and turned in a circle. Already we were surrounded by creatures, their weapons held aloft. The brochure had lied.

This was no island resort.

Brace was suddenly at my back. He reached out and took my hand.

As the Spurns moved closer, Brace leaned in to me.

"I need to tell you something, Red, in case we don't make it off this beach." Despite the situation, his low voice and close proximity sent shivers down my spine. "When I crashed into you in the forest, that wasn't the first time I saw you."

I stiffened as the rest of our group gained their feet. Our circle was pushed in tighter by the advancing men, all with flowing locks of dark-blue hair.

"What do you mean?" I finally spat out between clenched teeth.

His grip tightened. "I dreamed of you too."

***

Please, if you loved this book, could you do me a huge favor and post a review on Amazon and/or Goodreads. Reviews are so valuable to independent authors and I'd appreciate your feedback. – Jaymin ☺

https://www.facebook.com/JayminEve.Author
mailing list jaymineve@gmail.com
Or email jaymineve@gmail.com

About the Author

Jaymin Eve loves surrounding herself with the best things in life: a good book, chocolate and her two little girls. She's been writing for about ten years and now it has settled into her blood and she can't get it out. Not that she wants to.

She'd love to hear from you, so find her at
https://www.facebook.com/JayminEve.Author
mailing list www.jaymineve.com
Or email jaymineve@gmail.com

CPSIA information can be obtained at www.ICGtesting.com
Printed in the USA
LVOW04s1456100915

453651LV00008B/151/P